HURAGO

ALSO BY CATHERINE SNODGRASS

Another Chance, Another Time
Circle In The Sand
Feather On The Wind
Silk Dreams & Satin Lies
The Quest For Gillian's Heart
Seven Rings Binding
Smoke And Shadow
The Wishing Tree

With Bryndis Rubin

Always Faithful
Ice Princess
Judging Ellie

HURAGO

BY

CATHERINE SNODGRASS

AMBER QUILL PRESS, LLC
http://www.amberquill.com

HURAGO
AN AMBER QUILL PRESS BOOK

Amber Quill Press, LLC
P.O. Box 50251
Bellevue, Washington 98015

Copyright © 2002 by Catherine Snodgrass
ISBN 1-59279-971-X
Cover Art © 2002 Trace Edward Zaber

Rating: R

Layout and Formatting provided by: ElementalAlchemy.com

PUBLISHED IN THE UNITED STATES OF AMERICA

CHAPTER 1

Jessica Martin turned her gaze to the statues poised on the edge of the lagoon. One stood at the western point where the shallow azure waters met the deeper midnight blue of the Pacific. The other was near the first one, but closer inshore—almost halfway to the apex of the lagoon where a peninsula divided the waters into two equal sections. Over thirty-feet tall, they looked like gigantic ceramic dolls. As blasphemous as it sounded, Jessica likened them to the Virgin Mary.

Their hair was long and painted dark brown, the eyes a cerulean blue. Robes of blue edged in a thin line of red with a larger band of white on the outside showed the detail the ancient, mysterious craftsman put in his work that time could not erase. A glossy sheen of enamel covered the surface. Both gazed serenely down upon the lagoon. With arms crossed over their hearts, benevolent smiles danced upon their lips. A smile Jessica normally returned. Today she did not; she could not.

The tropical breeze stirred her hair until the copper-colored tendrils licked her cheeks. Jessica ignored the attempt to cheer her. The giant ladies were going to have to do more than that to pull her from her fear and depression.

Why? she silently demanded. But no explanation came. The statues were mute. Jessica wanted to scream out her frustration. Since the day she arrived on the island seven years ago, they had been a part of her heart, a part of her soul. They saved her from death, and once she put all her faith in their abilities, saved her from the horror of an abusive marriage.

So why this? Why now? Have I done something to displease them?

Hadn't she always touted their abilities, even to the extent of being teased by others on the island? How many times had people rolled their eyes and placated her with "Yes, Jessica." She brushed it all aside for them—Hurago's lovely ladies.

Now joy over the arrival of a much-needed doctor and two wildlife biologists was marred by the arrival of another—a presence so evil he could only have been spawned by the devil.

"Why?" she whispered on a choked sob.

She heard footsteps smush the grass behind her and blinked away her tears. It wouldn't do to have someone see her this upset. That would involve too much explanation.

"Meredith sent me to check on you. You okay?"

Jessica glanced over her shoulder to Leia Chamberlain. A smile dredged from the pit of her stomach never made it to her lips. "Meredith worries too much."

Leia sat beside her on the grass and dug her tanned toes in the sand that bordered it. Her sun-lightened brown hair dangled to her shoulders in a long ponytail.

"A regular mother hen. I was tempted to tell her to check herself, but I couldn't stand to see her waddle all the way over here."

This time Jessica did smile. Her friend was close to delivering her third child. The doctor was arriving none too soon. "This doctor is certainly a blessing. What do you know about him?"

Leia shrugged and stared at the waves gently washing to shore. "Nothing you don't already know. Divorced. His one child died in an accident. He's supposed to be very good…good looking, too, so Gina says. She doesn't know his brother or the other wildlife biologist, but they come highly recommended."

Of course they did. Leia's father wouldn't let them on the island otherwise. Too bad Edward wasn't as selective with members of his own family.

"Well, that's good. We sure need that doctor, and it'll be interesting to have wildlife biologists study the island. We've never had that before."

Leia hugged her knees and let her gaze follow Jessica's to the statutes. "Amazing how things worked. Just think, if I hadn't met Gina in college, she never would have come here to be our nurse. And she certainly wouldn't have been able to convince Chris Matthews to be our doctor. Guess everything happens for a reason."

Silence fell between them. Obviously Leia realized the phrase was frightening under the circumstances. What reason would Eddie Chambers have for coming to Hurago after all these years? The possibilities scared Jessica half to death.

"You won't like him, Jessica. I can't believe Daddy is actually allowing him to come here."

No, Jessica didn't like Eddie Chamberlain. She hated him to the very core of her being. She knew him more than she cared to. That had been and always would be her horrible secret.

"It's a pity Edward hasn't taken the same precaution with his own son as he does with everyone else on Hurago."

Edward's background investigations for anyone coming to live on the island rivaled anything the government could do. But when his oldest son was the subject, he turned a blind eye to his faults. And Eddie had a million of them.

"Or to listen to what Bobby had to say about it. They've argued and argued. I still think about that time at the waterfall. If Bobby and Dan hadn't come when they did, Jackie and I would have..." Leia broke off with a shudder.

Jessica touched Leia's arm lightly. "Tell your father about it." *Someone had to make Edward listen. Maybe he'd listen to his daughter.* God knew, Jessica couldn't begin to tell Edward how evil Eddie was. That would involve dredging up more nightmares than Jessica cared to relive.

Leia shook her head. Sunlight glinted off the highlights in her hair. "I can't. I just can't."

Jessica couldn't condemn her; not when she felt the same way. She dropped her hand to the statue's foot and traced each toe with a blade of grass. "It's hard to believe he came from the same parents as you and Bobby. He's so different...doesn't even look like you."

Puzzlement clouded Leia's face. "How did you know?"

Jessica longed to bite her tongue in two. How could she have slipped so easily? "Oh, your mother showed me family pictures."

"Oh..." She rested her chin on her knees and stared at the lagoon. "Keep your doors locked and your windows shut, Jess."

But Jessica knew even that wasn't enough to keep out a determined man. "You could stay with me and William."

"I'll be fine." Leia rocked herself and focused on the blue horizon. "I have a gun, Jessica."

She jerked her head around. "Leia!"

"I do. I borrowed it from Dan. I'll use it, too, if that bastard lays one finger on me."

Jessica gently touched her arm again. This time Leia looked at her. "Think of what you're saying."

"I want him dead." Her brown eyes clouded with tears. "I know it's wrong, but I want him dead. If Bobby weren't flying that plane, I'd wish it into the ocean so I'd never have to worry about Eddie again."

"And what about Bobby and those three innocent men on board?"

Leia sighed and looked back to the sapphire water. "I know...I know."

"It'll be all right." It was a lie, but it was all Jessica could think of to say. "We'll keep together. We'll watch the kids. We'll get through this."

"I hope you're right."

Jessica had no reassurances to give. She studied Leia for a moment, envying the way the sun shot streaks of gold through her long brown hair. Sparked by a touch of whimsy, she ruffled her own red hair. "You know, I think it's time I let my hair grow. What do you think?"

A smile brought Leia's head around. "You'll curse it when you're working at the farm."

"I curse it now 'cause it's always tickling my neck. It defies a ponytail."

Their shared laughter was interrupted by a shout from Meredith. "We could use a little help in here. There *is* an engagement ceremony tonight. There *are* new people arriving."

"Bossy, bossy, bossy," they said in unison, then laughed again.

A glance toward the community building and the sight of Meredith Chamberlain standing in the doorway with arms crossed over her belly set them off again. Before she could scold, they started her way.

Jessica lagged behind for a final look at the statues. This time she didn't ask them why, but neither did she arbitrarily accept whatever fate they were planning. Instead, she prayed for the strength to get through whatever was to come.

The sound of a small plane reached her. They were almost here and she hadn't realized it until now. Bobby was close enough to see her. Had he been alone he would have dipped the wings in greeting. Had Eddie not been on board she would have lifted a wave his way.

Instead, she ducked into the building to drown out the sound of the plane and smother the fear in her heart.

CHAPTER 2

"Would you look at that?"

Chris Matthews didn't need any encouragement from his brother to look out the airplane window. A mere hour before, they left Oahu. Chris didn't think anything could compare to the beauty of that tropical island. Now this.

The gray-green island jutted out of a sapphire ocean. Waves ringed its shores like the lace on a little girl's petticoat. Tufts of clouds were captured on peaks of the small mountain range.

Then there were the statues—giant ladies, Bobby Chamberlain called them. Description and photographs didn't do them justice. They took Chris's breath away. The midday sun bathed them in a glowing aura, adding a spiritual tone to their mystery.

Legend had it that for those who believed, true love was theirs and protection forever. A quaint superstition. But seeing the statues now Chris could see it was easy to get caught up in it. True love? Maybe it did exist...for some people.

He focused on the island once more. He heard the story of Hurago only once, but already knew it by heart. He memorized it like a well-worn fairytale told over and over to a child at bedtime. He could recite it by rout, on command, in his sleep if need be. He knew it all.

Of how, forty years ago Edward Chamberlain and three friends were fishing off Oahu when a storm blew them off course. When the storm passed, they were in the lagoon of this beautiful island. That very lagoon below that beckoned to him now. Elderly islanders, the last of their people, greeted the men. Bonds were formed when Edward and his friends repaired the islanders' storm-damaged homes. The native chief was so grateful, he bequeathed the island to them. He didn't want Hurago to die and claimed the island and the statues needed people to care for.

A lesser group of men would have turned the place into a haven for tourists. Instead, the four refused to allow exploitation. Edward was now the only one who remained. And here Chris was to add to the legend, tempted by a medical practice on a privately-owned island.

He smiled. Bullied by Gina was a more appropriate term. She'd written that Hurago was just the balm she needed to heal her fractured soul. That true magic lived here. Then she blatantly told him it was time he stopped feeling sorry for himself.

That stung. But the more Chris thought about it, the more he realized that was exactly what he had been doing the last six months— feeling sorry for himself. He wasn't the first man to go through a divorce. He wasn't the first father to lose a child. It was time he built a new life for himself; time for a change—a positive change. And who knew? Maybe true love waited for him there.

He stretched the kinks out of his back and smiled. Hurago. The name even sounded mystical. If half of what Gina said was true, he had nothing to lose and his peace of mind to gain. An island strictly devoted to scientific research. An island untouched by the trappings of tourism. It seemed almost too good to be true.

Judging from the tension between their pilot and fourth passenger left behind in Honolulu, he was beginning to wonder if there was a touch of trouble in paradise. He couldn't fathom such animosity between brothers and blessed whatever powers that be that he and Sean were close.

Chris tore himself away from the view below and looked over at Sean and Sean's best friend, Mark Simpson. Although alike in personalities, they were almost physical opposites. Both were six feet tall, but Sean had the Matthews' coloring—blond, blue-eyed, solidly built, while Mark was slender with dark brown hair and eyes.

"Better buckle up," Bobby Chamberlain called from the cockpit. "We're going in."

With his attention riveted on the island below, Chris double-checked his belt. Bobby guided the Cessna over a runway situated in the valley. The mountains enveloped them in a blanket of green as the plane landed. Minutes later Bobby opened the hatch and dropped the steps. A man who could only be Edward Chamberlain stepped forward to greet them. Chris got a good picture of what Bobby would look like when time grayed his brown head and added a few pounds.

"Welcome...Welcome to Hurago." Edward clasped each man's hand in a double-handed shake, then turned to his son. "Didn't Eddie arrive?"

Bobby turned his back to him and unloaded the luggage. "He arrived."

"Then where is he?"

He slammed the hatch closed and faced his father. "I thought I made myself clear on this. I left him."

Edward's back stiffened as his chin tilted up a notch. "All right...have it your way. That's why we have more than one pilot. I'll have Roger go get him."

They loaded into the passenger truck and drove toward the settlement in awkward silence. Chris studied father and son for a few minutes, then shrugged the incident aside. Whatever was going on, he knew he'd find out sooner or later. Living in a small community made it hard to hide secrets.

He admired the lush tropical foliage as they wound their way down the small mountain to the settlement. Other than palm and banana trees, he couldn't identify what he saw. A canvas of flowers—red, yellow, orange, and white—decorated bushes and trees along the roadside. From time to time he heard a chorus of birds above the hum of the engine.

"This is wonderful. And you built this all by hand?" Mark Simpson already had a pad out, scribbling notes as fast as his hand allowed. Obviously he didn't have any trouble identifying the plants.

"Well, not quite." In the front passenger seat, Edward twisted around until he could see them. The chance to talk about his island brightened his face and washed away the family tension.

"At first, yes, we worked with just simple tools. Then, when we built the landing strip and paved the road, we had equipment flown in. This road to the airstrip is the only paved road we have. Our other road leads to the farm in the center of the island. I've suggested paving it, too, but Jessica says it's not necessary."

"Jessica? Your daughter?" Chris asked.

"No. Jessica is in charge of the farm. Does one hell of a job. She's the widow of Bill Martin, Jr., Dr. Martin's son."

"One of the founders," Chris said, although he already knew the answer.

"Yes. Both were killed about six years ago. Jessica stayed on. She said this was her home—the only home she'd ever really known."

"It's beautiful." Sean edged a bit closer to his brother and rested his forearms on his knees. "For some reason, I thought it would be a little more rugged living here. I mean, you even have transportation. I was expecting…" He laughed, plopped back in his seat, and lifted his palms. "I don't know. Horse and wagon?"

Edward chuckled. "It took us awhile, but we're very civilized, and we try to conserve the resources. You'll find we have all the amenities here. Telephone, satellite dish. Anything to make our residents and visitors comfortable."

"How many people live here?" Mark added sketches of flowers to his notes. Chris admired how he managed to catch the tiniest details with only a glance. A real gift.

"Right now one hundred, but that fluctuates from time to time. People come and go," Edward said.

"Hard to believe when it seems so inviting." Sean waved his hand to the window. "The weather is beautiful, and I saw no evidence of volcanic activity from the air. Not even an old crater. Yet the rocks are clearly volcanic."

Edward shrugged. "I don't know what to say about that."

"Maybe there's a blown-out crater beneath the water," Mark said without looking up from his work. "Ever explore under water?"

"A little scuba diving offshore. Except for the lagoon, the current around the island is rough and swift," Bobby tossed over his shoulder.

"So, I don't know what to tell you," Edward said. "Other than a spurt of mild earthquake activity six years ago, it's been ideal."

"Yet people choose to leave." Chris meant to keep the comment to himself; it slipped out of its own volition.

If Edward was offended, he either chose to ignore it or chalked it up to newcomer ignorance. His casual, tell-you-all-about-it openness never faltered.

"Scientists are a transient bunch. They get what they want and go. As for doctors—we've had a hard time keeping one. They just don't want to stay, and big hospitals lure them away. That's why we sure were glad to get you. I was grateful Gina Monroe suggested it to you and me."

"She's a good nurse." And Chris had to admit he missed her. They'd helped each other through some hard times.

They rounded the last curve and the settlement came into view. Coconut palms dotted the sandy shore between the statues. The coastal lowland was narrow, no more than fifty feet from shore to the mountain base in some areas, but here in the lagoon settlement that expanded easily to two miles. Several varieties of trees shaded homes scattered through the area—nestled nice and cozy between the mountains and the lagoon.

Chris decided he liked the banyan tree the most. The branches sent out shoots that grew downward and formed secondary trunks. A natural fort. Apparently the island children felt that way, too. Several ducked in and out of the branches.

Bobby pulled to a stopped in front of a large house of pale yellow. A deep porch invited visitors to the front door. White patio furniture dotting the lawn matched the scalloped trim around the tall windows.

Edward waved his arm toward it. "We call this the doctor's house. Only our doctors have lived here. It's three bedrooms, so big enough for all of you. If you don't care to live together, there are single room cabanas by the beach. The dispensary is next door."

He flicked his finger to a long building, then to the house by the banyan tree. "My house is over there. Come on over when you get settled. I have maps of the island, and my wife, Elaine, has a light lunch waiting for you."

After another round of handshakes and Edward's, "Welcome again," Chris followed Sean and Mark into the house.

A spacious living room greeted them. A white ceiling fan stirred the trade wind caught by the open windows. Powder blue carpet accentuated bookshelves of dark walnut lining one wall. A pale blue sofa with matching arm chairs made a cozy circle before the picture window. An arched doorway opened to the harvest gold kitchen, and a short hallway beckoned them to the bedrooms and bath. It felt like home.

"Nice place for three bachelors, wouldn't you say?" Mark dropped his duffel bag in the middle of the floor.

Almost too nice. Chris stared at the instant clutter and bit back a comment. But the look was enough to make Mark retrieve the bag.

"Did you tell Carolyn you were leaving?" Mark asked.

Just thinking about his ex-wife made Chris's skin crawl and Mark knew it. Chris wondered if it was his way of getting even for Chris's look. He snatched up his luggage.

"My attorney knows. That's all that needs to happen. Master

bedroom's mine. You two can fight over the others."

As he walked away, Chris heard Sean smack Mark. "Idiot. You know how mad he gets whenever Carolyn's name comes up."

Mark was instantly on the defensive and Chris knew if he turned around right then he'd find the two nose to nose.

"Yeah, I know," said Mark. "But you know how Carolyn is when she doesn't get her way. I don't want her coming here and stirring up shit again. It's bad enough we have this problem with Angela. We don't need Carolyn here, too."

Chris managed a smile and turned around. Angela was Sean's problem. Carolyn was his. Yet because it was happening to them—his extended family—Mark considered it his problem, too. Chris felt guilty for wanting to snap at him about the duffel bag.

"We'll get through it, Mark. As for Carolyn... Just let it go. The divorce is almost final. Nothing will happen. Don't worry."

In the privacy of his room, Chris let his forced humor fade. He tossed his suitcases to the bed, then plopped down beside them.

It was Carolyn's dark Hispanic looks that had immediately attracted him—and every other man within her scope. He remembered the first time he made love to her, tangling his fingers through that mass of long, black hair.

It was only later, after they were married, that he realized the truth. He should have left her then, but the child, the boy she claimed was his, kept him with her. Though he knew the truth, Chris loved Brian, and Carolyn had managed to destroy that, too. Chris hated her...hated her so much at times he felt it threatened his sanity.

He pulled in a few deep, cleansing breaths and renewed his vow to start fresh. A glance around the room put a smile back on his face. Creamy sheers covered a bank of windows overlooking the infirmary. The cherry wood furniture gleamed from recent polishing. The scent of fresh-washed linen drifted to him. Obviously someone wanted to make him welcome. *Gina or someone else?*

He caressed the head of the sleigh bed. The wood was smooth under his touch. Night stands with candlestick lamps stood on either side. A chest of drawers and bureau also filled the room. And, finally, a walk-in closet was open and ready.

Anxious now to settle in, Chris snapped open his suitcases and unpacked. The past was just that.

* * *

The door to the Chamberlain house opened as Chris, Sean, and

Mark cut across the grass. Bobby invited them in with a sweeping wave of his arm. A tall, dark blonde woman stood beside him gently rubbing a belly swollen in the advanced stage of pregnancy.

"My wife, Meredith."

Her misty gray eyes crinkled with a smile. "Thank goodness. A doctor. And just in time." She patted her belly. "Number three is due very soon, Dr. Matthews."

"Chris, please. How soon?" He placed a hand on her stomach. It tightened beneath his touch. He smiled. "I see. Very soon. You're in labor."

"Don't worry." Meredith patted his hand. "We know the drill by now. We'll tell you when. Come on, Bobby, let's go check on that pig."

Chris watched them walked away hand in hand, laughing like newlyweds. Two children, a boy and girl, ran up to them. Each grabbed a parent's hand to hurry their pace.

That's what marriage should be like.

Edward edged up beside him. "They're calmer than I ever was."

"For now." Chris followed him inside where Sean and Mark already sat devouring sandwiches and ice tea.

"As you could see from the air"—Edward pulled out a chair—"Hurago is a small island only about twenty-five miles in diameter. Much of it is still unexplored. Most of the researchers who come here only study for about a year—just long enough to work on a thesis—then they go."

"Does anyone ever stay permanently?" Mark asked through a mouthful of potato salad.

"A few, but as I said earlier, it's a transient community. You'll find a general store down the road near the community building as well as a laundromat. If there's something special you need or just want, let my daughter know. Leia will see that you get it."

As if on cue a young woman poked her head through the doorway. "I just came by to get the bandeau for Jackie." She held up a headband made of fiber with long strings of beads attached to it. "I thought I'd say hi to our arrivals."

Chris choked back his laughter as he watched his younger brother's reaction to the woman. Sean's sandwich was poised halfway to his mouth while he stared in dumbfounded shock.

She was beautiful, Chris readily agreed. The sun had kissed her skin with a golden tan. Her golden brown hair dusted her back where her halter top had left it bare. Deep brown eyes studied Sean exclusively as his did her. A moment suspended in time...for Sean and Leia anyway.

It was she who finally broke the spell when she stepped backward toward the door and bumped into the frame. A blush covered her cheeks. "Sorry I can't stay and visit, but I've got a lot to do before the dinner tonight and I want to check on that pig."

Sean's gaze saw her to the door. When he looked back, it was all Chris could do to resist the impulse to tease him.

Edward cleared his throat, pulling their attention his way once more. "I don't think I mentioned it, but whenever new arrivals come to Hurago we welcome them with a feast. There'll be one tonight to welcome you. When the four of us arrived, that's how we were welcomed. It's a tradition I do my best to keep up."

He laced his fingers together and leaned forward on the table. "Actually, the party tonight has a dual purpose. The dinner and the dance following it will also be to recognize the engagement of Jackie Sinclair and Dan Daniels."

The children of the final two founders, Chris noted. All present and accounted for—Chamberlain, Martin, Sinclair, and Daniels.

"Their engagement ceremony tonight will be based on island tradition. I'll explain it all as it happens. For now"—he pushed himself to his feet—"let me give you maps of Hurago. It shows some of the landmarks and will help you to orient yourself when you're out backpacking. If you find a landmark that isn't on the map, please note it. It helps to get all the information we can. Come on. I'll give you a quick tour of the settlement."

Edward pointed out the general store and the other services available as they strolled around. No one said much, just listened. The last building on the tour was the one Chris had been impatiently waiting to see—the infirmary. The second he stepped over the threshold, he felt a rush of joy, just as he had when he started his first practice. Yep...he'd definitely made the right decision.

The facility was divided into separate rooms—waiting room, doctor's office, examination room, laboratory, a six-bed convalescing area, and a private room for delivering babies. Everything white, clean, and fresh.

Chris stopped before the medicine cabinet to study the contents. It seemed they were well-prepared for just about anything. There was just one thing missing—his nurse.

"Where's Gina?"

"Probably with everyone else checking on the pig," Edward said.

Mark screwed up his face in a mask of confusion. "What is it about this pig that everyone wants to check on?"

"I'll show you." Smiling, Edward led them to the community building across the road.

Off to the side of the long building, a group of people sat talking and joking. Chris spied Gina's mane of corn silk tamed by a French braid. Before he could call a greeting, she turned their way. With a wave, she hopped up and closed the distance between them with her long-legged stride.

"You made it." She tossed a tight hug around Chris's neck.

"Safe and sound. I don't believe you've met my brother, Sean. And this is Mark Simpson."

She nodded to each of them, adding a smile when she greeted Mark.

He pushed to the forefront. "We came to see this pig."

Laughing, Gina pointed to the ground. "There it is."

He looked even more confused. "That's the pig? What did you do, bury it?"

She laughed again. "As a matter of fact...yes."

"We dig a pit and build a fire in the bottom." Edward squatted down and waved his hand over the palm leaves. "The hot coals and stones are covered with leaves and grasses then the pig goes in. We cover it with more leaves and grasses, then wet sand. It's one of the traditions we learned from the islanders. We 'check on it'"—he drew quote marks in the air—"by sitting around drinking berry mash. Every once in awhile someone will poke a stick down through the sand to see if the pig's done."

Mark scrunched up his face again. "Berry mash?"

"Here, try it." Gina handed him a cup of liquid. Mark sniffed it tentatively, then cautiously sipped. "Ah...sweet nectar of the gods...booze." Laughter tittered through the group.

"But it's not that potent," Gina said.

"All the better." Mark gave her a wink. "I think I'm going to like checking on the pig."

The others laughed again and while they settled down to continue their vigil, Gina sidled up to Chris. "Well, what do you think?"

"Impressive. I'd like to look at everyone's medical records."

Gina's smile faded. "Chris, I know you're anxious, but can't it wait until tomorrow? The party's getting ready to start."

As if her shorts and T-shirt weren't clue enough. He smiled and gave her shoulder a squeeze. "I understand. Tomorrow's fine."

"Thanks." On impulse, she kissed his cheek, then sat on the grass beside Mark.

Chris gave a silent nod of approval. They looked good together, and something deep inside told him this was going to last. He regretted he had never thought to introduce them before now. Happiness was finally going to enter Gina's life. She deserved it after that disastrous engagement of hers and the emptiness of their own fleeting affair.

He propped himself against a nearby palm tree and stared out at the lagoon and the giant statues. *This place might be paradise after all.*

"Beautiful, aren't they?"

He glanced around to Leia Chamberlain, standing on the porch behind him. "They are."

"The islanders worshipped them. There are some here who believe in their magic."

"Are you one of them?"

She gave a soft laugh. "There are times... But then I'm a bit superstitious. And you?"

"Not really. Sean's the superstitious one in our family. He had to bring an extra suitcase along just for all his lucky charms."

She giggled. "Guess we'll have to see what we can do to change your mind then. Maybe we'll sic Jessica on you. No one knows those ladies better."

He questioned her with a raised eyebrow, and she pointed to a petite redhead toting a basket of fruit through a side door to the building. When he looked back, Leia was gone.

Curious about Jessica's insight into the statues, Chris wandered into the community building. A large buffet was set against one wall, laden with vegetables, fruits, breads, and platters for the pig.

Chris watched Jessica dart from the kitchen with yet another tray of food. She was trim and tight. And judging from the way she bustled around the table, used to keeping busy. Shorts showed off a nice set of legs and a heart-shaped bottom. Her hair was tucked behind one ear, inviting him to trace the shell with his tongue.

He shook himself back to his senses and tamped down his raging libido. And he had the nerve to want to tease Sean? Fortunately, Jessica was too absorbed in her work to notice him. She stayed only long enough to load the table before scurrying back to the kitchen.

In control once more, Chris ventured into the kitchen to lend a hand. He found her hard at work scrubbing a pot almost as big as she.

"Mind if I help?"

She whirled around to face him, hand clutched to her throat. "Who are you and what do you want?"

"I didn't mean to frighten you." He splayed his fingers across his chest. "Chris Matthews. I thought I could give you a hand. You look like you could use it." He motioned to the pot behind her and took a step forward.

Jessica backed away as far as the sink allowed. "I don't need your help and I don't want your help."

Talk about throwing cold water on lust. Any interest he had was definitely gone. Before he could react to her brusqueness, the door behind him opened.

"Chris, it's time. Meredith and I could use your help now," Bobby said.

"On my way." He brushed past Bobby, anxious to put as much distance as possible between himself and the redheaded ball of flame.

*   *   *

Jessica forced her heart to start beating again. She'd overreacted. She just couldn't help it. It was instinct.

"Jess, you'll watch the kids?" Bobby asked.

"Of course," she replied, then wished she had nodded instead when her shaking voice gave her away. She prayed Bobby wouldn't notice. He did.

"You did it again, didn't you?"

His hands on hips stance annoyed her. The last thing she felt like was a lecture.

Feigning interest in her work, she turned her back to him. "I thought he was Eddie, that's all."

"Yeah...right. I didn't bring Eddie. I told you I wouldn't."

"But he's still coming."

"There's nothing I can do about that. But there is something I can do about you."

Here it was—the lecture.

"How about putting a little life back into Jessica Martin? How much longer are you going to act this way? I know it was horrible, but it's in the past. Leave it there. Chris seems like a nice man. Why not give him a chance? You can't be afraid of men the rest of your life."

Her shoulders sagged. He was right, of course, but she kept her reply noncommittal. "We'll see, Bobby."

"Guess that's all I can ask for now." He ducked out the door.

Jessica threw open the windows the moment he left, inhaling the crisp ocean breeze. She needed something to calm her jangled nerves.

True, she had thought Eddie had snuck up on her, but that was no excuse for her rudeness to a man she didn't know. The reason came quicker than she wanted. It was he who set her on alert—not because of anything he had done, but because of her reaction to his presence.

Good looking was a poor choice of words for the man. He was gorgeous. In the space of a heartbeat, she'd memorized his features. A golden man. Hair that captured the sun. Not too short. Not too long. It tempted her fingers to ruffle their way through its thickness. And his eyes—the color of the ocean with the blue darkening the further it went from the iris.

His smile had faded too quickly. It was her fault she knew. As much as she'd wanted that heart-stopping grin to return, Jessica couldn't calm down enough to urge it back. Long, strong fingers had reached out to her, then dropped. His shoulders had filled the white golf shirt and his shorts...

Jessica bit her bottom lip. *How could a man have such great looking legs? There ought to be a law against it.*

Positively the most handsome man she had ever seen. And she wanted him. For the first time in her life, she experienced lust. Instead of reveling in the fact, it scared the hell out of her.

Sex wasn't something she relished. Life with Bill had taught her that. So why this wanton attraction to Chris Matthews? She didn't trust it.

So what's the harm? her conscience nagged. What *was* the harm? Bobby was right. It was time to live.

The determination was swept away once more by fear and uncertainty. She couldn't take that risk again. She was fortunate to have been released from one bad relationship. She certainly didn't need another.

She attacked her chores with a vengeance only a madman could appreciate. Nothing helped. By the time night closed in and the party began, all she wanted was to close herself behind the safety of her walls. Far away from the noise and handsome man who tempted her away from her safe, happy home. Knowing the early departure would upset her son and lead to more questions, Jessica resigned herself to a long night.

She ducked out the side door and sucked in a breath. A shaft of moonlight pierced the drifting clouds, illuminating the closest statue. From deep inside herself Jessica heard a single word—*go.*

"All right, all ready," she said into the night. "I'll take him dinner…but that's it."

A newborn's cry cut the air.

"Tomorrow… I'll do it tomorrow."

CHAPTER 3

For what must have been the hundredth time Leia told herself there was no such thing as love at first sight. That still didn't keep her from ogling Sean Matthews every time he was in the same room with her. She was worse than a love-sick teenager mooning over a movie star.

Worse still, more than a time or two he caught her staring. It was a devastating experience, as if he could read her thoughts and know exactly where they led. Each time she had to duck from the room before her flushed cheeks gave her away.

The whole thing unnerved her to the point of clumsiness. She bumped into the wall five times, tripped over two chairs, spilled three cups of punch, and dumped a tray of fruit. Her mother and Jessica banished her from the kitchen when she reached for a platter of roasted pig.

That was fine while the crowd was still eating, but now the engagement ceremony was over and the room cleared to dance, Leia didn't know what to do with herself. Cleaning up the kitchen seemed a good idea until Jessica shooed her away once more. Considering her unusually grumpy mood, Leia was glad to leave her alone.

Any children she might have kept corralled were either asleep in the adjoining nap room or being coddled by the island's few teenagers. There was nothing to occupy her mind and keep her gaze from wandering where it should not. No leftovers to put away, no floor to sweep, no trash to take out. She stood in the doorway, hugging her midsection while she watched couples pair off to dance.

Her parents. Jackie and Dan. Gina with Mark Simpson. Only she and Jessica were alone, and Jessica was up to her elbows in dish soap. It seemed the best place for her now was home.

She chanced a look across the room. Sean stood by himself. Their gazes met. Leia couldn't breathe. She forced herself to hold the look, and in doing so, felt he had touched her soul. It was a union as intimate as if he had physically joined with her. She couldn't break that mystical hold.

Before she realized what was happening, Gina grabbed her wrist and dragged her to the center of the room. Mark did the same to Sean. Suddenly they were face to face—alone in a room full of people.

"Would you like to dance?" He looked as puzzled as she. That had to be a good sign.

A mute nod was all Leia could manage before she stepped into his arms. Was he shaking or was that her? They smiled together, then his arms closed around her as he swept her away.

*   *   *

How was it possible to feel awkward and graceful at the same time? Sean asked himself a thousand times over. They moved in unison as if they had danced this way hundreds of times, yet they still hadn't managed to say more than a few words. He wanted to share his every thought and experience with her. The words stayed frozen in his throat. So they glided in harmony, moving from one dance to the next until they were breathless from the exertion.

"Enough." Leia laughed and pulled away. "I'm exhausted. Fresh air, please."

Sean pulled her hand through the crook in his arm. "Your wish is my command." He reprimanded himself for the silliness, then complimented his quick thinking when she giggled over the comment.

Leia cursed her immature response and prayed he hadn't noticed. Gina's knowing grin didn't help. Outside was never so inviting.

The stars greeted them warmly as they stepped from the building. A gentle breeze blew in from the ocean rustling the palm trees. Sounds of waves rushing to the shore eased his nerves. Sean absorbed the peace offered while he struggled for something to say to dispel the awkwardness that had grown between them.

Leia toed off her shoes and set her feet on the cool ground. "Ahh, that feels much better. I've never danced so much in my life. I had such a good time, but I should go home. I have an early morning."

"Me, too. I'll walk with you...if you don't mind." *Anything to keep her with me a little while longer.*

"Not at all."

They strolled on, her arm still laced through his. It was a good feeling.

"I'm glad you enjoyed yourself. I know I did. You people really know how to make a person feel welcome." *Stupid, stupid, stupid. Can't you think of anything intelligent to say?*

"Well, we do try our best." She giggled and cringed. She sounded just like an air head.

"From what I've seen, Hurago is beautiful. I can't wait to start exploring it. Mark and I are going to go out tomorrow for a few days of backpacking." Work seemed a good, safe subject. Still, it did nothing to ease Sean's tension.

"What will you be doing?"

Finally, something he could talk about with some level of intelligence. "Initially, just cataloging what we see. Later on we'll concentrate on a particular animal or species for a while, and watch how it lives and interacts with other things in its environment. We'll also try to determine how its daily doings affect our own environment."

"It all sounds so fascinating. There are a lot of feral pigs here. My father is torn between having them removed from the island or letting them stay. They're a nuisance to the wildlife, but were a big part of the islanders' culture. Personally, I'd like to see them all gone. They can have a nasty disposition."

Sean nodded. "You're welcome to join us if you like. All you need to do is be quiet."

He wanted to slap himself the minute the words left his mouth. He came to this island to work and here he was setting himself up with the owner's daughter. *What must she think? What would her father think?* A chance of a lifetime thrown away on a whim. Yet, he couldn't help the tug that pulled him to her.

"I have to go to Honolulu tomorrow for supplies," she said.

What he hoped would be a silent sigh of relief felt more like a heave of disappointment. "Well, that's too bad. Maybe another time."

"I think I'd like that." She slipped her arm from his. "Well, here's my house."

He looked up to see a small house of an indeterminate light color. Three steps led up to the darkened porch.

"Well, I guess I'll be going. Thanks again for such a good time."

"Thank you. I guess I'll see you when you get back. Good night."

She extended her hand.

A handshake seemed relatively safe under the circumstances. But all he wanted to do was crush her body to his and claim that beautiful mouth.

"Good night." He slipped his fingers around hers.

For a moment it was as if a magnet locked them together. Neither spoke. He looked into the depths of her eyes, feeling things no words could describe.

Just as quickly, they dropped their hands and backed away. But the magic lingered.

"I have to go." Leia ducked into her house.

Sean sprinted to the lagoon, hoping the spurt of activity would rid him of the hardness that had existed since his gaze first captured Leia's across the room. He jerked to a stop at the edge of the water and let the waves spend themselves on the toes of his sneakers. It didn't help. He could still feel where her hand had touched his, still see her big brown eyes, still feel her body as they danced.

With a sigh he wandered over to the lagoon statue and leaned against it while he pondered the wealth of bizarre emotions that had assaulted him since he first met Leia Chamberlain.

It was crazy. Not that he hadn't been attracted to a woman before, but because it went beyond anything he'd ever felt. It wasn't lust—that was too base a term. It couldn't be love—it was too soon. So that made it... What? Confusing, intriguing...unsettling.

He needed answers to questions he didn't know how to put into words. At least he was calmer now. A little tired, in fact, now that his body was relaxed.

He turned back to the settlement. The party was still in full swing, but with Leia gone he had no interest in returning. The lights in the infirmary caught his eye. There wasn't anyone better than Chris to talk to when his mind was a jumbled mess of thoughts and emotion.

He was almost to the door when he saw a petite redhead hurry toward the building with a plate of food. She paused when she saw him, glanced at the building, then looked at him again.

"Here." She shoved the plate into his hands. "Give this to your brother."

Before he could ask her name, she dashed back to the community building and slammed the door behind her. He frowned in puzzlement, then shrugged it off and walked inside.

Chris's smile greeted him when Sean stepped into his office.

"Thanks. I'm starving."

Sean placed the plate on the desk before him. "Don't thank me. Some redhead shoved it in my hands outside."

His smiled widened. "Really?"

"Yeah...really." He sank into a worn vinyl chair across from his brother and propped his feet upon the desk. "How's mother and baby?"

With the plate in his lap, Chris mirrored his actions. "Doing very well. Baby girl. Easy birth. Once I was certain everything was fine, I let them go home. They'll rest better there and undisturbed. How was the party?"

"Okay, I guess. Too bad you missed the engagement ceremony."

"Well, I did have other things to do." He tossed a grape in the air and caught it in his mouth.

"In your element, I know. And totally oblivious to anything else going on."

Chris grinned. "Something like that. So tell me about it."

"It was interesting." Sean smoothed the crease in his Dockers. "Although you'll never convince Mark of that. Part of the ceremony says the couple have to wait for the wedding night. Mark said there was no way he'd ever be able to do that."

"Could you?" Chris asked.

Sean considered that for a minute. Even in light of his attraction to Leia, the answer was easy. "Yeah, I think I could. Edward said the islanders believed that a lasting relationship should be based on more than just sex. If I loved a woman, sex just wouldn't matter. Well, it would matter, but it would be secondary."

"I see. And when did you become so wise?" Chris asked.

He shrugged. "I guess I've always felt that way. I just never bothered to say it out loud."

"Are you sure this doesn't have something to do with Angela's claims?"

His mood soured. "Absolutely nothing. Her claims are bogus and it won't be long before I can prove it. I don't think about her. I don't worry about her. She's a girl in trouble, looking for a way out."

"So...who *do* you think about?"

Somehow Sean suspected Chris already knew the answer, but his need to confide in his brother had disappeared. "No one for the moment. And you?"

Chris shrugged. "Hard to say."

"The redhead?"

He laughed. "Awfully anxious to get me hooked up, aren't you?"

"Maybe I just want to see you happy for a change."

Sean expected to see Chris glower over the reminder of Carolyn. Instead, he chuckled.

"Me, too. But I'm not sure chasing redheads is the answer. At least, not ones who bite off your head one minute, then offer you food the next. Let's go home. I'm beat. And maybe you can tell me what's really on your mind."

Sean sighed. Chris knew him too well.

CHAPTER 4

Jessica drew a brush through her hair for what must have been the tenth time. Then, even though it wasn't wrinkled, she smoothed her tank top over her shorts. This time there was no backing out. She was going to go over to that house and make amends—even if it killed her. And it just might. She was so nervous she'd swear heart palpitations were about to do her in.

She tousled her red hair in frustration. "Oh, why did I have to cut it in the first place?" She knew the reason better than anyone, and it wasn't something she needed to be reminded of now. Still, the memory, the horror, came back.

Jessica had loved having long hair. The shimmering mass of curls was the one thing she could actually believe was beautiful on her. For Bill, it was nothing more than a tool for abuse. If Jessica tried to escape him, he grabbed her hair and yanked her back.

She cut it, crying inside with every lock that fell. She believed she was helping herself. It only made matters worse. When Bill discovered what she'd done, he used it as another excuse to lash out at her.

Jessica blinked back tears. Now was no time to think about the past; it was time for the future. Bobby was right. She had to start living again. The past *was* the past.

"William, are you just about ready?"

"Aw, Mom, I don't want to go visiting. I want to go play with Jeff and Amanda," he said from the living room.

She found the five-year-old sprawled in front of the television watching cartoons. "You can play later. Come on, it won't take long. It's polite to welcome your neighbors."

She retrieved an oven-warm coffee cake from the kitchen and returned to the living room. "Let's go." She walked out the door with William grudgingly beside her.

Welcome your neighbors. Now there's a ruse if ever I heard one. But it would get her in Chris's house where she could apologize for her rudeness the night before.

She was five feet from the door when she saw Leia walking toward the house, a covered pan also in her hands. They stopped and appraised each other.

"I'd just thought I'd..." Jessica clamped her mouth shut. If Leia was interested in Chris, perhaps it would be a good idea to simply step aside and let her have him.

"Mine's for Sean." Leia's tone dared Jessica to interfere.

Jessica smiled and lifted her pan. "Chris."

Leia returned the smile. "Well, let's go."

They stepped up to the door, but moved no further.

"I'm scared." And Jessica wasn't afraid to admit it. The courage she'd dredged up had stayed home.

"Me too," Leia mumbled. "But someone has to knock on the door."

"I'll do it." William pounded his small fist on the screen door before Jessica could stop him.

Chris was there a half a heartbeat later. His gaze caressed her face. His ready smile warmed her heart and put butterflies in her stomach. At least he wasn't too mad about last night.

"Good morning. This is a nice surprise."

Leia poked her head between them. "We're the welcome wagon. We brought treats for breakfast. Have you eaten yet?"

"No, come in." He held the door while they stepped inside. "Bring those in the kitchen. Smells great. You'll join us won't you?"

"Of course," they replied together.

"Aw, Mom, you said just a minute." William scuffed his feet against the carpet. "I want to go play."

Jessica looked from her son to Chris to Leia and back again. *With Leia for moral support, what's the harm?*

"Go then."

The boy skipped from the house without a second's hesitation.

"Sean, pour a couple cups of coffee. We have guests," Chris called out.

Sean's jaw dropped as he glanced up from his paper. When Leia set the blueberry muffins on the table before him, he jumped up for the coffee. His hand shook so badly the carafe clattered against the first mug.

Fighting a smile, Chris slipped the pot from his fingers and filled four yellow mugs. Sean managed to put two on the table without sloshing, although Jessica wondered how when his hands shook so. Then he reached for a muffin. Leia did the same. Their arms brushed and the two jerked back as if they'd been electrically shocked.

Leia jumped up, rubbing her arm where he had touched her. "I just wanted to bring that over. I have to go to Honolulu. Enjoy it. See you later." She dashed out the front door without another word.

Sean snatched up a couple of the muffins and darted for the opposite door with his backpack in his hand. "I'm going to get Mark so we can start exploring. See you later."

Jessica drummed her fingers on the table. The whole thing would have been comical if she weren't so nervous; if she weren't alone with a man with a killer body and a smile to match.

Now what am I going to do? She'd depended on the presence of others to ease the conversation. Everyone had deserted her. Should she run too, or awkwardly sit here and hope she could think of something intelligent to say?

"Well, that was interesting," she managed to say.

"Very." Chris set a mug of coffee next to her hand, then pushed the creamer and sugar her way.

"Black, thank you. Where's Mark? I thought he was going to live here with you."

"He...uh...spent the night with Gina."

Jessica felt heat creep to her cheeks. "Oh." She'd never understand how people could rush into...

"I understand you're widowed."

"Yes, a relieved widow." She longed to bite her tongue in two. He'd definitely caught her off guard.

Chris cocked his head. "Excuse me?"

She jumped up to retrieve a knife and napkins from the drawer. True, it wasn't her house, but she knew the place by heart. At least Chris didn't seem to mind her making herself at home. Another plus in his favor. That gave her confidence she sorely needed.

"I... It... We didn't have a good marriage."

"Yeah? Neither did I." He stirred the hot from his coffee.

She cut two slabs of cake for them and sat back down. This wasn't so bad after all. They were just friends, sharing. "Yes. I heard. I was sorry to hear about your son. Do you mind me asking what happened?"

Chris pinched off a piece of cake and popped it in his mouth. Did she realize how much compassion he saw in her expression? Probably not. One thing he'd learned about Jessica Martin in his very brief association with her was that she wasn't phony. What she felt was what you saw. The last thing he wanted from that beautiful face was pity. Still, he'd rather her hear from him than someone else. And it was a small island.

"Brian was four. One day while I was at work, Carolyn went to visit a friend on Catalina Island and took Brian with her. They took the ferry. Somehow or other he fell overboard. Brian's body was never recovered."

Jessica's eyes filmed over with tears. "I'm so sorry. I know how much that must've hurt."

She dusted her hand over Chris's arm sending shock waves throughout his body.

Her sympathy was almost more than he could bear. So was her sweetly innocent touch. She could have danced naked and not affected him as much. His body would have been plenty happy, that's for sure. But this? This touched his heart.

Chris managed a small smile. "More than I can say, but I've learned to deal with it." He slipped his hand over hers and gave it a squeeze. "Thanks for listening."

Jessica averted her eyes and slipped her hand from his. "I was wondering...I'm cooking dinner for Bobby, Meredith, and the kids tonight. Would you like to join us?"

Only a fool would say no. "I'd love to. But you have to do something for me."

"What's that?"

"Walk me all the way to work."

Jessica laughed—a bright, sparkly giggle that tickled Chris's spine. "All the way, huh?"

"Yes, ma'am."

"Deal."

They stepped outside and found a small gathering of friends just outside the infirmary. Sean and Mark stood with Gina and Leia talking to Bobby and the children. With them were the couple Jessica told Chris were the ones who had become engaged the night before.

27

"Looks like a party," he said as they joined the group.

"We were just making plans for a backpacking trip," Sean told him.

"Yeah, we're going to take Dan out to keep his mind off his lovely bride," Bobby said.

"His mind and his hands," Leia added, to the young couple's delight and embarrassment.

Suddenly the smile faded from Dan Daniels's angular face. "Damn it, Bobby, look," he said with a jerk of his head.

Chris followed the direction indicated and saw the elder Chamberlains walking toward them with the infamous Eddie. He felt Jessica's hand on his back and looked around to find her hiding behind him, her green eyes wide with fear. Instinct screamed at him to wrap his arms around her; propriety and the newness of their friendship refused to let him.

Eddie sauntered up to his younger brother with a cocky grin, and in that instant, Chris could see why he was so disliked.

"Bobby, good to see you again."

A cold glare was Bobby's only answer as he picked up his daughter.

"Who's the pretty little girl?" Eddie reached out to caress Amanda's cheek. The man oozed sleaze. Hustler, pimp also came to mind.

Dan grabbed Eddie's arm and yanked him back. "You dare lay a finger on her, and I'll see you regret it."

"It's good to see you, too, Dan." Sarcasm erased his smirk. He glanced at Jessica behind Chris, but said nothing. Instead, he turned to Leia.

"Well, you certainly have grown into a beautiful young woman." He reached out to touch her arm.

She slapped his hand away. "Don't come near me."

Eddie backed away. "It feels great to be so welcome." He gave a humorless snort, then walked away. Edward and Elaine Chamberlain slashed a look to their children and Dan, then followed their eldest child.

"This is too much." Chris tossed up his hands. "I know it's none of my business, but I've got to know what this is all about. My God, he's your brother."

"And we wish he wasn't," Leia told him.

Jessica eased out from behind Chris. "Bobby will tell you tonight before dinner...while the kids are busy playing. Sean and Mark, you come, too. Nothing I like more than cooking a big dinner."

"We'll be there," Sean told her. Then he and Mark swung on their backpacks and walked off to begin their explorations.

"Bobby...okay?" Jessica asked.

He tore his gaze from Eddie's back. "It's okay with me. They need to know. Come on, kids, if we're going to work at the hotel, we'd better get going. Leia, you about ready?"

"Yeah." After a backward glance to Sean, she followed Bobby and his two children.

"We'd better go, too, William." Jessica tucked him under her arm. "I still have work to do at the farm, and I'm sure Dr. Matthews has a lot he needs to do, too."

William's tousled brown head whipped around to Chris. "You're the new doctor?"

Chris squatted down to his level. "I sure am."

"Wow..." he stuck out his hand, "I'm William Robert Martin."

Chris shook his hand. "Very pleased to meet you, Billy."

"William, not Billy...after my grandpa. He was a doctor, too, but I never met him 'cause he and my dad died when I was a baby. I want to be a doctor when I grow up. Can I watch you do doctor stuff today?" With each word the boy got closer until he was almost in Chris's lap.

Jessica gently pulled him back. "William, Chris just got here. He's very busy."

"It's all right, Jess." Chris cupped the boy's head. "He's welcome to spend the day with me."

He sensed her hesitation and wished he hadn't offered. He'd feel the same way about leaving a child with someone he'd only just met.

"I'll help keep an eye on him," Gina said.

With a smile Chris sensed she didn't quite feel, Jessica agreed. He made a mental note to thank Gina later. William slipped his small hand into Chris's and looked up at him with all the trust and worship a five-year-old has to offer.

Jessica watched the three of them walk away. Bobby and Meredith were right—Chris was a nice man. But then so was Bill Martin until she married him. That thought alone made Jessica want to run as far as she could from Chris Matthews, but she remembered her promise to Bobby.

CHAPTER 5

From his office window, Chris watched Jessica drive up the road to Hurago's farm. He hated to see her go. In fact, he missed her company and she hadn't even been gone five minutes. Silly, he knew, but her smile, her openness embraced him. Chris wanted to get to know her better. A lot better. And not just in the baser sense of the word, although he'd been hard for her the second she flashed him that smile.

No, this went beyond the physical. He already wanted to share everything with her. From the beauty of a flower to the deepest secrets of his heart. Things had been going along pretty good too until...

Chris's jaw tightened at the thought of Eddie Chamberlain. Jessica's openness was also her vulnerability. She was scared to death. What tiny pleasure Chris might have gotten over her trusting him to protect her was washed away by the unbridled fear in her eyes. Now she was driving away...alone. Chris's only peace of mind was that Eddie was with his parents. He'd milk the first day of his visit for all it was worth. And they, blinded to what others saw, would let him.

At least Jessica was safe for now. There was little more Chris could do.

He turned around to William, who sat on the floor playing with two Matchbox cars he had pulled from the pockets of his shorts. Chris smiled. So much like Brian and yet so very different. He wondered if Brian...

Chris forced the thought away. It was too late to dwell on what he should have done.

"Well, William, let's get to work."

The boy bounced to his feet.

Before Chris realized it, the day was over. At the first sight of Bobby's kids on Jessica's front porch, William raced home ahead of Chris to share his day with them.

Chris chuckled. He knew how the boy felt. Jessica was only a few yards away. It'd been hard as hell to stay at work when he saw her come home. The scent of garlic wafted to him on the breeze. *Pasta.* She was cooking some sort of pasta tonight. Onions, the hint of oregano, bread baking. By the time he reached her door, his mouth was watering.

On impulse he ducked around to the kitchen door, then almost chickened out when he saw the women crowded around the table cooing over the new baby. He was ready to sneak off when Meredith waved him in. All heads turned his way, but Chris was only interested in one.

Jessica's eyes lit up when she saw him. A smile followed, drawing him right to her side.

"Dinner smells great." He lifted the lid on one of the pots.

Jessica tapped the back of his hand with a wooden spoon. "No cheating. Out with the other men." Her eyes danced with mischief.

Chris grabbed his hand and dredged up the most innocent look he could muster. "But I'm starving."

She pulled a carrot from the relish tray. "Eat this."

Eyes focused on hers, Chris wrapped his hand around hers, bit off a chunk of carrot, then turned it her way. She looked at it, then at him, and took a bite. If they hadn't been in a room full of people, he would have wrapped his arms around her and kissed her.

He pointed to the tray. "Is that for the hoard of starving men in the next room?"

When she nodded, he gave her a wink and carried it to the living room.

*   *   *

Jessica clutched the edge of the counter and willed her knees to stop shaking. He could have stripped her naked and had her right there on the floor in front of everyone and it wouldn't have been as intimate as sharing that carrot. She swallowed hard. The carrot was still lodged in her throat. She washed it down with a glass of water.

So far no one had said anything. They still chatted over baby Rachel. Maybe they hadn't noticed anything.

Jessica laughed at herself. They saw all right. How could they not?

Chris was standing so close. He and she were so quiet. Goodness, she could still feel the heat of his body surround her. How could no one notice that when it was all she could think about?

She reached for another glass of water then opted for the bottle of Chianti instead. That should settle her nerves and get her through the evening. *And after everyone left?* Jessica took a big sip of the wine. She'd cross that bridge later.

"Lasagna's almost done," she told the others over her shoulder.

"Whenever you're ready."

Jessica didn't know if there was hidden meaning in Meredith's words or not, and she sure wasn't going to ask her.

*   *   *

Bobby looked up when Chris walked in the room. A map of the island lay on the coffee table. The men hovered over it, making plans for the next day.

"I think this is what you wanted to know about. It'll make your stomach turn." Bobby tossed a manila envelope to the table. Its contents spilled over the map.

"It's all in there if you want to read it. Child molestation, sexual assault, attempted rape. There's even one charge of statutory rape with a twelve-year-old." Bobby snorted and stared at the far corner of the room. "He's been charged a lot of times, but the charges were always dismissed for lack of evidence or other technicalities."

Chris wasn't sure he wanted to read it. Just hearing about it was enough to make him sick. He set Jessica's relish tray on an end table and sat down.

"Don't your parents know about this?" Sean fingered the reports, but didn't pick them up.

"They refuse to believe a son of theirs could be so bad. If I told them about the reports, they wouldn't look at them."

"What made you ask for them in the first place?" Chris scanned the report on top and cringed. The man needed to be locked up.

"When Leia and Jackie Sinclair were thirteen, Bill Martin and Eddie tried to...corner them. They were twenty. Fortunately, Dan and I came along before the girls were hurt. Leia and I had never really liked Eddie very much, but after that, we hated him. What bothers me now is that after all these years, he's decided to come back. I want to know what he's been doing the last twelve years."

Chris passed the report to Mark without reading any further. *Twelve years ago? Eddie Chamberlain had been away from Hurago for twelve years?* Something didn't mesh.

"When did Jessica move here?"

"About seven years ago. Why?

"Did she ever meet Eddie?"

"No. He left long before she got here."

Chris raked his fingers through his hair. "Then why is she so afraid of him?"

Bobby shrugged. "Probably because she knows what he's done. Anyway, now you all know about this, you can help me keep a eye on him. I really don't know what else to do."

Chris felt his stomach knot. A rapist and child molester here? Not exactly the idealistic paradise he'd imagined. Well, he'd wanted to know what was going on. Now that he did, it sickened him. That Bobby shared so quickly with three men he'd just met underlined the threat.

Again he felt an overwhelming need to protect Jessica. This time he didn't shove it aside.

He stayed at Jessica's long after everyone else had gone. He used the ruse of helping her with the dishes, but he mainly wanted to assure her she was safe.

Chris laughed at himself. Who was he kidding? He just wanted time alone with her. To warm himself in the light of her smile.

"That was an excellent meal," he said as he began scrubbing the plates.

"I'm glad you enjoyed it. I think the others did." She beamed that smile his way.

Chris felt like a king. "I would say so, since there isn't a bite left." He leaned closer and lowered his voice. "Can William hear us in here?"

She pulled back. Puzzlement wrinkled her brow. Curiosity brightened her emerald green eyes. "No. He's should be asleep by now. Why?"

"His birthday is about a month away. So he tells me."

"Yes...he'll be six. He's been reminding *everyone*." She rolled her gaze to the ceiling.

"I wanted to get him something I know he's been wanting, since he mentioned it *several* times today. But I thought I'd ask you first. I wouldn't want to get on your bad side. Especially after getting whacked on the hand by that wooden spoon of yours."

Her laughter filled the room. "That's for severe behavioral problems. And it was hardly more than a tap."

Chris slowly shook his head and made a big show of studying his hand. "I don't know. I'm thinking I might need a doctor."

"Good luck finding a good one on this island," she shot back.

The jab caught him by surprise. So…she could give as good as she got. He liked that, too—a lot. Dredging up the most indignant expression he could muster, he looked down at her. "I'm the best doctor around."

"You're the *only* doctor around."

He laughed. God, he loved the mischief in her eyes. Each second he spent with Jessica, the more she wriggled under his skin and into his blood. No doubt about it. He wanted this woman and he was damn sure going to have her.

"So, what is it you want to get him?"

He turned back to the dishes to hide his pulsing interest. "A puppy."

"Oh, Chris, he'd love that." The words came out in a rush of breath as she grabbed his arm.

"You don't mind?"

"Not as long as you don't give him a Great Dane," she said, laughing.

It was contagious. The best aphrodisiac a man could ask for. His erection throbbed.

"I was thinking more along the lines of a cocker spaniel." Did she have any idea how desirable she was? Did she have a clue how he ached to have her?

She clapped her hands and gave a little hop. "I can't wait to see his face." Her happiness faded. "I don't know how you bear it without Brian. If anything happened to William, I don't know what I'd do."

That threw ice water on his libido. Chris shoved his hands beneath the suds. "You go crazy for a while. At least that's what I did. Yes, I miss him very much. I wish he could've met everyone here. I think he'd have had a great time. I'd like to think he and William would have been great friends."

She rested her elbow on the counter, her chin on the palm of her hand. "Was he a lot like William?"

Chris cocked his head to one side and rinsed the last of the pots. "He liked playing with his little cars and having his stories read to him. But Brian was real quiet. Almost too quiet. William's all boy. All kid just like Bobby's two.

"Brian never misbehaved…and it scared me, Jess. For awhile I thought maybe Carolyn was physically abusing him. Every night when I gave him his bath, I'd check to see if he had any unexplained marks on him. But...I never found a thing."

The sadness in his voice twisted her heart. "Could you have been wrong?"

"I hoped so, but I wasn't. Her abuse was psychological. Right before Brian died, I came home early one day. There was a fire going in the fireplace. She and Brian were standing in front of it. She had his teddy bear in her hand. He was crying and begging for it. I heard her tell that four-year-old baby he was too old for a teddy bear and she was going to see to it he never had it again. Jessica, she was going to burn it."

She scanned his face while he pulled the plug and watched the sink drain. Her heart felt as if it would break listening to him talk. As long as she lived she'd never understand how people could be so cruel. And she had lived with the master of cruelty. It sounded like Chris had lived with its mistress.

"I never felt like killing someone before but, God forgive me, I wanted to kill her then. I grabbed the teddy bear and Brian, and told her she'd better never pull anything like that again. That's when I decided to divorce her. Ironically, the day before I was going to serve papers on her, I lost Brian."

"How in the world did you ever fall in love with someone so hateful, Chris?"

He looked at her deep and steady. "That, Jessica, was the biggest mistake of all. I married someone I wasn't in love with."

She frowned. "I don't understand."

"Well, after I got my MD, I got it into my head it was time to settle down. Get a wife. Have some kids. Along came Carolyn and we got married, but we didn't love each other. And we never told each other we did. I was fascinated by her.

"I guess I thought love would grow in time. I was wrong. I know it's something you've got to feel inside. Without it, no marriage will last. Next time for me love first, marriage second." He dried his hands and tossed the towel onto the counter. "Have I completely depressed you?"

She reached up to cup his cheek, then pulled back and offered a smile instead. "No, not at all. I think I know how you feel. I've come to realize I married Bill out of desperation. I guess I was afraid no one else would ask me. I wanted babies. Lots and lots of babies. I didn't want to be an old maid. I made a big mistake, too, Chris."

He looked at her and felt himself drawn into those deep green eyes of hers. If he stayed much longer, he might not be able to trust himself alone with her, and it was too soon for that—for both of them.

"I guess I'd better be going. Jess, I want you to know I wouldn't let anyone hurt you."

He placed the softest of kisses on her lips and walked out the door, leaving Jessica to deal with the whirlpool of emotions that simple kiss left.

CHAPTER 6

Jessica twisted the corn off the stalk with a vengeance normally reserved for butchering chickens. She slammed the cob into the basket beside her.

Running away. That's all you're doing. And for what? All because he gave you a peck on the lips.

But simple affection had escalated emotional contradictions within her. Jessica didn't know what she wanted, and knew her indecision must be just as confusing to Chris.

First, she shoves him away. The next morning she's at his house with breakfast. A tiny kiss and she runs away. Yes, I'm interested. No, I'm not.

"Damn it all!" One yank and she stumbled backward.

"You okay?" Dan called from the next plot.

Jessica glanced his way. Not only was Dan staring at her, but so were Jackie and William.

"I'm fine. Just lost my balance."

Dan returned to the tomatoes while Jackie and William went back to picking peas. Jessica was grateful for their company, even if she hadn't told them so. Since Bill's death, she'd never had reason to be afraid. But Eddie's arrival changed that. Dan and Jackie hadn't hesitated to come with her to the farm. Nor did they complain when Jessica decided to remain for the week rather than return home each night.

Jackie was sweet enough to thank Jessica for giving her and Dan something to do to keep their minds off each other. Just like her. Not only did she look like an angel with her long blonde hair and clear blue eyes, she acted like one, too. She and Dan were going to make a great couple.

"Look who's here." Jackie grabbed the basket of peas and started toward the truck.

Jessica's heart raced with anticipation. She poked her head through the rows of corn. Her spirits sagged. It was only Meredith. She waved to Dan and Jackie, and walked straight to Jessica who considered hiding in the corn, but it was too late for that. She dusted her hands on her jeans and met Meredith halfway.

"I was just going in for some lemonade. Care to join me?"

Meredith fell in step beside her as they walked to the small farmhouse.

"Where's the baby?" Jessica asked.

"The kids are with Edward and Elaine. Rachel's nursed and has a spare bottle of breast milk on hand just in case. I was on my way to pick up Bobby at the airstrip, then decided to stop by and see how you're doing."

"We've been real busy with the crops. But those damn chickens aren't laying their quota of eggs. If they don't start laying soon, I'll butcher every last one of them."

"Well, you're certainly in the mood for it."

Jessica shot her an ugly glare from the corner of her eyes.

"I wasn't asking about the farm," Meredith said. "I was asking about you."

"I'm fine."

"Then why are you hiding out?"

In the shade of the porch, Jessica spun around. "I am *not* hiding out."

She crossed her arms and arched a brow. "What would you call it?"

"Why are you here? If it's to butt in—"

Meredith laughed. "My goodness, you're grumpy. I've never seen you like this."

"Stop teasing me." Jessica wasn't in the mood for this.

Meredith's smile faded. She pulled a piece of corn husk from Jessica's hair and flicked it to the ground. "I'm sorry, Jess. Bobby and I were just worried about you."

"I'm fine...really. I just have a lot of things on my mind."

"Things like Chris?"

Jessica sighed. Meredith knew her too well. "I'm just a little confused and afraid that's all."

"Why don't you tell that to Chris?"

"I…I couldn't do that."

"Then I'll tell him."

"No… I mean…" She ducked into the house and marched to the kitchen.

Meredith followed. "I know what you mean. I just want you to know Bobby and I are always there to help you."

"I know that." Jessica set glasses on a tray and pulled a pitcher of lemonade from the refrigerator.

"We've gotten to know Chris pretty well since he's been here. He has dinner with us every night. If it matters, I don't think he's the type of man to rush you. Sean and Leia have been spending a lot of time together, and he doesn't rush her. How much different can brothers be?"

When Jessica lifted an eyebrow, Meredith avoided her gaze.

"I guess that wasn't a good example."

"Not when you look at Bobby and Eddie. How can two brothers be more different?"

"Sorry, Jess. I'd better get going. Don't forget, Dan and Jackie have a wedding to plan."

For the first time since Meredith's arrival Jessica smiled. "I won't forget."

She watched Meredith walk to the van, waving when she drove away. Then she hugged herself. If only she could be as decisive about going after her man—like Leia was.

Jessica laughed. *Her* man. She'd already tagged Chris. She wondered how he'd feel about that.

William sidled up to her and cuddled under her arm. "Mom, I don't feel so good."

Jessica felt his forehead, then picked him up. "You need to rest." She kissed his cheek and carried him inside.

*   *   *

Sean sat at the base of the statue next to the lagoon. Since they'd arrived, this spot had become his favorite refuge. No matter how many times he looked at these giant ladies, they never ceased to amaze him. He found peace here. A chance to sort out his feelings about Leia.

They hadn't progressed beyond the bounds of normal friendship, but each time he was near her, he felt a tug in his heart. He enjoyed

39

being around her, her bubbly laughter, the swirl of her golden brown hair in the wind, the sound of her voice.

She wasn't afraid to let the tomboy out. In the blink of an eye she'd jump into a game of softball with the kids or shimmy up a palm tree for a coconut. Yet she could be a lady, too, and a determined businesswoman when called upon to handle a problem for her father's company. At twenty-five, Leia Chamberlain had more self-confidence than most women twice her age.

He wanted her in a way that was hard for him to understand. He wanted her not for her body, but for her mind, her heart, and her soul. It was a strange emotion for him to deal with since there was nothing previous in his life to compare this to.

Sean missed her when she wasn't around. At times he discovered that simply by willing her to come to him, she would appear within a few minutes' time. It was almost like a psychic link between them. And now, as he waited for the other men to arrive for their backpacking trip, Sean wished she was there. Five minutes later, she walked toward him.

"Good morning," she called out with a smile.

"Good morning."

She sat in the niche beside him and stared out at the lagoon. It was quite large, but interrupted by a small peninsula in the center. A bridge built from the peninsula to the eastern edge of the lagoon met a pathway that disappeared up the mountain into the dense foliage. The bridge itself was simple construction, but unique because it was over ten feet above the water level. Steps allowed easy access.

Leia nudged his foot with hers. "I thought you were going backpacking."

"I'm waiting for the others. There's an overgrown path we want to explore."

"Who's going?"

"Mark, Bobby, and your dad."

Leia leaned against the statue. "I love these ladies, don't you?"

"Yeah." He craned his neck to look up at them. "They give me peace of mind. I feel an almost spiritual connection when I sit here."

"That's what Jessica's always saying."

"What did the original islanders tell your dad about them?"

She hugged her knees to her chest. "That the statues needed only people to love. They needed no care and demanded nothing in return. They believed the ladies protected them from harm and evil, and could help you find true love."

"Kind of like a totem." Sean brushed his hand over the surface.

"No, it was more than that. They said the ladies would give them the warning when there was great danger. Then the islanders said when they got the warning, they would go to the sacred place until all danger had passed."

"Where is this sacred place?"

"They never said and we never found it."

"I sure wish I could. I'd like to see it." Sean let his gaze travel up the other statue. Magnificent. "It's easy to understand why the islanders worshiped them."

"I know what you mean." Leia smiled. "I must've been here hundreds of times and they always leave me speechless."

Sean rubbed his palm across the surface once more. "It feels like enamel." He didn't know if it was his imagination or not, but he would swear he felt a tingly warmth from the statue. In his mind he called it the statue's energy. Reluctantly, he let his hand drop. He could sit here all day and not grow bored.

"And as far as we can tell they're one solid piece." She stood and brushed off her backside. "If you look in the eyes, it's almost as if they're looking directly at you."

"I noticed that, too. Jeez, these things are big." Sean pushed himself to his feet. "They would have to have a huge foundation."

"Granite pedestal straight down into the ground for who knows how far." She walked around it slowly. "There's no erosion around the feet either. Which is pretty amazing considering this one is virtually right on the beach. That other one over there doesn't even have any erosion of the rock around it. Now that is really a hard one to figure because... Well, come here, and I'll show you." Leia led him to the other statue on the rocky point.

"Now look...On this side, you've got the very edge of the lagoon. It's starting to get deeper, so there's not too much heavy wave action because the change is gradual. But look on this side." She led him to the other side of the statue, walked to the edge of the bluff, and pointed down over the edge.

"Look how blue it is!"

"And deep and turbulent and swift." As if to confirm her words, a wave rolled in and splashed the side of the bluff, dousing them with spray. "The tide's coming in now so it's pretty rough, but there's no erosion."

"That's kind of hard to believe. That ledge down there must have eroded some." Sean pointed to a two-foot wide shelf about five feet below them. "It looks like there was a path leading to it at one time, but that section of it's gone. Judging from the look of the rocks, I'd say it wasn't too many years ago. If that's not erosion, what would you call it?"

"Our fathers destroyed the path."

"Why?"

"When we were kids we were told never to go on this side without a parent. We did. What do parents know, right? Jackie and I were about six. The boys dared the girls we couldn't walk out on the ledge. You know how kids are. We did it. The tide started coming in and the waves were splashing a few feet below us. We got scared and started to walk back up, but Bill kicked rocks down the pathway so we'd lose our footing. We started crying. Bobby and Dan told him to quit, but he wouldn't. Next thing we knew our dads had snatched us up and took us all home. They destroyed the path so we couldn't go out on the ledge again."

"Boy, it would make me a little nervous to be down there." Since they'd been talking the waves were now almost over the ledge.

Leia stared down. "To this day, Jackie and I still get nervous and scared when we're around rough water. And I absolutely refuse to go out on Dad's boat."

"I can understand why." He looked up at the statue. "You know, from the way this one is situated on this point, it could almost be a lighthouse."

"We thought of that. They even took the boat out one night to check it out, but you can't see it. There's not a physical clue anywhere. Only what the islanders said."

Sean looked toward the peninsula. "Has the bridge always been here?"

"Yes, although we upgraded it structurally."

"What's its function? Maybe it has something to do with the statues."

"I don't think so. As far as we know it's just a shortcut across the lagoon to that path."

They returned to the base of the first statue and sat back down. They were quiet for several minutes, content to watch the waves slap the beach.

At the same moment, they turned to look at each other.

Leia had never been more aware of a man in her life. She searched his blue eyes, and in those depths, she found herself. The wind blew her hair across her face, and as she reached to pull it back, Sean did, too. They froze, their hands locked together. He caressed her cheek, and when his gaze fastened on her slightly parted lips, he brushed his thumb over them.

"I want to kiss you so badly," he whispered.

"Then do," she softly replied.

She closed her eyes as his head dipped nearer, waiting expectantly for his lips to touch hers. He was so close she could feel his breath against her cheek.

"Hey, Sean," Mark shouted. "Where are you?"

The spell was broken. In unison, they pulled back and stood.

"Over here," Sean called.

"Come on. We're ready if you are."

"I'll meet you at the bridge." He gave Leia a half-hearted smile. "Guess I'll see you later."

Leia watched him walked across the wooden bridge with the other men until they disappeared into the woods on the other side of the lagoon. Only then did she trust herself to move, for once Sean was out of sight, her thudding heart returned to a more normal beat.

*   *   *

Sean followed the men off the bridge and into the wooded hillside where trees masked the sounds of the ocean. They walked in silence, their footsteps muted on the leaf-covered trail. Only the island birds chattered above. Sean and Mark took their time, carefully observing their surroundings and noting any animal track or a specific bird they saw. So far the animals avoided them, but Sean knew once he and Mark set up a blind they'd hit pay dirt.

Mark tilted his ear into the breeze. "I hear the waterfall. I don't think the path we discovered the other day is much further."

"Let's stop at the falls for a moment. I want to see if those hummers are still there." Sean turned to the other two men. "When we were here before, there was a congregation of hummingbirds in the hibiscus by the waterfall." He took the lead and detoured down the path to the falls.

From the small mountain above them, a slender waterfall rained down to the canyon floor. Creating a large pool of water, the excess trickled gently into a stream and out of the canyon. The trees shielded the surrounding area, but opened at the top to allow a canopy of sun to warm the rocks.

There, among the hibiscus, ten hummingbirds sucked the nectar, oblivious to their audience. The men watched in silence as the hummers flitted from flower to flower. Then the tiny birds buzzed off in search of other blossoms.

"That was really something." Edward's grin was contagious.

Mark committed the moment to his sketch pad. "Kind of gives you a thrill, doesn't it? Now you know why Sean and I enjoy our work so much."

"It's really beautiful down here." Sean clicked away a few shots on his camera. Another place to find peace…and a bit of torment as well. All he could think about was being alone here with Leia, gliding through the crystal pool.

"Actually, what you're looking at is the old swimming hole." Bobby squatted down and tickled his fingers through the water.

"Really?" The revelation added to Sean's distress.

"Yeah. When we were kids, you'd always find us down here swimming. Every so often we still come down here."

"The water must be pretty cold." Mark tested his assumption with his fingers, then shrugged.

"A little, but it's not too bad on a hot summer day," Bobby said.

"It's getting late." Sean adjusted his backpack strap. "Let's get going." If he stayed there much longer, he'd have to jump in just to make it through the rest of the day.

He followed the others out of the canyon back to their original route. After about five minutes, they came upon the old, overgrown pathway he and Mark wanted to explore.

For the most part the tangle of foliage was easily yanked aside. With each step they took, Sean's excitement grew. From time to time he caught sight of a clearing through the trees. It called him closer, teasing him just enough so they'd keep up a steady pace. And just when he thought they would be rewarded, a clump of dense foliage blocked the way.

Hands splayed on hips, he surveyed the barrier. "This is going to take a bit. We'll take turns. I'll go first."

Sean slipped his machete from its sheath at his waist and hacked at the thick overgrowth. It was tough going. After fifteen minutes he was tempted to join the other men with a cool drink of water under one of the trees behind him.

One more foot.

He raised his machete and sliced through. The clearing opened before him. Success, however, was tainted by a wild pig rooting through the grass. So far it hadn't spied him.

He stepped back. His foot snapped a branch. The pig's head whipped around in his direction. The body followed.

"Jeez," he muttered under his breath.

"It's okay," Mark whispered from behind. "I'm here."

From the corner of his eye Sean saw Mark raise his own machete and move silently toward him. Sean edged back. The pig snorted and pawed the ground. Anger peaked, it charged.

He jumped aside too late. The tusk grazed his thigh, ripping a path through jeans and skin. The near-miss doubled its rage. The pig turned and charged again.

Mark slammed the knife into its back. The pig squealed and fell, taking the weapon with it. Sean jumped forward and jammed the machete deep into its heart to end its misery. Shaking from the ordeal, he and Mark slumped against the nearest tree as Bobby and Edward rushed to them.

Edward skidded to his knees beside him. "My God, son, are you all right?"

Sean nodded as he struggled for a normal breath.

"For a minute, I thought he had you for sure," Mark said.

"Well, he certainly didn't miss." Sean pointed to his upper thigh.

"Good God!" Mark cut away the blood-soaked jeans to use as a compress.

Sean gritted his teeth against the pain.

"Sorry."

"Just do what you have to do."

Mark nodded and pressed the material into the gash.

Sean drew in a sharp breath. This wasn't doing any good. The pain worsened with each second. "Just get me to Chris."

"Soon as the bleeding stops and I can be sure you won't pass out on the way back."

Sean nodded and leaned his head against the tree. Mark was right. The close call rattled his nerves and stole his common sense.

"You two work well together," Edward told them. "A real team. It was as if you could read each other's minds."

Talking was good. It kept him focused on something other than the searing pain. Still, it took a lot of effort to push words out.

"We have signals we've developed over the years to communicate when we're out in the field. We've also tried to plan ahead for emergencies like this one. Besides that...when you've been together as long as we have, you just kind of know when the other guy needs help."

Bobby pulled the machete from the pig's back. "He's a big one. Wonder what made him charge."

"Probably just pissed him off." Mark tied off the bandage. "No one's been here in decades."

"We might as well take him back," Bobby said. "We'll be needing a pig for the wedding party. He can stay in the meat locker until then. Don't worry, we'll be quick. When you're ready, we'll be ready."

Bobby gutted the pig while Edward and Mark cut saplings to use as poles. Then they buried the guts and tied the pig to the poles. By the time they were done, Sean's nerves had settled. He dared a peek under the compress. A gash stared back. The bleeding had subsided, but he knew a trek back to the settlement would start it again.

After tying the compress in place, he pushed himself to his feet and limped over to the clearing for his pack. Cautious in the event the boar had friends with him, Sean scanned the clearing.

He had to blink twice to make sure his eyes weren't playing tricks on him. Ten large caves were carved in the mountain at the opposite side of the clearing. Vines obscured the entrances like the web of a giant spider.

"I think you guys need to see this."

The brush rustled behind him as they hurried forward.

"Wow!" Mark said it for everyone. Grabbing Sean's machete, he dashed across the meadow and cleared one entrance. Slowly, reverently they followed, then stepped inside.

"These are man-made." Edward caressed the dark gray surface. "Anyone got a flashlight?"

Sean pulled his from the backpack and watched Edward disappear into the bowels of the cave.

"There are paintings on the walls," his voice echoed to them. "It's also not as dark as you'd expect it to be in here. Let's get Sean and the pig back home. We can come back later to explore."

Cursing his fate, blessing his luck, and grinning over his discovery, Sean slung his backpack over one shoulder and hobbled down the path. He couldn't wait to share this with Leia.

It was only when he saw the statues when he and the others stepped from the trees that the impact of what he'd found hit him. This was the sacred place. He'd wanted to find it and the ladies let him.

As Sean stared awestruck, he swore he saw their gazes shift his way. A voice touched his soul. *"For those who believe."*

He glanced around to see if any of the other men had heard it. Their steady trek across the bridge said no.

"I believe," he whispered.

A gentle breeze caressed him.

"You okay?" Frowning, Mark started back.

Sean nodded. "Yeah. Just..." He couldn't put the feeling into words. "Just resting a bit."

As they passed the closest statue, the breeze curled around him once more.

"Are you worthy?"

He glanced up and swore he saw the thing smirk.

CHAPTER 7

"Why the long face?"

Chris closed the medical record he was reviewing. Meredith stood in the doorway of his office, baby Rachel bundled securely in the carry pouch in front of her.

"I was just concentrating on this person's medical history."

Meredith's gray eyes crinkled with amusement. "Odd. I've been standing her for five minutes and you never once turned the page. I'd think you were a faster reader than that."

Chris tossed the folder aside. "What's up? Where are Jeff and Amanda?"

"Playing at a friend's house." She eased into the chair across from him. "As for what's up... Well, I was hoping you could tell me. You've been moping around here the last few days. And you weren't the best of company at dinner last night."

"Meredith, I have no idea..." The lift of one of her eyebrows made him stop. "If you *must* know, I was worried about Jessica. She's been at that farm for a week."

"That *is* her job. There's a small house up there. When she has a lot of work to do, she just stays there. If you're worried about Eddie bothering her, she isn't alone. Dan and Jackie are with her."

"Don't they have jobs?" He flicked a paperclip into its bowl.

"School's out for the summer."

"Well, the least she could've done was say goodbye before she left. How much longer is she going to be up there?" Even to his ears, he sounded like a petulant child. It didn't help when Meredith burst out with a laugh.

"Jessica isn't used to having to tell someone where she's going."

"Did she tell you?"

"Well, yes."

"See... I somehow get the impression Jessica went to the farm to get away from me."

Her smile faded.

"It's true, isn't it?" Chris pinched the bridge of his nose between his thumb and forefinger. "She wanted to get away from me."

It was the kiss. He'd jumped the bounds of friendship all for the whim of kissing her. It didn't matter how simple it was. He'd ruined everything. His punishment now was to not even have her around. No smile to brighten the room, no laughter to lighten his mood, no shared confidences. Nothing.

Meredith looked down at Rachel, avoiding his gaze. "Chris, Jessica's been through a lot. She just wants to make sure of herself and her emotions before she gets involved with a man again. She doesn't want to make a mistake or get hurt. Up at the farm, working with her crops, will give her time to get her bearings. Please be patient."

"Do you suppose she'd mind if I went up there?" He had to see her, if only to apologize.

A smile brought her head up. "I think she'd like that. Feel free to use the van."

Before Chris could speak, a man's voice boomed through the dispensary. "Where the hell's the damn doctor?"

Chris darted to the waiting room where Gina and Leia were desperately trying to calm two fathers and two teenagers. The young girl looked up at Chris with bloodshot eyes. Tears spiked her lashes. Grass and leaves clung to her hair. She clutched the edges of her shredded shirt together with quivering hands. Chris guessed her to be no more than fourteen. Even though he had a feeling he knew what had happened, he forced himself to ask.

"What's the problem?"

"What the hell do you think? He raped my little girl." The girl's father shook a chubby finger at the boy.

Chris studied the teenager. He hid behind his parents, eyes wide with fear. He looked like his biggest problem in life should be acne, not being accused of rape. He was barely older than the girl.

"And I'm telling you he didn't do it," the boy's father shouted.

Chris turned to the girl. All this screaming was doing her little good.

"Is this true?" He kept his voice soft, hoping she would realize he was her friend.

"No, sir," she replied through choked sobs.

"I swear I didn't do it," the boy cried.

"They're lying!" the girl's father shouted.

"Do you know who did this to you?" She looked so pathetic Chris longed to hug her and tell her everything would be all right.

The girl shook her head and twisted the edges of her blouse in her fists. "It was a man. But I couldn't see his face. He put something over my head. He was husky and not very tall."

"I'm telling you she's lying to protect him!" her father yelled.

She plucked at his sleeve. "No, Daddy. Please...listen. He stopped the man before...before..." She buried her face in her hands and cried.

Gina wrapped an arm around her.

Chris clasped the boy's shoulder. "You saved her from being hurt, didn't you?"

A single tear slipped down his cheek as he nodded. "We were gonna meet there, you know, to make out. I saw him... He... I hit him with a stick. He ran off. I was too worried... I never saw his face."

Chris patted him on the back. "That doesn't matter. You saved her and that's what counts."

The girl's father snapped his arms over his chest. "So now what?"

"Take your daughter home, seal everything she's wearing in a brown paper bag. The police will want it as evidence. Photograph any injuries of any kind. I'll make the report."

"Don't bother. You can tell Edward Chamberlain we'll be leaving." He stormed from the building, dragging his daughter with them. After a gracious thank you, the boy and his parents left.

Gina stared at the closed door. "We *know* who did it, Chris."

"Yes, but how do we prove it?"

"Bobby is going to be furious when he finds out about this." Meredith hugged the baby. "I don't know how to tell him."

Gina's gaze shifted to the window. "Well, you'd better think of something because here they come. Looks like Sean's been hurt."

A gasp yanked Leia to her feet. She would have run to Sean's side if Chris hadn't pulled her back. "Take it easy. He'll be here soon enough."

She wrung her hands while she watched Sean hobble toward the building. Once he stepped through the door, she sprinted to his side. Seeing his bloodied thigh, she gasped again and yanked his arm over her shoulder.

Chris didn't know what she hoped to do. Sean outweighed her by a good fifty pounds.

"Leia, please." Chris gently peeled her away and helped Sean to the examining table. "What happened?"

"Pig gored me," Sean pushed out through clenched teeth. "Hurts like hell, but you ought to see the caves we found."

"I'm sure I will. Let's have a look." He glanced at the gash in his brother's thigh. "Hmm. Nasty. It's going to hurt for awhile. I'm going to have to put some stitches in it. But you're lucky, just a few more inches up and over, and you'd have been singing soprano. Leia, you'll have to go."

"No." Sean braced himself on his elbows. "She can stay. I want her to stay."

Chris shrugged and went to work.

Every so often Chris caught a glimpse of Leia while he and Gina stitched up Sean. She nibbled her bottom lip, winced when Sean did, and unconsciously rubbed her thigh as if she were the one in pain. Once the last stitch was in place, a sigh released her psychic connection.

Chris straightened and let Gina clean the blood from Sean's leg. "Stay off this the rest of today and tomorrow. Keep it elevated. Mark and I will take you back home."

Leia tsked. "Chris, with you here all day and Mark living with Gina, there's no one to help Sean. He'll need help today, right? You said he had to stay off the leg."

"True. Well, you can stay here, Sean."

She tsked again. "It's so unprivate here."

He propped his hands on his hips. "Well, Leia, what do you suggest?"

She looked from one brother to the next. "I'll stay at your house."

"Leia, I don't think—"

She covered Sean's lips with her fingers. "Don't argue. It makes sense. You'll be comfortable if you don't have to move. I'll sleep in Mark's bedroom. He's obviously not using it." She arched her eyebrows while she waited for a response.

It was an argument Chris had no hope of winning—not when faced with such stalwart determination. "Well, all right. Let's go."

Leia released the breath she'd been holding. Why did men have to be so stubborn? Why did it take them so long to see the sense in what she was suggesting? She was trying to help—if they would simply stay out of the way and let her.

With victory hers, she trailed Sean to Chris's, ready to catch him should he slip from Chris's and Mark's steady hold. At the house, she dashed ahead and yanked the bedcovers down. He crawled into bed with a sigh. She truly felt his exhaustion.

Chris waited until he was settled, then headed for the door. "I'll be back in a little while. Sean, stay off that leg. Once that anesthetic wears off, you'll feel it."

Sean nodded and flopped against the pillows. "This stinks. I hate being stuck in bed." He shoved his elbows under him.

Leia pushed him down. "Chris said to stay off that leg."

An impish grin cut his glower. "You act as though you intend to make me."

"If you don't, I'll tape your chest hairs to the headboard."

He parked his arms behind his head. "You'd attack a helpless, innocent man?"

"You might be somewhat helpless at the moment, but I doubt there's much innocence left in you." She reached across him to fluff the pillows.

Her scent drifted over him, fresh as morning rain and spring flowers, as heady as fine wine.

"You could very well be right about that."

The words, spoken soft against her ear, sent shivers down to her toes. She turned her gaze to his and met his lips.

Sean cradled her in his arms as their tongues swirled in warm synchronicity. With her sigh, he deepened his kiss and let his fingers drift to the buttons on her shirt. When the last one was released, he shoved the material open and gazed at the rise of her breasts.

Leia curved her arm behind her back and released herself from the confining undergarment. Sean dipped forward to capture the treasure. Leia gasped aloud and pulled his head closer as he drew the soft flesh into his mouth.

A throat cleared behind them. Dazed with passion, she looked up to see Chris standing in the bedroom doorway. They yanked her blouse closed, then jerked apart.

"Mind telling me what's going on?" Chris turned his palms outward. "Yes, I know I'm a doctor and I'm supposed to know. I came back to give you some Motrin to help ease the pain." He plomped the bottle on the dresser near the door. "It's a good thing I came back when I did, or I'd have been putting new stitches in it. Damn it, when I said to take it easy and stay off that leg, I meant it."

Sean looked everywhere but at his brother, while Leia struggled to surreptitiously fasten her shirt.

"Now, let me be more specific. *Don't move.* If you two can't deal with that, then I'll send Gina over instead." He paused. "Do we understand each other?"

"Yes," they mumbled.

"Motrin," he repeated, and walked out the door.

Leia darted an embarrassed glance to Sean. How could concern have changed to passion in scant seconds?

"We have to talk." He patted the bed beside him, and when she sat down, laced his fingers through hers. "This thing between us—"

"Frightening...everything's happening so fast...too fast. I..."

He traced the curve of her jaw with his thumb. "I know. It feels right. It feels crazy. And strong. Very, very strong."

"So, how do we handle it? It's hard to know what to do. It's hard to resist." *Much too hard.*

"I don't want a fling with you, Leia."

Her heart thudded in a strange mix of anticipation and uncertainty, yet she wanted nothing more. This *was* too soon too quick.

"I don't know where this is leading, but as strong as this is, I have a feeling it won't die soon. That's why I want to be totally honest with you now—before we make any physical commitments."

Leia gave a single nod. It was all she could do since words could not be forced past the lump in her throat.

Sean pulled in a deep breath. "There's a girl, but she's not my girlfriend. Never was. She says I got her pregnant."

"I don't understand. If she's not your girlfriend..." A frown furrowed her forehead.

"This is where it gets crazy. She said I slept with her one night. All I can say is that I woke up naked in her bed. The night before I was at a party where she was. She was drunk and asked me for a ride. When I took her home, she wouldn't settle down unless I had a drink with her. Next thing I know, it's morning. A month later, she tells me she's pregnant."

"I guess I still don't understand. If you didn't do it—"

"That's just it. I don't know. I'm waiting right now for her baby to be born. Shouldn't be much longer. If the baby isn't mine, then fine."

"And if it is?"

"Now do you see the problem?"

Leia nodded. The child would always be there. And while Sean was willing to accept responsibility for it, Leia could not in good conscience say she was. "It's something that has to be considered."

When Leia made a move to leave, Sean curled his fingers around her wrist and held her in place. "I don't have any right to ask this of you, Leia, but...please stay here with me tonight. I just want to hold you. To talk with you. To have you by my side."

Leia looked into his eyes and knew nothing could make her refuse him. She stretched out beside him and rested her head on his shoulder.

*   *   *

Chris watched the anger build in Bobby's face. The last thing he wanted was to tell him about the attack on the young girl. Unfortunately, he had no choice. Seconds later, the rage burst into a full-blown explosion.

"Damnit! I knew it! I just fu—"

Meredith pressed her fingers to his lips. "Honey, please." She curled her arm around his shoulders in a vain effort to calm him. He shrugged her aside.

"Where's Amanda?"

"The children are playing at the Jensen's," Meredith said.

"Go get them! I want Amanda where I can watch her!"

"But, Bobby—"

"Damnit, Meredith! Do what I tell you!"

Shock at his own behavior sobered him. He raked furrows through his hair and buried his head in his hands. "God, honey, I'm sorry."

"It's okay." She wrapped her arms around him once more. "I know how you feel."

"What can we do, Chris?" Mark paced a groove in the linoleum. "We can't let this happen again."

Castration came to mind. Tar and feathers. Drawn and quartered. "I personally think we should call the police in and give them the evidence. But the Fosters refuse to cooperate."

The screen door creaked open. Edward stepped inside, but moved no further. His lips were drawn in a tight line; his jaw clenched. "I just spoke to the Fosters. Is it true? Was their daughter attacked today?"

If telling Bobby was hard, this was excruciating. "Yes, Edward, it's true," Chris said. "Her boyfriend managed to stop the guy in time."

"Damn it all, we've never had anything like this happen here." His gaze fell to Mark Simpson. "When did this happen?"

Bobby snapped to his feet. "Don't even suggest it, Dad. Mark and Sean were with us all day, remember? And Chris was here."

Edward's gaze flicked to his son. "I wasn't accusing anyone. I just want to get to the bottom of this."

"I'm not so sure you do, Dad. You might find the truth a little hard to take. But keep this in mind... Chris, Sean, and Mark aren't the only ones who just arrived." He draped a protective arm around Meredith and brushed past his father as they walked out the door.

"What was that all about?" Edward turned on Chris. "Is there someone you suspect?"

"Yes, there is." Chris braced himself for making the revelation Edward's oldest son was a rapist.

Without another word, Edward walked away. He was no more ready to hear the truth than Chris was to tell him.

Chris breathed a sigh of relief. He looked down and saw the keys to the van on the desk before him. Meredith hadn't forgotten, but his mood had soured since his initial decision to visit Jessica. He picked up the keys and jiggled them.

"Why not?" He still owed her that apology.

He drove the winding road up to the farm, rehearsing several scenarios of conversation. They all disappeared when he arrived.

Jessica's farm was nestled in a small valley. He guessed it to be twenty acres. Vegetables grew in abundant variety with fruit trees ringing the far end. A small red and white house was perched on the edge near the end of the road. Trees shaded it as well as the hen house a few yards away. He scanned the field, but saw no sign of Jessica, Dan, Jackie, or William.

"Hello, stranger." Dan waved from the house. His lanky frame propped up the porch rail. "Come for a visit?"

"Just thought I'd get a look at the place. It's huge."

"Sure is. Come on in. Jessica's in the shower. Jackie and I are just finishing supper dishes."

Chris stepped inside the cool house. Although sparsely furnished, the living room was bright and inviting. He sat down while Dan returned to his chores.

Jessica stopped short when she walked from the bathroom and found Chris sitting on the couch reading one of her farm journals. Her heart leaped to her throat, and for a moment, all she could hear was the pounding in her ears. Then his blue gaze flicked up to hers. He smiled, and Jessica felt warmth creep to her cheeks.

"You must've badly wanted something to read." She motioned to the magazine.

He tossed the journal to the small, white coffee table. "I just read that article on corn hybrids."

"You read it all?" Her eyes widened. "I wasn't in the shower more than fifteen minutes."

"In medical school, there's a lot of stuff to read. I took a speed reading course to help me keep up. It was one of the best things I could've done. Just thought I'd stop by and see how you're doing."

Jessica sat down next to him, shoving her hands between her knees to hide their shaking. "I'm glad you did."

"How have things been up here?"

"We've been busy. Got some of the legumes processed and dried. Zucchini needs more time. A few more days and we'll have squashes. There'll be a big batch of tomatoes soon, too."

"Sounds pretty hectic to me."

"It is, but I'm gradually getting the crops to grow on a staggering basis so we have something every month, instead of everything all at once. With this climate, it's easy enough to do if you plan right."

"Do you can most of the harvest?"

"I used to, but Bobby and Dan put in cool bins at the general store. Bobby uses some of the excess at his hotel. Now people do their own canning."

"I don't know how you do it. I mean, you know what to grow, how to grow it, and how much to grow. You plant it, you harvest it, you test the soil. It truly amazes me." *Get to the point.*

She beamed a smile his way, chasing away his worries. "Well, thank you. My next project is honeybees. I want to make our own honey for the island. I've got everything I need. There's only one thing stopping me."

"What's that?"

"Fear of being stung."

"Now that I'm here, you don't have to be afraid of being stung."

Was there a hidden meaning in his words? Jessica wanted to believe so. "Now that you're here, maybe I'll take that chance."

Chris's skin tingled. Was she talking about him and her or honeybees? He felt like a kid on his first date. What should he say or do next? Where was his carefully rehearsed apology? Gone. With everything else coherent in his brain.

"Well, I guess I'll be going."

Jessica stood as he did and walked him to the door.

"When will you be home?"

"Sometime tomorrow. Dan and Jackie need time for last minute wedding details."

"Well, then, I'll see you tomorrow."

They paused in the doorway, each waiting for the other to say or do something more.

Jessica popped to her tiptoes and kissed his lips. "Yes, I'll see you then."

Chris smiled and Jessica felt like singing.

"'Bye, Jess."

He whistled as he walked away. It was all he could do to keep from kicking up his heels. She had kissed him! It seemed a perfectly natural thing. Like something they did everyday. It was a good start. He couldn't wait to see her the next day. As he drove off, he waved.

Jessica returned his wave. Her spur-of-the-moment kiss had been right. She was glad she'd done it. She hugged herself to ease her goosebumps.

A cry from the bathroom shattered her euphoria. "Mom, come quick. I'm throwing up."

She stopped her daydreaming and hurried to her son.

*   *   *

The telephone blasted Chris from sweet dreams of Jessica shortly before midnight. He snatched the receiver off the hook, afraid the call would be from another of Eddie's victims. He realized he must have snapped out a greeting, for the caller paused overly long.

"It's only me," Jessica finally said.

Chris tossed the sheet over him, as if she could see through the phone. "Jessica? Is something wrong?"

"William and I got back from the farm about an hour ago. He's really sick. Can you come over and take a look at him?"

"Of course I will. What's the matter with him?" He whipped back the covers and began to dress.

"He's been feeling bad all day. He started throwing up right after you left. I haven't been able to get him to stop. He seemed to be getting worse, so I brought him home."

"Fever?"

"He feels like he's hot, but I haven't taken his temperature because of the vomiting. When I kiss his forehead it feels about one hundred two."

"Well, I've been a doctor long enough to know not to argue with a mother about temperature readings. I'll be right over."

Jessica returned to the bathroom where William rested against the cool bathtub. He hadn't budged since she left him to call Chris. She pulled him to her. Overcome by illness and exhaustion, he leaned into her chest and started to cry.

That's how Chris found them when he walked in.

"Shh," she brushed a kiss against his forehead, "Chris is here now. He can help you feel better."

William looked up when Chris knelt down beside them. "I don't feel good."

"I know, buddy." He cupped his fever-warm cheek. "Don't worry. We'll make you feel better. I know it's scary when you're sick, but try to stop crying. It'll make you feel worse."

"Okay." William sniffled and crawled onto Chris's lap.

"Jessica, let's try to get his pajamas on him first. He'll be more comfortable."

By the time she returned with the pajamas, William was having another bout of the heaves. When he recuperated, they dressed him together.

"Now, William, let your mom hold you while I take your temperature and check you over. Just relax. Everything will be all right."

Jessica watched Chris examine William. His compassion tugged at her heart and brought a smile to her lips. He was a good man. She could see it. She could *feel* it.

Chris studied the thermometer. "Jessica, if I ever run out of thermometers, I'm going to come over here and borrow your lips. You were right—one hundred two. William, where does it hurt most?"

"My side."

"Which side?"

William clutched his right side. "This one."

"It's the hospital for you, little buddy. I'll bet that nasty old appendix has to come out. Jessica, call Bobby and tell him we have to fly out."

The last thing Jessica heard before she hurried out the door was William ask, "Chris, am I going to die?"

Chris chuckled. "No, William, you're not going to die." She glanced over her shoulder in time to see William hug Chris. "I love you, Chris."

"I love you, too. Now just rest. We'll be on our way soon. I'll be with you the whole time."

*   *   *

Bobby twisted along the winding road with a skill usually reserved for race car drivers. Jessica sat on one side of William's stretcher while Chris cared for him on the other. He must have sensed her rising fear, for when they reached the airstrip, he took a moment to whisper, "Calm, Jess. Don't panic. It'll frighten him."

He was right, of course. She took a deep breath and nodded as Chris and Bobby carried the stretcher onto the plane.

Once the plane was airborne, she rushed to William's side. Chris sat on the floor of the plane comforting him with soothing words and a gentle caress across the forehead.

"I love you, Chris."

Chris combed his hair back. "I love you too."

Jessica's heart ached as she saw the tears fill Chris's eyes. She knew he was thinking of Brian. *How could he not?* Even the thought of losing William was enough to drive her crazy. She didn't know how Chris could bear having actually lost his son.

At the hospital, Jessica was left in the waiting room while Chris and the hospital staff wheeled her son away. With a sigh, she sat down, wishing she had let Bobby come along instead of insisting he return home. It was going to be a long, lonely wait. She had been there no more than half an hour when the desk nurse plopped a stack of forms beside her.

"Admissions forms. Fill them out and return them to me at the desk. Make sure you write hard for the carbon."

It was then Jessica realized she had left her purse at home. A request to borrow a pen earned her an irritated "hmph" before the young nurse slammed a pen on the desk.

Before her tongue vented sarcasm, Jessica took the forms back to the waiting room to complete. When they were done, she returned them and the pen to the nurse, resisting the urge to smack them onto the desk.

The nurse snatched both from her and scanned the forms. "That'll be fifteen hundred dollars. It should've been paid before the child was admitted."

Jessica couldn't believe the woman's gall. What had happened to compassion? "You mean you want fifteen hundred dollars right now?"

"That's right." The nurse curled her lip.

"But I don't have it, I left my purse at—"

The nurse snorted. "You charity cases are all alike, always making excuses."

Jessica jammed her fists onto her hips. "Charity case? Lady, I'll have you know I have more money than you could hope to earn in a lifetime at this place. If you don't believe me, you can call the head of your board of directors and ask him. Edward Chamberlain will readily verify my financial status for you. Would you like his number?"

When the young woman didn't answer, Jessica spun around and returned to the waiting room to pace off her anger and frustration. She was still pacing an hour later when Chris returned from surgery. He was in his hospital greens, and for one tiny second, Jessica almost didn't recognize him. When she did, she hurried toward him.

"How is he? Is he okay? Can I see him?"

Chris grasped her shoulders in a gentle hold. "Yes, you can see him, but I doubt he'll know you're there. He's out of the recovery room and in a room with three other children—to keep the lonelies away. He's still groggy from the anesthetic and will probably sleep 'til noon tomorrow."

Jessica tossed her arms around his neck. "Oh, Chris, I'm so glad you were there."

Chris returned her hug, closing his eyes as he memorized the feel of her curves against him. "I'm glad I was, too." He reluctantly set her back from him. "Ready to see that boy of yours?"

Jessica smiled. "Yes."

They crept into William's room where a grandmotherly nurse stood vigil over the boy. She smiled when she saw doctor and mother, then scooted aside to let Jessica near her son.

Chris watched Jessica smooth William's brown hair away from his forehead and brush a kiss against his brow. The tender affection squeezed his heart. It was what he'd always expected from a mother, not the cold indifference Carolyn showed. There was enough love in Jessica for many children, while Carolyn didn't even deserve the child she'd had.

Was that why Brian died? Because God felt Carolyn didn't deserve to have him? Chris shook his head slowly. His parents always said there was a reason for everything that happened, and this was the only explanation he could find that made sense.

With that revelation, Chris felt some of his own guilt lessen. If he was to truly believe, as his mother did, that a person died when it was their time, then Brian would have died at the prescribed time, no matter where Chris was or what he could have done. As for the reason why— maybe the answer was right here before his eyes.

He studied Jessica once more. This was a woman to love, a woman to spend a lifetime with, a woman to raise children with. Both of them had disappointing past marriages to forget, but could they put them aside enough to build a life together? He didn't know, but he was willing to give it a try.

"Jess, we should go. You need your rest, too." He cupped her elbow in a gentle hold.

She nodded, dropped one last kiss to William's forehead, and stood. Chris rested his hand on the small of her back and guided her from the room.

Jessica kept the smile she felt inside. It was a gentle touch from a gentle man. Maybe this time she *could* put her fears aside and try life with a man again.

"I need to stop at the nurse's station and let them know where they can reach me."

Jessica snorted. "Better watch out. She accused me of being a charity case. Do you honestly think she'll believe it when you tell her you're staying in the penthouse at the Bed Chambers Resort? Then try telling her you know the owner. She'll never believe Bobby Chamberlain is your friend."

"Gave you a hard time, did she?" Chris asked with a lift of his brow. "Well, we'll just see about that."

They stopped long enough for Chris to leave his surgical greens in the recovery room laundry. Then they walked up to the nurse. Jessica could swear she saw the woman preen when Chris approached, and for the first time in her life, she felt a tinge of jealousy.

Chris scribbled out an address and phone number, then slid the paper to the nurse. "I'm Dr. Christopher Matthews. William Martin is my patient. This is where I can be reached. Mrs. Martin will be there, too."

Her smile faded. "Thank you, doctor. I'll let the next shift know."

Jessica felt her gaze follow them to the elevator. A glance over her shoulder confirmed the glare she felt piercing her back. It didn't end until the doors began to close and the nurse yanked up the telephone.

*   *   *

Carolyn Matthews hung up her bedside telephone with a triumphant laugh. With a toss of her long black hair, she bounced from bed to do a seductive flamenco around the room. She'd known all she had to do was bide her time and Chris would eventually turn up at one of Honolulu's hospitals. Her patient waiting game, and her offer of money for information, was finally being rewarded. The nurse was generous with her information. Now it would be a simple matter to win back her soon-to-be ex-husband; at least she hoped it would be simple.

She flopped back onto the bed. He was becoming more elusive than ever. Six months before she had hoped grief over losing Brian would have brought them together; instead it caused him to divorce her. She cursed herself then and now for seriously misjudging him. Divorce was certainly something that didn't fit into her lifestyle. She needed the prestige and money that came with being a doctor's wife.

Without that title, she was a pariah among her social groups. Yes, she'd win him over, just like she did when they first met. And when they were back together, she would confess all she had done out of *love* for him. He'd be overcome with emotion and Carolyn would have him in her control once more.

She thought of the little boy she had so callously used as a pawn in her game and smiled. "Yes, my little man, you served me well after all."

Then with conquests and victory on her mind, Carolyn snuggled under her sheets to dream of revenge.

CHAPTER 8

"Wake up, sleepy-head." Meredith invited the day into the room with a jerk of the drapery cord.

Jessica squinted against the sunlight. "When did you get here?"

"A little while ago. We brought you and Chris a change of clothes for the next few days. We have some business to take care of here, so we left the kids with Leia. We'll head back in the morning."

"What about nursing the baby?"

"Shoot, I've got enough breast milk to feed ten babies. I made up some bottles before I left. Rachel's got plenty to see her through until I get back."

"Yeah, but do you think Leia can handle the baby?" Jessica rubbed the sleep from her eyes and sat up, yawning.

"If she can't, it's not for lack of help. Gina and Mark are there to pitch in…Sean, too. I think there's something there."

"Yes, I think so, too." Jessica smiled as she recalled the morning she and Leia took breakfast to Chris's. Her smile faded, and she smoothed the bedspread to avoid Meredith's gaze.

"What do you really think about Chris?"

"I think he's a kind and gentle man, a compassionate doctor, and he'd make a good family man. He loves kids and is great with them. And he's got great legs."

She jerked her head up. "Meredith!" Feigned shock turned to laughter.

"Well, he does. I can't help it. Haven't you seen him in those tennis shorts he wears?"

Yes, she had definitely noticed. When Meredith laughed at her, Jessica leveled a glare in her direction.

"I'm sorry, Jess, but you did ask for my opinion."

"I did. You'd think I'd know better by now." She fluffed the pillows behind her. "I wonder... I wonder what it would be like with him. You know..."

Meredith sat beside her and covered her hand with hers. "Yeah, I know. It's a decision only you can make. Give it a chance. Like I said before, I don't think Chris is the type of man to rush you into doing something you don't want to do."

"It's just that I'm so scared."

Meredith squeezed her hand. "You have every right to be. Just relax and let things happen the way they're supposed to. No one's going to force you...especially Chris. Come on, we'll have breakfast on the lanai. The coffee's already out there."

"I'll be along shortly."

*   *   *

It was a beautiful view from the penthouse patio. *Lanai*, Chris corrected himself. In Hawaii, patios were called lanais. He'd have to get used to that. From this height, the white sands of Waikiki Beach were in clear view as they stretched toward gray-green Diamond Head. Even at this early hour, tourists dotted the area, ready for a day in the sun and a dip in the crystal clear ocean. By noon, all the people would make the sand invisible.

"It's pretty, isn't it?" Jessica slipped into the chair beside him, poured coffee for herself and freshened Chris's cup. "You know, I've lived in these islands almost all my life and I still can't get enough of the view."

"It is beautiful," Chris said. "Did your parents move here?"

"When I was eight, Daddy was transferred to Pearl Harbor."

"A Navy man?"

"Yes. Four years later, he and my older sister were killed in a car accident. My mother went crazy and was put in a hospital on Maui. My grandparents sent me to live in a convent. They're gone now, too. When I was old enough, I left and went to college right here. University of Hawaii. Then to Hurago. I've been there ever since. Wouldn't want to live anywhere else."

"And what about your Mom?"

"She died of a stroke two years ago. It was a blessing in disguise, I guess you'd call it. She had Alzheimer's and really had no inkling about what was going on around her. She was more helpless than a baby."

"I'm sorry."

Jessica offered a smile to reassure him. "Don't be. I feel like I lost my mother the day I lost my Dad and sister. Her death just made it official."

The glass door slid open, and Meredith and Bobby walked out with a platter of waffles.

"Hope you're hungry. Meredith made enough to feed an army." Bobby was about to spear one for himself when the doorbell chimed. With a light-hearted curse, he went to answer it.

There were two things Jessica knew she'd remember for the rest of her life. Chris's unmitigated look of hatred when the door opened, and the Hispanic beauty who walked through that same door. She was dressed in a bright yellow sun dress with a halter top that accentuated her full figure. Her long hair was a mass of black waves that draped around her like a cape. She was model-perfect and by far the most beautiful woman Jessica had ever seen. Jessica felt like a paltry tomboy in comparison.

Chris slammed his napkin to the table with a curse far less tame than the one Bobby had uttered only moments before. He pushed from the table and stomped toward the woman.

*   *   *

A dozen questions ran through Chris's head, all starting with who, what, where, when, and, most importantly…why. His best guess was that Carolyn wanted money.

She oozed with cocktail party charm. "Christopher, darling, how wonderful to see you." She made a move to toss herself into Chris's arms.

He pushed her back, gently but firmly. "Cut the crap. What the hell are you doing here? How the hell did you get up here?"

Carolyn put on her best pout. "I told the clerk I was your wife and was here to see you. He let me up."

Stay calm. Don't let her bait you. "You've got a lot of nerve passing yourself off as my wife. When were you ever a wife to me, Carolyn, in any sense of the word? I don't know how you found out I was here, but I want you gone."

"I know it's a surprise to find me here. I've been doing a lot of thinking the last few months. I think we should give our marriage another try."

Chris tossed back a humorless laugh. "I thought so. You're broke. Now the divorce is almost final, you won't be getting that very generous support check and you'll miss it. Right, Carolyn?"

"No, it isn't that at all. I miss you." She drew a playful circle on his shirt. "I miss your company, and I miss you making love to me."

Chris shoved her hand away. "You really have got balls, Carolyn. I'm surprised you can remember back that far. What was it? Over five years ago? And there've been so many others for you since then."

She ignored the sarcasm and slithered closer. "Christopher, I can understand you're upset. You're still surprised to see me. Please, I beg you, let's give it another try. After all, we did have a child together."

"Get out." He grabbed her by the elbow and pushed her toward the door. "Find someone else to leech off. Don't bother me again."

She jerked free. "Let go of me. I'm quite capable of seeing myself out."

"The only thing you're capable of doing is signing your name to checks and credit card receipts." He whipped open the door. "Goodbye, Carolyn."

With a toss of her hair, she stormed away. Chris quietly shut the door behind her, then took several deep breaths to calm himself.

Bobby came up behind him. "I'm sorry. I didn't know who she was. She shoved her way in when I opened the door. I've already called the desk and told them not to let her up here again."

"It's okay." Chris tried to assure him with a smile he didn't feel. "Let's finish breakfast. I'm anxious to check on William."

He tried another smile when they reached the lanai. "Sorry for the interruption."

"Was that…" Jessica let the question die.

Chris squeezed her hand. "My soon-to-be ex-wife. Or as Sean calls her—the bitch." He waved it away like the pesky insect the subject was. "She's gone. Let's just forget she was even here. In fact, why don't we all go to dinner and a movie tonight. My treat."

Meredith clinked her fork against her glass. "Shopping. New outfit."

"I should've known." Bobby cast a dramatic look heavenward.

Jessica giggled and Chris laughed. This was exactly what he needed. The light-hearted joking between Bobby and Meredith, Jessica's sparkling laugh—already the sour feeling Carolyn gave him was dissipating. Nothing was going to spoil his evening with Jessica.

He wanted to give her the moon, the world—anything to have her smile, that laughter surrounding him.

*   *   *

For Jessica, it was a magical night. Dressed in sea-foam green silk skirt with a matching sleeveless shirt, she felt like a princess on the town. If hard-pressed, she doubted she could tell anyone about the meal or the movie. She never laughed so hard in her life.

All too soon, it was over. The four of them chattered about the movie during the ride back to the hotel. Once there, Bobby and Meredith said their good nights, and she found herself awkwardly alone with Chris.

She paced around the sunken living room of grays and creams, straightening a pillow here, wiping a speck of dust there, until she found the courage to sit beside him. Even then, it took her a few seconds more to relax enough to lean back.

"I had a lovely evening. Thank you."

"It was fun, wasn't it? Want another drink?"

"Oh no…no. I've definitely had enough." She stared down at her hands. "I had a wonderful evening."

He lifted her chin on the pads of his fingers. "And you were the most beautiful woman wherever we went."

He traced her bare arm with the backs of his fingers, from the shoulder to wrist, then back again. The gentle caress left goosebumps on her flesh. When he reached her elbow, Chris slipped his hands to her waist. He pulled her forward, then bent to taste her lips.

Chris's kiss was as simple as it had been before, yet Jessica felt as if her heart would burst from the pounding excitement. Unsure of what to do, she rested her palms on his chest and curled her fingers into his shirt.

He drew her closer and kissed her again. Jessica slowly slid her arms around his neck as she returned his kiss. He kissed her a third time, this time lightly flicking his tongue across her lips. The sensation sent shivers down her spine, and she opened her lips to him.

Chris slid into the warmth of her mouth and caressed her velvety tongue with his own. His breath quickened as Jessica joined him in the oral dance. He sealed their kiss with another smaller one, then pulled back to look at her. Staring into her green eyes, he felt as if he would drown with desire. He wrapped his arms around her and explored her mouth once more, giving her one long, lingering kiss after the other. He could kiss her for a thousand years and never get enough.

Jessica felt light-headed and dizzy. Her pulse raced as if she were running a marathon. She eagerly accepted each kiss he gave, wanting him to never stop.

Chris tried to take his time, but he couldn't remember ever wanting a woman as much as he wanted her. He moved his hands to her rib cage and rubbed her sides with a gentle circle of his thumbs. With each kiss he inched upward. When he reached her breasts, he deepened his kiss and traced the outer circumference.

His touch was like an electric shock. With a gasp, she pulled away and put her hands on his to restrain him.

His forehead furrowed with concern. "Did I hurt you?"

"N…no."

He bent and kissed the nape of her neck with a wispy kiss. "Do you want me to leave?"

"No," she whispered, and closed her eyes as bliss enveloped her.

He rubbed the sides of her breasts once more, even though her hands were still on his. Again his kiss relaxed her and her breath quickened with his. She dusted her hands up his biceps and around his neck. Encouraged, Chris pulled her to his lap. With her cradled in his arms, he molded one kiss after another onto her lips.

His fingers found her buttons and flicked them open to his questing hand. He slipped inside and felt her tense. When no protest left her throat, he danced his thumb over her bra. Her nipple hardened, begging for more attention.

He shoved the shirt away, and watched her face as he slipped one bra strap down and nudged the cup with it. Her eyes were closed, her lips parted as sounds of excitement whispered out. His body throbbed in response. He couldn't wait. He dipped his head to the rounded flesh and took it fully in his mouth.

Jessica gasped for breath. She wanted to tell him to stop, but couldn't get the words out.

Chris ran his hand down the length of her body. Her skirt had inched up to her thighs. He slid his hand between them. Her heat beckoned. He moved his hand to her moist center and touched her tenderly.

"No!" She leaped to her feet and snatched the edges of her shirt closed.

Chris was shocked and hurt by the fear in her eyes. At that moment, all he wanted was to reassure her. He stood and took her into his arms. "I'm sorry, Jess. I just want to be with you."

She shoved him back. "I can't. I just can't."

"I didn't hurt you, did I?" He cupped her cheek.

"No. I just...can't give you what you want."

He bent to kiss her again.

"Don't...please." She turned her head away. "Meredith said you wouldn't rush me."

"Meredith's right. I would never rush you and I'd never hurt you. Please don't be afraid of me." He caught her chin and turned her face to his. "Good night, Jess." He kissed her forehead and walked to his room.

CHAPTER 9

Chris couldn't wait to get home. The days in Honolulu had been lonely and confusing ones after Jessica made every effort to avoid him. The day after their dinner date, she moved to a hotel closer to the hospital to be with William. Her excuse was that she was relieving the nurse and assuring William she was nearby, but Chris knew that was only a ruse.

It wasn't what she said; it was more the way she acted when he came around. She would refuse to meet his gaze, hug herself, and step away, almost as if she were afraid contact with him would contaminate her. It hurt Chris more than he thought possible, but there seemed no rational explanation for her behavior.

He longed to talk it over with someone. But who? Bobby was too close to Jessica to be objective. His father? Chris tossed that idea aside, too. What would his dad think of a long distance plea for help with woman problems? Then there was his friend and former partner—Chris shook his head over that idea. Kevin Samuels would think Chris was crazy for getting involved with another woman so soon after his divorce.

Sean? Chris hesitated on that one. All these years Chris had been the advice giver; maybe it was time for a little role reversal. The idea appealed to him. The more he thought about it, the more anxious he became.

On the return trip to Hurago, while making sure William was comfortable, Chris rehearsed questions to ask his younger brother.

Once William was settled in his own bedroom and Jessica awkwardly showed Chris to the door, Chris hurried home. But Sean wasn't there. With a muttered expletive and a pout any three-year-old could have mimicked, he stomped to the infirmary.

Instead of stopping at his office, he continued on to the lab area to see if Gina had run any tests in his absence. He was surprised to find her seated on a stool with rubber tubing wrapped around her upper arm, trying to draw a vial of blood from her arm. She looked up when she heard him enter. Her eyes were red-rimmed from crying.

Gina thrust the syringe toward him. "Here…you do it. I can't get the angle right."

"Mind telling me what we're doing?" He took it from her.

"I'll tell you, but you aren't going to like it."

"Well?"

She stared at the wall behind him. "I think I'm pregnant."

It was all he could do to keep from dropping the syringe. "What? You told me you couldn't get pregnant. That was why Todd left you."

Gina nodded. "I know. That's what my doctor told me." She flicked tear-filled crystal eyes up at him. "But, Chris, I've missed a period. What else could it be?"

"How late are you?"

"Just a week."

"Don't you think you're panicking a bit early?"

Gina vehemently shook her head. "I'm always on time. Every twenty-eight days since I was twelve. I'm never, never late."

"All right. We'll do a blood serum and see."

When the results came in, Chris paled while Gina mopped up a fresh batch of tears.

"Hell, Gina." He rubbed the tension from his neck.

"I'm sorry, Chris." She sniffled. "I didn't know."

"When I think of all the times we were together—"

She jerked her head up. "I don't know what you're freaking out about. We used condoms."

"Too bad you didn't think to do that now."

"We did." She clenched her fist on the arm of the chair, then sagged. "Mostly. Except for one time up at those caves. He took me on a tour inside. We got caught up in a moment." She hugged her midsection and rocked herself to and fro. "Chris, what am I going to do?"

"It might be nice if you told Mark."

"I can't do that." She covered her face and sobbed.

"Aw, Gina... Come here." Chris wrapped his arms around her. She clung to him until she cried herself out.

"This is how we wound up in bed in the first place." She sniffled against his shoulder.

"Yeah, I know." He gently pushed her back. "You have to tell him."

She shook her head. "No...at least...not yet."

"Why?"

"I love him. I'd like to know he loves me. For me, not because I'm carrying his child. Does that make any sense to you?"

Chris handed her a box of tissues. "But this isn't something you can hide forever."

Gina dabbed her cheeks dry. "I'll tell him, but only when I'm ready, and when I think the time is right. Promise me as my friend and as my doctor..."

He raised his hand. "You don't have to say any more. I won't say a word to anyone. But let me tell you something. I've known Mark Simpson all his life, and if you don't tell him, all hell will break loose."

"I understand." She blew her nose. "But the more time he spends out in the field, the less time I have to find out how he feels about me. He and Sean have been up at those damn caves for a week now. Leia, too. They came down long enough to attend Dan and Jackie's wedding yesterday, then went right back. It's not fair."

"It's his job, Gina." He rubbed the tension from her shoulders. "And you'd better get used to it. If you really love him, it might help if you show you support him."

"How?"

"By going up to those caves and showing a little interest in his work. Change into some messing around clothes and we'll go right now."

Gina's shoulders slumped. "I'll be ready in five minutes."

*   *   *

From her porch, Jessica watched Chris and Gina cross the lagoon bridge and disappear into the woods. She hugged her body to quell the butterflies in her stomach. They came to life every time she looked at Chris lately. All she had to do was close her eyes to relive that night when he had tried to make love to her. Her breath quickened at the mere thought of his hands roaming her body.

"Are you ready to go to the farm?"

The question jerked Jessica from her thoughts. She glanced to the bottom of her porch steps and saw Bobby standing there. "I guess so."

"You guess so? Jess, you left William at our house ten minutes ago. You aren't ready yet?"

"Yeah, I'm ready." She locked her front door and walked to the truck with him. "It's a shame we have to lock our doors now."

"It'd be an even worse shame if you didn't and came home to find Eddie in your house."

Jessica shuddered. "I wish he'd leave."

"We all do. Jessica, what happened the other night between you and Chris? You've been distant. He's been professional. Did you have a fight or something?"

"No, no fight. Nothing went wrong. I just... We were just...kissing and...stuff and—"

"You got scared."

Jessica nodded.

"Maybe it's time you and Chris sat down and had a good, long talk. Tell him exactly what living with Bill was like."

"I couldn't do that, Bobby. I'd be too ashamed."

"You've got nothing to be ashamed about. It wasn't your fault. Honey, if you care for Chris, and Meredith and I think you do, then you're going to have to tell him. If you like, we'll be there with you when you do."

"I'll think about it. That's the best I can do for now." And about the only thing she could think of.

*   *   *

It didn't look like Sean, Mark, and Leia were planning to come home any time soon. A large tent dominated the clearing in front of the caves. A makeshift laundry line was strung between two trees. There was even a small cook fire going with three canvas chairs nearby. A peek inside the tent revealed three sleeping bags neatly arranged side by side, backpacks stowed in the corner.

"Cozy, isn't it?" Gina's tone indicated otherwise.

Chris was beginning to wonder if bringing her up here was such a good idea. "They look like they're enjoying themselves. Anybody here?" he called out.

Leia poked her head out of the last cave. "Hey, guys, look who's here." She lifted a wave to Chris and Gina. Sean and Mark ducked their heads out.

Chris had to laugh; all three were smudged with dirt and sweat. "What're you doing? This doesn't look like wildlife biology to me." He gave Gina a little nudge and walked toward them.

"We're flexing our scientific muscles as amateur archaeologists," Mark said.

"And we think we're doing pretty good." Sean blotted the sweat from his face with a worn pink towel.

"But why?" Chris asked.

"Gina, didn't you tell him?" Before she could answer, Leia went on, "Dan's father arrived shortly after you left. Oh, Chris, you should've seen the wedding yesterday. It was beautiful. The flowers. The ceremony..."

Sean cleared his throat.

She laughed. "Sorry. Anyway, Joe offered Sean and Mark a temporary teaching job this fall semester about this island, the original inhabitants and their culture, the wildlife, the statues."

Sean picked up the story. "He was particularly interested in the discovery of these caves. He spent a few days with us before he left. We were able to clean the foliage away and look inside each one. That was when he made his offer."

"We have to leave the end of August," Mark said. "So we're trying to piece together all we can. Come take a look." He slipped an arm around Gina's shoulders and pulled her inside while Sean and Leia tugged Chris along.

"It's not as dark as I thought it would be," Chris said.

"No, in fact, you can see all the way to the back." Sean pointed to the ceiling, then the walls. "It's nice and cozy inside. The walls are dry. From the paintings on the wall and other indications, we believe these were used as a shelter of some kind. This is the sacred place the islanders spoke of."

"We even spent one night in here ourselves," Mark said. "It's as comfortable as our tent and a lot more secure."

Gina shivered. "What about bugs and wild animals?"

Mark laughed and tucked her against him. "Don't worry. I'd protect you." He dropped a kiss to the tip of her nose.

Chris studied the hieroglyphics on the walls. He had no idea how to begin deciphering them, but it did look like the fledgling archaeologists were correct about it being used as a shelter.

The cave was about ten feet high, twenty feet wide, and over fifty feet deep. Niches in the walls showed the remains of what could have been candles. Several small pits had been dug in the center aisle of the cave and were equally spaced apart. These were lined with rock and contained ashes from campfires.

"Look back here." Leia waved him over to another discovery. Tucked away in the back of the cave were remnants of blankets, grass mats, clay jars, wooden bowls, and baskets. "We found water in the jars and it looks like dried fruit in the baskets."

Chris picked up one of the wooden bowls and examined it. "Fantastic."

"Joe said it's the same kind of bowl the islanders were using when they got here," Sean told him. "Each cave is an exact duplicate of the other. Except in here." He led the way down a narrow passage to a small, secluded room off the main area. Candles situated in the walls lit the room.

"What do you suppose this was for?" Gina glanced around.

Sean, Leia, and Mark smiled, triumphant in their discovery.

Leia lowered her voice. "It's a fertility room. See the goddesses." She pointed to the floor and ceiling. "This is where the islanders went after they were married. Other paintings on the walls in here seem to indicate that whomever consummated their marriage between these goddesses would be blessed with many children."

"Fantastic." Chris gazed around the room in awestruck wonder.

Eyes wide, Gina hugged herself, then focused on Mark. "How much longer are you three going to be here?"

"Oh, about a week more. We're taking pictures, doing tracings and drawings."

"I couldn't stand being out that long without a bath." She rubbed her arms as if to ward off a chill or bugs.

"Oh, we wash everyday in the waterfall," Leia quickly answered.

Gina narrowed her eyes. "Together, I suppose, like all good buddies."

Mark laughed. "Don't be silly. We're gentlemen. We sit with our backs to Leia until she's done."

Leia stared at her. All humor was gone. "I'm hurt you'd think I'm that kind of person, Gina."

"Sorry. I guess I'm just a little tired."

"A cool dip will fix that." Mark wrapped an arm around her waist. "Come on. Just me and you."

Before she could protest, he grabbed her by the hand and led her down the trail to the waterfall. The other three returned to the camp.

"William okay?" Leia asked.

"Fine. Another week of recuperation at home and he'll be as good as new." Chris waved away Leia's offer of water.

"We missed you around here. Too bad you missed that wedding," Sean said. "Leia's right. It was beautiful."

Chris stared absentmindedly into their cold campfire. It wasn't that he hadn't heard them or didn't care, it was simply that Jessica was too much on his mind. Being here, seeing the discoveries, doubled that feeling. He wanted to share the experience with her.

"I need some advice."

Sean's eyes flew open. He splayed his fingers across his chest. "From me? You want advice from me?"

"Yes. Does that surprise you?"

"Shock is more like it, but I'm ready." He scooted closer.

Leia made a move to leave. "Stay." Chris waved her down. "Maybe you can help. It's about Jessica."

Leia stared at the water bottle in her hand. "She's afraid every time you try to love her, isn't she?"

Chris's gaze flicked up. "Yes, and I don't know what I'm doing wrong."

"Probably not a thing. She had a bad marriage. Very bad."

"That's an understatement," Sean said. "Chris, Bill Martin used to beat her."

"Just about everyday," Leia added. "Poor little thing was so scared she didn't know what to do. He threatened to kill her if she ever left him, and she believed him. Besides, she had nowhere else to go. We tried to help her all we could, but they lived up at the farm. We never knew when there was trouble. The day he fell over that cliff, she went straight to the statues. We found her sitting at the base of the farthest one clutching her hands under her chin and thanking them for helping her."

"Good God." He rubbed away an onslaught of tears. Jessica. His sweet, loving Jessica. "How can I make up for that? How could I possibly convince her I'd never hurt her?"

"By talking to her. Tell her how you feel." Sean cupped his knee. "By taking things one step at a time."

Chris nodded. "That's good advice."

"Hey!" Sean clapped his brother on the shoulder. "I learned from the best."

Chris stood. "I'd better go. I'll stop by the waterfall on my way and get Gina. See you both when you get back."

They listened as his footsteps disappeared down the path then Sean reached out to cup Leia's cheek.

"Was it good advice?" he asked her.

Her deep brown eyes searched his. "It has to be since that's what we agreed on."

It was a moment suspended in time, his work-roughened hand against her silky skin. They had decided to take things slowly, each afraid a romantic relationship would only be torn apart by Angela and her baby. But there was a force here stronger than either of them, a force that pulled them closer with each day that passed.

Their lips touched and Sean swore a spark ignited. Their kiss lasted for one long, glorious minute, then they pulled apart and quietly tried to convince themselves there was no magic.

CHAPTER 10

"Looks like someone is waiting to see you."

Jessica's gaze followed Bobby's point. Her stomach did somersaults. Chris sat on the top step of her porch. Bobby pulled the truck to a stop on the road in front of him.

"We're taking the harvest to the store. Want to ride along and help unload?" He jerked his head, inviting him in.

With a smile, Chris walked over and slid onto the seat beside Jessica. She was more than aware of his nearness, and painfully aware of the stench pouring from her body.

"How'd things go at the farm?" Chris's voice was low, seemingly for her alone even though Bobby was right there.

"See for yourself." She waved her hand to the truck bed filled with baskets of lettuce, tomatoes, melons, different varieties of peas, asparagus, and string beans.

Chris smiled, warming her pounding heart. "You've been busy as usual. Maybe I should go with you one day and help."

"Be careful, Chris." Bobby backed up to the door of the small grocery store. "She'll get you there under the pretense of showing you around, and the next thing you know, she's working you like a dog."

Jessica gave him a playful nudge in the ribs. "Oh, you. Quit teasing me and help me unload this stuff."

"See what I mean?" Bobby's eyes were wide with feigned horror. "Woman's a slave driver."

"If she wasn't, we probably wouldn't eat as well as we do." Chris gave her a wink.

It took only a few minutes to unload the truck, and once they were done and the truck back to the community building, the three walked to Bobby's house to get William. Jessica spied Eddie lounging against a palm tree and moved in between Chris and Bobby.

Eddie burst out in a laugh and stepped in front of them. "How cute. Out for a walk with your guard dogs, Jessica?"

"Attack any little girls lately?" Bobby ground out the words through bared teeth.

Chris nudged Bobby forward. They pushed past Eddie and walked on.

"Must get mighty lonely at nights without a man, huh, Jessica?" he called to their backs.

Unbidden, a little squeak left her throat. She would have run if Chris hadn't slipped his arm around her. When she turned to look at him, Chris had to see the fear in her eyes. There was nothing she could do to hide it.

"No one's going to hurt you, honey, I swear it." He brushed his thumb against her cheek, easing her panic, giving her a safe harbor. He dropped a kiss to her lips, then tucked her under his arm and leveled a glare toward Eddie.

"She has a man. One who will do whatever it takes to protect her."

Jessica's heart swelled with love. She stared at Chris in awestruck wonder.

Eddie snickered, ruining the moment. Clutching Chris's arm, she glanced his way.

Eddie looked her up and down, stripping her naked with his leer. "But is one enough?"

Bobby shoved his face within inches of his older brother. "Stay away, or you'll regret it."

He merely grinned and stuck a cigarette in his mouth before sauntering away. Bobby spun around and stomped into his house.

Chris gave her quivering shoulders a squeeze and kissed her temple. "He won't hurt you, Jessica. I swear it. Come on. You've worked hard all day. Time for a treat."

She leaned into him and let him lead the way.

* * *

Jessica couldn't recall when, if ever, she had felt so spoiled. She had intended to cook a nice dinner for Chris and William, but the second they stepped into her house, Chris took over. With William stretched out on the couch, Chris escorted Jessica to an easy chair, propped up her feet, and turned on the television. Thirty minutes later she was enjoying a meal any woman would have craved—broiled chicken breasts with pesto noodles and steamed vegetables.

"Be careful," she called over her shoulder as he washed dishes. "I could get used to this. It was nice…homey."

Chris laughed. "Good. You deserve it."

She wasn't sure about that, considering the mixed signals poor Chris got from her. Maybe tonight she could make up for that.

But once William was tucked into bed, her courage started to fail her. She felt awkward being alone with Chris. She did her best to shake it off and sat beside him on the sofa. *Now what?*

"It's been a busy day. I feel all tense." Jessica rubbed her neck and stretched her lower back, knowing well any tension was due to Chris's presence, not from work.

"Turn around and I'll massage your neck for you."

"You're too good to me." Smiling, she turned her back to him.

Long fingers kneaded her neck and shoulders with gentle precision until Jessica wanted to melt into the cushions. She closed her eyes and let the feeling absorb her. "That does feel good."

"I'd never do anything to hurt you, Jess. I just want you to know that."

A sigh drew her further into contentment. "I know that, but sometimes I just get scared."

"When I think about the way that bastard treated you, I…Well, if he were still around, I'd probably kill him."

Her eyes flashed open. "Who told you?"

"Leia and Sean. I went up to the caves and talked to them."

She didn't know whether to curse their big mouths or bless them from relieving her of the burden of telling him. But even they didn't know the full extent of Bill's abuse. No one did except Meredith. And Jessica knew she would take that secret to the grave rather than tell a soul.

Jessica twisted around to face him, resting her hand on his thigh. The muscle flexed beneath her touch.

"I'm scared, Chris, there's no denying that. But I'm damn tired of being scared. I know you'd never hurt me, but you have to be patient with me. I love being with you and I miss you when you're not around. I love the way you kiss me and hold me and touch me." She slowly brought her lips to his and kissed him, exploring the warmth of his mouth.

Feeling as if his heart would burst, Chris pulled her close and deepened the caress. All too soon it ended. His body pulsed with need.

"Jessica, I care about you. I want to see you smiling and happy. I want to please you so much. But I have to admit I don't know how fast or how slow to move. I don't want to do something that frightens you. I guess what I'm trying to say is—you lead the way and I'll follow. You tell me what you want and I'll do it."

She cocked her head to one side. A smile sparkled her eyes. "Really?"

"Really."

"No matter how odd it might sound?"

"That's right."

The whole room lit up with her smile. "Meredith says it's very romantic to take a bubble bath together. Since I met you, I've often wondered if that's true." Suddenly shy, she averted her eyes.

"We won't know unless we give it a try." He patted her thigh. "You get the bubbles ready, and I'll get that bottle of wine from your fridge."

"Don't come in until I tell you." She hurried to the bathroom before her courage deserted her.

Jessica trembled with anticipation as she tossed William's toys to the far corner of the room. She couldn't begin to guess why she had suggested something so bold, but since she had, nothing was going to hold her back. The thought of lying in a tub of hot water across from Chris made her giddy, breathless, and just a little bit naughty. Even the bottle of chardonnay in her refrigerator was bought weeks ago with this moment in mind.

Nothing she didn't want to happen would happen. Chris had already promised her that. With a pounding heart, she stripped her clothes away and slid into a sea of steaming bubbles under the faucet. After a deep breath, she called to Chris.

He opened the door. The chilled bottle of wine and two glasses were in his hand. With that gentle smile Jessica had grown to love, he locked the door and sat on the floor beside her.

Chris tried his best to concentrate on pouring the wine and not what was hidden beneath those bubbles. But when he handed a glass to her, he couldn't help sneaking a peek at the curve of her breasts where an island of suds rested. It was too tempting to resist. With the back of his index finger he brushed her skin clear.

Jessica shivered. "Aren't you going to join me?"

"Do you have any idea what you're doing to me?" he asked in a husky whisper.

"To be honest...no."

Chris didn't doubt she was telling the truth. "You're killing me," he said with a smile.

"I hope not. I'd have a heck of a time explaining your dead body in my bathroom." A mischievous twinkle lit her green eyes.

Chris chuckled, raised his glass in mock toast, and sipped.

"You're as nervous as I am." The thought delighted her.

"Yes, I am."

She giggled. "I promise I won't bite."

"Well, if you promise..."

Chris kicked off his shoes, peeled off his socks, then stood. Jessica watched him pull his shirt over his head. Her breath caught at the carpet of blond curls which spread across his chest and tapered down to the band of his jeans. There was no sign of a paunch, no love handles, only a broad expanse of smooth muscle and a huge bulge in his pants.

Her gaze darted away. The past had shown her this part of a man was nothing but a weapon, now Chris intended to use it as a tool of love.

Chris paused at the snap of his jeans. He was so hard it hurt, yet he wasn't certain she was really ready for this. "Jess, are you sure you want to do this?"

Her voice came out in a whisper. "Yes."

She nervously drew her finger around the rim of her glass while Chris finished undressing. She couldn't look. Out of the corner of her eye she saw his bare leg reach into the water.

"Holy cow!" Chris jerked his toe out of the water.

Jessica's head snapped up. She focused on his face. "What's wrong?"

"Can you get the water any hotter? I sterilize my instruments in cooler water."

Jessica laughed until tears came to her eyes. "Just get in here."

"Well, I'll try, but it won't be easy." He slid into the tub, complaining with each inch of flesh that was immersed. His antics set Jessica off again.

"Go ahead and laugh. I'll remember this day for the rest of my life—the day you tried to boil me."

Jessica would remember this day, too. Never had she felt more comfortable and at ease with a man. As he settled into the water, he stretched his legs out to either side of her. Jessica draped her legs over his.

For several minutes, they quietly sipped their wine. Jessica kept her eyes from straying to the part of Chris that peeked up through the bubbles. Big as it was, that was hard to do.

Chris watched the flush creep to Jessica's cheeks. Her bashfulness was endearing, but it made him feel like an awkward schoolboy. He longed to love her, to join their bodies together, yet didn't have the first clue where to begin. The last thing he wanted to do was frighten her away again. Being with her and not having her was agony for sure, but it was nothing compared to being without her.

"This is kinda nice. Comfortable. Relaxing." Somehow he had to break this excruciating silence. "I don't think I've taken a bubble bath since I was a little kid."

"You want to make love to me, don't you?" Jessica stared into her wine.

"More than I can say." It was the truth. He couldn't remember ever wanting a woman more than he wanted Jessica. But passion had to take a back seat here.

She set her glass aside and draped her arms on the rim of the tub. "The last few years I've read a lot of romance novels. The authors always make it sound so wonderful, so exciting. For once I'd like to know—" A blush heated her cheeks. She struggled to finish her sentence. "I'd like to know what it feels like to have an orgasm."

There, she'd said it. She half-expected Chris to laugh at her. When he didn't, Jessica wanted to fling her arms around him and tell him how grateful she was.

Chris drained his glass and placed it beside hers. What kind of bastard was Bill Martin? Chris hated the man. Here was a beautiful, caring, intelligent woman who deserved nothing but the best. He respected the courage it took her to share this secret part of herself with him. He laced his fingers through hers and pulled her over his body.

Jessica readily glided to him, but when her stomach pressed against his hardness, every muscle in her body tensed. She jerked back, her eyes wide with fear as memory after memory slammed into her.

"Jessica?"

"I'm scared." The quiver in her voice verified that. "I don't think I can do this."

"Honey, I swear I'd never hurt you. Don't you believe me?"

Jessica nodded, but tears still sprang to her eyes. He clasped her shoulders in a gentle hold and forced her to look at him. "Honey, did Bill…" The thought was too horrible to mention. Somehow Chris had to get it out, to breach this awful wall between them. "…force himself on you?"

A tear slid down her cheek. *Force himself? That was an understatement.* "From the night we got married until the day he died."

Shocked rattled his soul. "My God, Jessica." He gathered her into his arms. This time she didn't jerk away. There was no longer anything hard pressing against her belly. Chris was so disgusted with Bill Martin's abuse, he'd lost it.

"The first time it hurt, but he wouldn't stop. He went crazy and started hitting me. He said I was his wife and it was my duty. Every night he'd start by knocking me around, then making me go to bed with him. It always hurt so bad. I tried to fight him once. It only made matters worse."

Chris squeezed his eyes against tears. He couldn't bear the thought of Jessica living with such horror. No wonder she was afraid—she had every right to be. He cuddled her as she cried into his shoulder, his tears finally spilling onto her head.

"I was so afraid of him, Chris. Too afraid to even leave. Then I found out I was pregnant. I cried so hard. I always wanted babies, lots and lots of babies—a houseful. But not any baby of Bill's. I didn't tell him. I couldn't tell him. When I was four months along, he said I was getting fat and punched me in the stomach. That's when I told him. He was furious—called me every name in the book. Said he'd kill it the minute it came out."

Chris nestled his fingers in her hair. He didn't want to hear any more, but the gates he'd longed to open were shoved wide now and all the horror they guarded poured out.

"Bobby beat the hell out of him when he heard. When I went into labor, I was so afraid Bill would kill my baby. I remember him shouting at me—and the earthquakes.

"After William was born, I lived with Bobby and Meredith. I never even got a say in naming him. Bill filled out the birth certificate information and convinced his father it was what I wanted. He kept calling him little Bill. God, how I hated that. I refused and called him William. I should've known better. I should've known how furious it would make him. I guess being with Bobby and Meredith made me braver.

"When William was six weeks old, the whole island had a picnic on the mesa meadow. Bill demanded I come home. I refused. He called William a bastard and started knocking me around. Dr. Martin came to help me. Bill took a swing at his father, but missed. There was another quake—bigger than the ones before. The edge of the bluff gave way and Bill fell. Dr. Martin tried to catch him, but..."

She looked up at him. Tears spiked her lashes. "Chris, I was never so glad to see someone die in my whole life. He was pure evil...like Eddie. And they found his father, but they never found him. I used to have nightmares about him coming back until I realized how silly I was being."

Chris brushed a kiss against her temple. "Well, honey, I'd say you have a damn fine reason for being afraid. I won't hurt you—not ever. And I'll be damned if I'll ever let anyone else hurt you."

"You mean, you still want me after knowing all of this?" A frown inched her eyebrows together.

"Of course, I do. Now more than ever, I want to show you what it can really be like. But not here. Not in this bathtub. And definitely not tonight. Tonight all I want to do is sleep in your bed with you in my arms."

CHAPTER 11

As he had done every sunrise for a week, Chris slipped from Jessica's bed to dress. And, as always, even though he tried to keep from waking her, Jessica stretched herself awake and gave him a lazy good morning smile. Her eyes grazed over him.

Despite the fact they had not yet made love, she knew his body well. Each night they spent their time exchanging heated kisses, their hands softly exploring the contours of the other's body. She had to know he wanted her. There was no way he could hide that. Yet every night they merely snuggled together and slept. It was killing him, but if that's what it took to make her feel safe, to build their relationship, he'd do it. They'd be together one day. Jessica was well worth waiting for.

"I wish you didn't have to go." She pursed her lips in a pout.

Chris chuckled. "You wish that every morning."

"That's how I feel every morning."

The mattress dipped with his weight as he parked his hands on either side of her. "I'll make a deal with you. As soon as you can explain to William why I'm sleeping with you. Naked–" he added with a playful whisper, and Jessica giggled, "—then I won't leave at the crack of dawn."

"I'll work on it." She ruffled her fingers through his blond hair.

He leaned closer. "Do you suppose you could spare time at the party tonight for a dance with me?"

"Well, now"—she drew circles on his chest—"maybe I could if you could think of an answer for William."

"Bribery. I love it. I'll see what I can do." He dropped a kiss to her lips. "See you later."

Jessica watched until he walked out the door. Normally she curled against his pillow and drifted back to sleep, but there was a lot to do for Dan and Jackie's welcome back party. After a final cat-like stretch, she slipped from bed to start cooking.

* * *

Chris was surprised to find the lights blazing at his house. He didn't think he'd left them on. In fact, he was sure of that since he hadn't had a reason to use them. When he walked into the living room, he found his brother bent over his laptop computer diligently working away.

Sean looked up when he heard the door open. "Hi. I was wondering where you were. Someone sick?"

"Nope." Chris flopped into a nearby chair. "When did you get back?"

"Last night. We wanted to go to the party tonight. Our work was essentially done, so..." He shrugged a shoulder.

"What are you doing up so early?"

Sean looked away. "Well, actually, I never went to sleep."

"Why not? Too much work to do?"

"Well, not exactly." He set the computer aside and leaned back. "Promise you won't laugh?"

"Sure."

Sean scratched the side of his neck. "I couldn't sleep without Leia. I know it sounds silly," he quickly added. "It's not like we've been *sleeping* together. It's just that the last couple of weeks she's been beside me in that tent. Now she's not. I miss her."

Chris couldn't help it—he laughed.

Sean's look screamed of betrayal. "You promised."

"I'm sorry. Do you know what I've been doing the last week? Sleeping with Jessica. Just sleeping."

Sean smiled. "What's the matter with us? This can't be normal."

Chris rested his forearms on his knees. "It's normal when you love someone."

"You love Jessica?"

Chris didn't hesitate. "Yeah, I do. For the first time in my life, I can honestly say I'm in love with someone."

Sean nodded. "I'm beginning to feel the same way about Leia. We have so much in common. Mark accused her once of being a female Sean in disguise. She's everything I've ever wanted in a woman. All I want to do is sweep her away and make love to her all night long. Then I think of Angela—"

"You can't let Angela run your life."

"I know that, but I do have to consider how Angela's baby will affect my life. If that child is mine, you know I'll take the responsibility for it. I guess that's why Leia and I are so cautious. She's just as unsure of this as I am."

"Leia knows?"

Sean looked at him like he was crazy. "Of course, she knows. I wouldn't keep something this important from her. No, that's not quite true. I think I was actually warning her. Maybe I was even trying to scare her away. The funny thing is, once I told her, the last thing I wanted was for her to go away."

Looked like Chris wasn't the only one falling in love. "Why don't you call her and tell her how you feel?"

Sean stared at the telephone. It seemed a simple thing to do. Dial her number, tell her he just about worshiped the ground around her slender feet. He thought about the times at the waterfall when the three of them would bathe. Even though he wasn't supposed to look at her, he couldn't help but sneak sidelong glances her way. Her upturned breasts, the curve of her hips, the golden glow of her skin all urged him to dive back into the water after her. Just imagining the two of them under the fall in each other's arms was almost more than he could take. He wiped his sweaty palms on his trousers. All he had to do was pick up the phone.

He glanced over at Chris. "What did Jessica say when you told her how you feel?"

His brother picked imaginary lint off his shirt, brushed a nonexistent speck from his jeans, checked the time, and scratched his morning beard; anything to avoid looking at Sean.

"You didn't tell her." A wide grin broke his face.

Chris coughed into his fist. "No, I didn't."

"There's the phone." Sean shook his finger toward it.

It was Chris's turn to stare at the object. His feelings were clear, yet he hesitated. Jessica had been through so much heartache in her life— her tragic family circumstances, that disastrous marriage to Bill Martin.

He ground his teeth. Just thinking of the bastard made him want to choke the life out of him. *What would my declaration of love do to Jessica?* Would she crawl back into herself, afraid his next move would be to force himself on her? Isn't that exactly what Bill had done? *"I love you. You're my wife. You'll do what I want or else."*

Chris held a clenched fist on his thigh. All he wanted was to love Jessica, emotionally and physically, but before that could happen she had to know she could trust him. Hadn't that been the whole purpose of his nightly sleep-overs? She had to know by now he wouldn't hurt her.

"All right, I'll tell her." He reached for the telephone. As he laid his hand on the receiver, it blasted out a ring. He and Sean jumped, then laughed.

Chris's smile faded to confusion when he answered the call. Why in the world would Edward want to see him this early in the morning? He posed the same question to Sean. His brother shrugged and went back to his laptop.

*   *   *

Edward opened the door before Chris could knock and led him to the kitchen without a word. Elaine sat at the table, a cup of coffee clutched in her hands. Her eyes were puffy and swollen. She'd been crying for a while. A manila envelope and a pile of papers were spread out before her. Edward sat down beside her. He'd done his share of crying, too.

He motioned Chris to a chair and waved his hand over the papers before him. "We got these reports last night."

"I couldn't believe it." Elaine bit back a sob. She looked like she'd aged twenty years overnight. They both did. "We tried so hard," she said, chin quivering. "All he ever did was throw back our help in our faces. We forgave his disrespect, the money he stole, but this…this… It's just too horrible. Those poor little girls."

Edward circled her shoulders with his arm. Chris longed to give them comfort, but they were so immersed in comforting each other he was afraid to interrupt.

"Did Bobby give you the reports?"

Edward blinked back tears. "No. I sent for them after the girl was attacked. It was the argument with Bobby that made me do it. I was trying to prove to him he was wrong about Eddie. Instead, I got a shock of my own. Chris, if Bobby had a copy of these reports, why in the hell didn't he give them to me?"

He waited until his gaze caught the older man's. "Would you have read them if he had?"

He closed his eyes and sadly shook his head. "I honestly don't know."

"I don't understand." Elaine dabbed away tears. "What made Bobby suspect? How could he have guessed at such a thing?"

"I don't know." A lie, of course, but what good would it do to tell them Eddie and Bill Martin had almost attacked Leia and Jackie all those years ago? They were hurting enough. They didn't need to hear any more. "What's important now is that he be turned over to the police."

"I called them this morning. They said that as soon as we find him, to let them know and they'll send a chopper to pick him up," Edward said.

"What do you mean, 'find him'?" Chris's thoughts raced to Jessica. She was alone. Had he locked the house when he left? He calmed down right away. Yes, he'd locked the door and double-checked it afterward.

Edward drew in a shaky breath. "We haven't seen him since last night. We have no idea where he could've gone."

Fresh tears sprung to Elaine's eyes. "God, I hope he's not hurting someone else."

Chris gave her hand a reassuring pat. "I'll talk to Sean. He and Mark can find Eddie."

Edward offered a weak smile. "That's why we called you. I don't want a panic, and I don't want this turned into a man-hunt. He'll turn up. With everyone on their guard, I don't think he'll have the chance to hurt another girl. I trust your cool head and common sense to pass the word."

Chris's head was anything but cool. He wanted to hunt Eddie down like a...like a... Words weren't enough to describe how he felt. Somehow he forced himself to tell the Chamberlains he'd take care of it, then blindly walked from the house. How could common sense prevail when all he wanted was to see Eddie locked away for life?

*   *   *

Leia stood outside her house for nearly five minutes trying unsuccessfully to deal with the fury inside her. A madman was loose on her island, an island she used to think of as sanctuary. He'd think nothing of attacking another young girl. No matter how careful people were being, Leia knew there were times you just couldn't be careful enough. Eddie was evil, as evil as Bill Martin had been. The friendship between those two could only have been spawned by the Devil himself.

It was the island that had chosen to deal with Bill. Jessica often said the island dealt with true evil, destroying it forever. Leia wanted to believe the island would take care of Eddie, too. She just wasn't willing to leave that up to chance.

Her father had wanted no man hunt. Perhaps that was right. This *was* a family matter. Leia would deal with it on her own. With her purpose firmly set, she marched to Dan and Jackie's house. Using the key they'd left her, she walked inside.

*   *   *

Jessica watched from her kitchen window, wondering why Leia would be in the Daniels's home this time of day. She remembered the countless numbers of plants Jackie owned and realized Leia was probably there to water them all. A few seconds later, she glanced up again to see Leia leaving with Dan's rifle clutched in her hand. Leia looked angry enough to kill. Only minutes before Meredith had phoned about Eddie. *Surely Leia wouldn't...*

"Good heavens!" She tossed her paring knife aside and raced outside. "Leia, what do you think you're doing?"

"Stay out of it, Jess. This is something I have to do." Leia's lips were tight with determination.

Jessica grabbed her arm and jerked her to a stop. "You're acting crazy. I know you're upset. We all are, but this isn't the way to handle it."

Leia faced her, tears pooled in her deep brown eyes. "Jess, you don't understand."

"*I* don't understand?" Jessica gave a humorless laugh. "Leia, I understand better than anyone else on this island. Don't you think I want him gone? Don't you think the idea of him being here scares the living hell out of me?"

"Oh, Jess, I'm so sorry. I forgot." A single tear slipped down her cheek.

"I know. But I never forget. I live with that nightmare almost constantly." She pulled Leia toward her house. "Come inside and have some breakfast with me. Once William wakes up, we can go to the community building to set up for tonight's party. That way maybe we can both forget about this for awhile. Come on. Just me and you."

A nod dropped Leia's head. The fight went out of her. Common sense slipped in. "I'll put this back and be right over."

*   *   *

Chris was certain Bobby's anger matched his own. Neither of them spoke nor did they touch the lunch Meredith put before them.

Chris finally broke the silence. "What about Dan and Jackie?"

"Roger picked them up a few hours ago." Bobby stared at the table. "They should be at home right now getting ready for the party."

91

"The last thing I feel like right now is going to a party." Chris picked at his salad. It was no use. His appetite was gone.

"Yeah. Know exactly how you feel, but it's probably just what I need. Besides if I don't go, you'll wind up with a patient you might not want to treat."

Chris thought about that. He'd taken an oath to help people—all people. Yet how could he justify helping an individual who by all rights should be left to die? It was a difficult decision to make, and he prayed he wouldn't have to do so.

He shoved away from the table and left Bobby's house without a word. Already people gathered at the community building. He wasn't ready to be with anyone, and Jessica sure couldn't see him this way.

He hooked his thumbs in his pockets and wandered to the lagoon. Edward's boat bobbed at anchor in the deeper water. Today was one of the few days Edward hadn't taken it out fishing. The dingy was tied up at the dock waiting to carry someone to the boat. Chris was one of the privileged few who received an open invitation to use it whenever he wished. So far he hadn't taken Edward up on his offer. Now seemed the perfect time to get away.

He jumped into the dingy and cast off. In less time than it took to think about it, he had tied up to the boat and was climbing over the rail. The key was in the ignition as Edward said it was. The engine cranked with the first turn, and he slowly made his way into the ocean. He had no goal in mind, just a lazy tour around the island.

The view from the sea was just as impressive as the one from the air. Chris wished he had his camera along and made a mental note to come back with one.

With the exception of a tiny secluded beach here and there, the island offered no place to land a vessel. It swept directly into the ocean leaving only the gray jagged rocks dotting its shores, discouraging potential invaders. It was almost as if the island itself only allowed access at one point—the lagoon. A great defense advantage for the original islanders.

Chris spotted a high flat bluff a few miles away. A green meadow swept from it into the mountain. A ribbon of road cut through it. This had to be the bluff the Martins fell from.

He stared at the bluff as the boat motored by. The greenness of the meadow gave way to the stark gray rocks at the side of the bluff and below. Survival from a fall was impossible.

Small caves now dotted the coastline as the boat continued by the bluff. Most of the caves were no more than small indentations in the rock—hardly worth anyone's attention. Chris turned instead to the ocean where six porpoises cavorted.

The sun was edging toward the horizon by the time he poked back to anchorage. The sky was an artist's dream of pinks, golds, blues, and purples. It made him want to pick up a brush and give it a try. Unfortunately, the best compliment anyone could make to him about his artistic ability was that he made good stick people.

After tying the dingy to the dock, Chris wandered to the farthest statue to watch the sunset. He was halfway there when he saw Jessica coming toward him. That smile he thought of as just for him brightened her face.

"Would you like some company?" She wrapped her arm around his waist.

"Nope...just you." He draped his arm around her and they walked on.

At the statue, he sat in the niche and nestled her between his legs.

"Look at this." She picked up something from the ground and held it up.

At first Chris thought it was a heart-shaped seashell, but it glowed with an iridescence that hinted otherwise. "It looks like it came from the statue."

Jessica held it up to catch the light. "It would make a pretty necklace."

"Allow me." He tucked it in his shirt pocket and cuddled her to him.

Jessica sighed with contentment. Inch by inch the sun fell until it reached its goal and disappeared. "What a beautiful sunset."

"But not as beautiful as you." He kissed her then, deeply, slowly, his tongue dancing with hers until she was breathless with what he prayed was anticipation.

"I love you, Jessica."

The words were so soft she thought for a moment she had misunderstood.

"All I want to do is take you home and make love to you until the sun comes up again."

She wanted to tell him she loved him. She wanted to tell him to sweep her away. But his lips, those deliciously marauding lips of his, captured hers once more, leaving her words unsaid. There was a noise behind them. Chris reluctantly released her mouth.

Sean scuffed the sand. "Sorry, Chris. I heard Jessica came this way and…"

He wanted to see she was safe. Jessica resisted the urge to jump up and hug him.

She scrambled to her feet. "Come on. We've got a party to put together."

As they reached the community building, she whispered to Chris, "Hopefully, it won't last long. I'll see if Meredith will let William spend the night."

"You wouldn't tease me now, would you?"

"Only if you want me to." She gave him a sassy wink and ducked inside.

The party lasted forever. At least it seemed so to Jessica. Many times she longed to grab Chris by the hand and sneak off. Each dance, each touch was a promise of what was to come. She could hardly bear the wait. Finally, people started to leave.

The hardest part was asking Meredith. Once she agreed, Jessica thanked her, then ducked into the kitchen before anyone could see the flush of her face. As Leia stacked the dishes and pans, Gina wiped down the counters and stove. Jessica would take all the help she could get tonight. Anything to be done and alone with Chris. Even the men worked on cleaning the main room.

"Where's the soap?" Leia searched through the lower cabinets.

"I used the last of it this morning." Jessica whipped open the back door. "I'll get some from my house." *Anything to get done.*

*   *   *

Leia almost called her back, but shoved her worries aside. Jessica was only running next door and right back. She'd be gone less than two minutes. What could happen?

Fear nagged at her. Eddie was out there somewhere waiting. It'd take only a second to grab a victim. A scream could be muffled. Jessica would be gone.

Leia threw the dishrag aside and dashed to the door. No sense alarming anyone else, but she was determined to wait there until Jessica returned. Her gaze followed Jessica's shadowy figure across the grass and into her house. She ticked the seconds off until she heard Jessica's door open again.

*   *   *

Jessica paused with her hand on the door knob, wishing she had sent Chris for the soap. The moonless night smothered her like a heavy blanket. She walked home as fast as her legs could carry her. Even now her heart was ready to race her back to the community building. She looked up to see Leia standing in the doorway like a candle in the window to guide her. A grateful smile quivered on her lips. She pushed away from the door and trotted down the steps.

She'd gone no more than three feet when she felt a presence beside her. Jessica looked over her shoulder. A Cheshire cat smile cut the darkness.

"How nice. Alone at last."

Before she could shout for help, Eddie clamped a hand over her mouth and dragged her against him. Jessica struggled, smashing the bottle of dish soap into his head. Eddie ducked the blows, laughing at her efforts. Jessica kicked his shins, then sank her teeth into his finger. He let out a yelp, shaking pain from his hand.

She was free. Jessica sucked in a breath and let out a blood-curdling scream.

Leia broke into a run, the men close behind her.

"Still got fight in you," Eddie said. "I thought Bill would've beaten that out of you long ago." He lunged for her.

His hands swished the air in front of her. She snatched a fallen palm frond from the ground and lashed out at him. "Son of a bitch! You leave me alone!"

He shielded his face with his arms. "Cut it out, Jessica!"

"What's the matter? Can't take it when a woman fights back? It's only fair when a woman's tied down and can't defend herself?" She sliced the frond across his skin, back and forth.

"I'm warning you."

"Or what?"

Eddie whirled around to face his father. "Dad, I... She—"

Edward backhanded him as hard as he could. Eddie fell into Jessica. Together they tumbled to the ground. He scrambled to his feet, pulling her with him. Jessica raked her nails across his face, then beat the frond against him wherever she could reach, over and over again until all he could do was curl in a ball and take it. An arm of steel snapped around her waist.

"It's okay, honey. We've got him. It's okay." Chris's voice was a sweet caress against her shattered senses, a lifeline against the nightmare she replayed in her mind.

His arms engulfed her in a loving embrace, and Jessica dropped her weapon and fell against him. Tears of relief, fear, and remembrance of a time long ago overwhelmed her.

"What the hell's going on?" Bobby ran up to them. It took only a second for him to piece the events together. Another second later, he hauled Eddie to his feet and smashed a fist into his jaw. Eddie sprawled to the grass.

"I'm going to call the police." Edward jerked his thumb at his eldest son. "Watch him. I want to make sure the law gets him."

"My pleasure." Sean yanked Eddie to his feet, and with Mark's help, hauled him to the community building.

Gina rested her hand on Jessica's back. "Maybe a sedative would help."

Jessica snapped around. "I don't want a sedative. What I want is to not be used as an outlet for a man's revenge."

Chris tensed and pulled away. Jessica whirled around, balling his shirt in her hands.

"Not you, Chris. I could never mean that about you."

Her tears heightened the green of her eyes, and for a moment, Chris could almost imagine himself looking into a sea of sparkling gems. He'd never seen such fear or rage pent up in one person. He was frightened for Jessica, agonized for the pain she was going through, and utterly helpless to know what to do.

"I know, honey." He traced the tracks of her tears with a gentle caress of his thumb. "Please don't be upset with Gina. She was only trying to help. Maybe a glass of wine would help."

She nodded against his chest, then let him lead her back home. When Leia tried to follow, Bobby slipped his arm through his sister's and tugged her back. Chris was on his own and scared to death.

With a flick of his wrist, he flooded the living room with light. Jessica eased onto the sofa.

"I'll get the wine and be right back."

"No." She clutched his arm. "I don't need the wine. I just need to be with you."

He sat on the coffee table before her, taking her hands in his. "Look at you. You're shaking like a leaf. A little wine will help you calm down."

"I'm not shaking." She offered a tiny smile. "You are."

Chris looked at their hands. He couldn't deny it. He was trembling as much as she. "Then we can both use the wine. Humor me."

He retrieved the bottle and glasses and returned before she had the chance to miss him. With great effort, he managed to pour.

"Reminds me of Sean and Leia a few weeks ago." Her laughter was forced.

"Yeah. I guess so." He sat beside her, and gulped the glass down. With elbows on knees he dangled the empty glass in his fingers.

"I've known hate before, Jess. Living with Carolyn taught me that. I remember that incident with Brian's teddy bear. I wanted to kill her then, but not as much as I wanted to kill Eddie tonight. When I heard you scream and saw what was going on, I was never so scared in my life. If Edward hadn't gotten to you first..."

She dragged her arm over his shoulders and kissed his temple.

"I've never felt that strongly about anyone else. I love you, Jess. I love you more than life itself."

Jessica swallowed the emotion welling up in her throat. "Then show me, Chris. Show me what it's like to be truly loved. I want to know. I need to know. Now. Tonight. Every night we lie in bed. You give me those delicious kisses. We touch each other. I know you want me and I know you hold back for me. Don't hold back anymore. Love me the way you want to love me. The way I need to be loved."

Chris stretched out on the sofa, pulling her with him until she was nestled in the cushions beneath him. He had to shove the nightmare away...for her...for both of them.

He combed his fingers through her coppery hair. The fresh-washed scent chased away the demons.

Jessica's breath exhaled in a sigh. She closed her eyes and tilted her head back. He nuzzled his way to her ear, nipping at the soft flesh. Jessica cried out, gathering him close.

"Lights on or off, Jess?"

Green eyes opened to his. "On. I want to see the man making love to me."

"I'd prefer the bedroom. There's more room. And, just in case you wear me out, we'll be comfortable enough to sleep."

Jessica giggled. "Wear you out?"

"That's right." He pushed up and swooped her into his arms. When he finally let her go, it was to place her feet firmly on the bedroom carpet.

Jessica slipped off her shirt and shorts. Her undergarments followed. His eyes devoured the view of creamy flesh. He'd seen her before, but always with the knowledge he had to restrain himself. Now that she was to be his to love as he had longed to do, he took the time to appreciate what he saw.

Peach colored nipples capped full ivory breasts that looked as if they were made to fit in the circle of his hand. The indentation of her tiny waist accentuated her narrow hips.

"You act as if you've never seen me before. Don't I look all right?"

Chris swallowed in a vain effort to ease a throat gone dry. "All right? Jessica, you're the most beautiful woman I've ever seen."

Her eyes dropped to the bulge in his pants. With one hand she reached for his fly button and tugged it open. Then came the slow hiss of his zipper as she pulled it down. She looked up at him as her fingers moved to the waistband of his briefs. He caught her wrist in a tender grip.

"If you touch me now, it'll be all over for me."

Her eyes widened with mischievous delight. "Really?"

"Really."

He gave her a playful nudge that sent her sprawling to the bed. She scooted to the headboard and whipped the covers back, never once taking her eyes from his body as he yanked off his clothing.

Jessica moistened her lips as she drank in the sight of him. This time instead of shy observations, her eyes boldly caressed every inch of him.

His skin was lightly bronzed, the area covered by his swimsuit a pale contrast. There was that soft covering of blond hair across his chest that Jessica loved to curl her fingers through. She followed its downward taper until it ended with his fullness proudly jutting out from a nest of coarse curls.

Jessica couldn't help herself. She had to discover for herself if he felt as hard as he looked.

She knelt before him, mesmerized by the beauty of his body. Her nails raked across his stomach, up through his chest hairs, and down his back. Muscles rippled beneath her touch and Chris's sharp intake of breath followed when she nuzzled her breasts against him.

He let her explore, content in the sensuous feeling of her touch. But when she wrapped a small hand around him and cupped the other between his thighs, it was almost the end for him.

"Honey!" He sucked in a breath, then pushed her away and crawled in bed beside her.

"Would you like to know what you're doing to me?" His fingers dipped between them to the apex of her thighs. There he slipped a gentle caress to her moist warmth.

Jessica fell back with a groan while places never before touched gently were lovingly awakened. His fingers brought sparks of fire she never before imagined. And when his lips circled her breasts, she thought she would surely die from pleasure. He urged her onward with kisses, caresses of hidden places, and tender words, never once giving Jessica a second to doubt she was loved.

When he was certain she could last no longer, he covered her body with his. Their lips locked together, tongues twisted and twined in sensual play. Then he plunged deep within her.

Jessica gasped for air. Her hands fanned out over his back, swooping low to knead his buttocks. They rocked together in that steady rhythm only lovers know. When her time came, Chris watched the frozen cry of ecstasy on her face, reveling in the knowledge he had been the one to give this to her. Then he closed his eyes as a convulsive shudder overtook him. He plunged once, twice, and a third time before collapsing in sated bliss.

Chris caught his breath slowly, as she did, then eased his weight from her and pulled her into the curve of his arm.

"I love you, Chris. I love you so much. You don't know how good it was. I never knew making love could be so wonderful."

He smiled and kissed her forehead. "Neither did I. I want to marry you, Jessica. I want to spend eternity in your arms."

She giggled. "And to have lots and lots of babies?"

He grinned. "A houseful."

"I can't wait. Too bad it takes nine months. We have a lot of catching up to do. Unless—"

"Unless what?"

She traced the laugh line in his cheek. "Maybe we can double up."

"As much as I love you, I doubt I'll be able to get pregnant."

Laughter absorbed her. "No, silly. The fertility caves."

Chris rolled to his back with an exaggerated groan. "I'd forgotten your superstitious streak."

Laughing, she crawled over him. "It's not superstition. It's real. Do you doubt the magic of Hurago? The power of the statues? I don't. They brought me you."

Chris tucked her hair behind her ear. "How can I argue with such logic? The fertility caves it is. But be careful what you ask for, you just might get it."

She hopped from bed. "Grab a blanket and a flashlight and let's go."

"Naked?" He tsked. "Jessica Martin, I'm appalled."

"No, you're Chris." Giddy with love and the happiness the future offered, she couldn't help the pun.

Chris rolled his eyes heavenward. "Let's go before you get any sillier...and bring some candles. If we're going to do this, we're going to do it right."

*   *   *

A circle of candlelight bathed their skin in a warm glow. They knelt before one another, fingers interlaced. Eyes said what their hearts felt—love. A love to last forever. The past problems seemed trivial when held up to the power it represented.

Here they were, naked before each other, nothing to hide, no secrets between them. The sacredness of this room was not lost on them. It pulsed with life from the walls to touch the center of their beings. They were like the islanders who came here so long ago. And like them, they were here to ask for the island's blessing.

They drew closer until their bodies touched. Each kiss lapped at the flames which burned inside, yet to rush seemed sacrilegious. They took their time, touching places already explored and memorizing new ones until every plane, angle, hollow, and curve had been caressed. Only then did they join, rocking together with love's ancient rhythm to reach that wondrous joy which awaited them. Once attained, they drifted back to earthly bounds to soar again until, finally, they were spent.

They dressed among the tender kisses and caresses of after-love, then returned, arm in arm, to the comfort of their bed. One last kiss settled them, spoon fashion. And with Chris's hand on her belly and Jessica's over his, they drifted to sleep to dream of the children hope would bring.

CHAPTER 12

Sean fingered the unopened envelope, afraid to open it, yet afraid not to. It was the long-awaited letter from Angela. It had been well over a month since the birth of her baby. Each day that passed with no word had given Sean hope she'd discovered he wasn't the father. Now this. It was the equivalent of having the wind knocked from your lungs.

He looked up to see Leia staring at the letter, her dark brown eyes wide and troubled. She sat across from him on the edge of Chris's easy chair, her hands clutched on her lap.

"Aren't you going to open it?"

"I'm scared to." There, he'd admitted it. Out loud. Now for the rest of it. He caught Leia's gaze with his own, looking deep into her eyes so there would be no misunderstanding.

"Right now I can hold your hand. I can kiss you when I want. Hold you in my arms while we stretch out on the couch to watch TV. Every night we fall asleep here. And every morning we wake up together. Opening this letter could change all that."

Leia's gaze was steady and unwavering. She'd had a long time to think about this. Months of anxiety. Months of guarding her heart and emotions. Months of telling herself that as hard as she tried, she couldn't keep from loving Sean.

"Nothing will change," she finally said. "Open it."

Sean slipped a finger under the flap.

"Wait!" She jerked his hand away and pointed to another letter on the table between them. "Let's take that to Chris and open your letter in front of him. Maybe with him there bad news will be easier to take."

Anxious to postpone what he felt was inevitable, Sean seized the idea. "Let's go."

They marched to the infirmary like two soldiers on a mission, startling Gina with their abrupt entrance. She jerked up from the book she was reading and hid it between a stack of papers.

"Chris here?" Sean asked.

"Yes, but he's with someone right now. He shouldn't be too much longer. Have a seat and I'll let him know you're here." She ducked into the adjoining room.

"Things must be going pretty good for her and Mark," Sean told Leia.

"Why do you say that?"

"Mark told me Gina's been feeding him so well, he's going to have to go on a diet. Looks like Gina's put on a few pounds herself. I notice it in her..." He gestured across his chest.

Leia laughed and punched his arm. "You would notice that. Sit down."

They sat on the worn vinyl sofa, and saw William on the floor playing with his cars.

"Hey, big guy, how you doin'?" Sean braced his forearms on his knees.

"Okay, I guess."

Sean glanced up at Leia. "I wonder what Gina's reading that's so private she had to hide."

William sat back on his heels to study the layout of his cars. "It's a book about babies."

"Babies?"

"Yeah, there was a picture of a baby on it."

Sean pulled back, mouth agape.

Leia stared into space. "Why the secret?" she whispered. "Do you suppose Mark knows?"

"You know Mark. He'd be too excited to keep it to himself."

"Do we tell him?"

That answer, too, was simple. "It's their business, not ours. We'll have to let them stumble along."

"Like us?"

He pulled her hand into his. "Yeah, like us. I wish Chris would hurry up. I wonder who's in there?"

"Mom's gettin' a check up," William told them.

"Is she sick?" Leia asked.

"Nope. Just gettin' a check up."

*   *   *

Jessica played with the necklace Chris had made for her. She hadn't taken it off since the day he gave it to her four weeks ago. To her, the heart-shaped piece was a sign from the statues that they blessed this love. Jessica couldn't contain her excitement any longer.

"Well? Well?" It was good news. She knew it. The smirk on Chris's face told her so.

A month of watching the calendar. A month of no period. Neither could wait to verify their suspicions. Now, knowing how anxious she was, he was dragging out *the* moment.

In the most professional manner he could muster, Chris studied the lab chit in his hand. If she had known what to look for, she would have snatched it from him.

"Let me see now. We mustn't be too hasty in reading these results."

She smacked his hand. "Stop it. You're not being fair. The woman's supposed to know before the man."

"Not when the man is the most diligent, conscientious, hard-working doctor in these parts."

"Not to mention the *only* doctor. Come on, honey, tell me."

Chris laughed. "Well, for a couple who have been as celibate as we've been this last month—"

"I'd hardly call that celibate."

"Do you want to hear this or not?"

"Go on."

"Sweetheart—," his smile widened. "—we're gonna have a baby."

Jessica squealed and threw herself into his arms. "This is wonderful! So wonderful! Want to feel around and see?"

Chris laughed as he hugged her. "At this stage, I doubt I'd feel much."

"See, I told you doing it between those fertility goddesses would get us pregnant. Maybe next you'll listen to me."

He laughed again. "I promise. Ready to start planning our wedding now?"

"Of course. Especially since we've already had the honeymoon. We'll announce it after William's birthday party tomorrow night. And," she drew her finger down his cheek, "let's wait awhile before we mention the baby."

"All we need now is my final divorce papers and we'll be good to go. Should arrive any day now."

"I'm so happy. Maybe it'll be twins. I've always wanted to have twins."

"When you're a little further along, I'll schedule an ultrasound and we'll just see." He patted her bottom and set her on her feet. ""For now, you take extra good care of yourself while you're working. No pesticides."

Jessica jammed her fists on her hips. "I am an *organic* farmer."

He laughed at the indignation blazing from her eyes. "I should've known. Sorry. Now, to work...for both of us."

After a tender exchange of kisses, he walked her to the waiting room.

William jumped to his feet and hurried to Chris. "Do you still love me?"

Chris knelt before him. "Of course I do."

Tears brimmed in the boy's brown eyes. "But you hollered at me this morning and made me sit in the corner for a long, long time."

"William, you were wrong and deserved it. If you pull something like that again, you'll sit in the corner for an even longer time."

"But you'll still love me?"

"Yes. Give me a hug?"

Reassured, William readily obliged. Then, with a smile, linked his small hand through Jessica's and left with her.

"What was that all about?" Sean asked.

"He was told to do something this morning, lost his temper and took a swing at his mother. So, I punished him," Chris said. "You two here to see me?"

"Yeah. Privately," Sean said.

Chris led them to his office and shut the door. Once they were seated, Sean slid Chris's mail across the desk.

Chris tore open the envelope and smiled. The final barrier was gone. "Good. My divorce from Carolyn is finally finished." He set the papers aside and folded his hands on the desk. "But this isn't something you had to give me in private."

"No, but this is." Sean slid Angela's letter across the desk. "We want you to open it and tell us what it says."

Chris slit the envelope open, much more slowly than he had opened his own, then pulled out the contents.

"It's a letter from her with a birth certificate. Baby girl born one-and-a-half months ago. Father is listed as unknown. She says she wanted to give you the benefit of the doubt. Baby's blood type is O positive. Mother's blood type is O positive—"

"And so is mine," Sean said.

Leia jumped to the edge of her chair, her spine ramrod stiff. "So is mine. It doesn't prove a damn thing. Every member of my family is O positive. Just about everyone I know is O positive. This isn't fair. What right does she have to interfere with two people in love?"

Sean jerked his head up from his thoughts. *Love? Did she really say love?* Those deep brown eyes of hers caught his and in them he saw the truth. Although neither of them had mentioned love, she felt it as much as he did.

Should he call her on it? Make her say it again? Make his own declaration? He looked to Chris for a decision.

Chris gave a single nod, but Sean couldn't say the words aloud.

Leia closed her eyes to squeeze back burning tears. It wasn't fair. She'd hoped this letter would end their suffering, but it only made her feel worse.

I don't want someone else to have Sean's children. I want to be the only one.

And now he knew the extent of her feelings and could only stare at her in dumbstruck silence.

Chris cleared his throat. "You know, most of the time I'm pretty good at minding my own business. But if one of you don't say something soon, I'm butting in."

Leia heard the chair creak and opened her eyes to find Sean standing before her.

"I love you, Leia."

"Oh, Sean, I love you, too." She stepped into the circle of his arms.

"Thank God that's finally out in the open," Chris said. "That has to have been one of the worst kept secrets on this island."

"What do you mean?" they asked.

"It seems as though everyone knew you were in love but the two of you," he said. "Now that you know, I'll bet you'll find this thing with Angela easier to handle."

They sat down, fingers interlaced.

"What happens now?" Sean asked.

"Paternity tests will have to be done. But be prepared. Sometimes it can take a long time."

"Is it something you can do?" Leia asked.

"Under the circumstances, it'd be best if I didn't. We don't want there to ever be any question raised about validity. When Sean and I are in Honolulu tomorrow, arrangements can be made there to do the tests."

Sean nodded. "Sounds good. Thanks." He stood, but Leia remained where she was.

"You go on. I want to talk to Chris about a few things. Female stuff," she added with a smile she didn't feel.

Sean gave her hand a squeeze before leaving. Leia looked up to see Chris questioning her with a slight lift of his eyebrows.

"I…I really didn't want to talk about female stuff."

"Somehow I'm not surprised."

She hesitated. Chris *was* Sean's brother. Could she really depend on him to be objective? Yet, she'd asked to see him. It would look funny if she didn't say something.

"Mom and Dad are really upset," she finally said.

"About what?"

"The Fosters still refuse to talk to the police about what happened. Looks like Eddie's going to get away with it again."

"I heard. But I understand the Los Angeles District Attorney has some charges against him. He's going to be extradited to California to face trial. The evidence is solid and the witnesses are more than willing to testify. He's going to jail this time, hopefully for a long time."

Leia nodded.

"Was that the private thing you wanted to discuss?"

"No." She stared at the floor. "Can I talk to you as a doctor and not as Sean's brother?"

It wasn't an easy thing to do, but he supposed it was something he'd have to get used to, being the only doctor. A complete division between his personal and professional life. *How can you do that with Jessica?* his conscience nagged. Chris smiled.

"What's so funny?"

He dropped the smile and leaned forward. "Nothing. I was thinking of something else. I'll be as objective as I can."

Leia took a deep breath, folding and unfolding her hands on her lap. "You punished William this morning. How did you feel about that? How did Jessica feel? I mean, he's not your son."

He leaned back in his chair. "Let's not use examples and other people or skirt the issue, Leia. Tell me, what's really on your mind?"

Tears she thought were dry, sprang to life. "If this child is Sean's, you know he'll be as much of a father as he can."

"That's true."

"I love him and I'd like to make a commitment to him, but I just don't know if I could handle—"

"The intrusion of a child who wasn't yours?"

Leia nodded and flicked away tears.

"This is a tough one. Only you know what you're capable of dealing with. I think you're wise to weigh your emotions. To take your time. I think Sean's also concerned about pushing another woman's child off on you."

"But isn't there a big difference between dealing with your own child and someone else's? I mean, it must've felt strange for you this morning."

Chris rested his chin on the points of his fingers. "Leia, I wouldn't know if there's a difference."

"But Brian—"

"Wasn't my son. Carolyn got pregnant by someone else. She spent our whole marriage screwing around. I stayed with her and accepted Brian as my own because..." He shrugged a shoulder. "Well, I was a fool, I guess. I could never believe she couldn't love her own son. I was wrong. I cared for him and I loved him. It killed me when he died. As for William..." There wasn't much more he could say without giving away his and Jessica's plans.

"I know I haven't helped much. But I'll tell you this much. If you and Sean really love each other, nothing can change that. Not even Angela's baby. It might not be easy, but the love will be there no matter what."

"So I guess we just have to find out if it's the real thing."

"I guess so."

"But how?"

"Leia, if I knew the answer to that one, I'd be on a mountaintop in Tibet," Chris said. "Nothing's a for-sure thing. Sometimes you just have to jump right in and take your chances."

"Jump in or fall in."

He chuckled. "Take your pick. You coming with us tomorrow?"

Leia pushed to her feet and walked to the door. "Might as well. I wouldn't call it jumping in though—just plodding along."

Outside the infirmary she glanced toward the statues. If she were to believe all Jessica said about the giant ladies, all the answers to her worries could be found there. She gave a humorless chuckle. It was superstition, that was all. But instead of walking away, she allowed her footsteps to carry her to the farthest statue. There she sat at the base and stared out at the ocean as she had seen Jessica do so many times in the past.

CHAPTER 13

Chris had what he hoped was the perfect engagement ring tucked in his pocket. The puppy he and Jessica had picked out was hidden at his house while Sean and Leia fussed over her. Now all he had to do was sneak into Jessica's house without William seeing him. He couldn't wait to see her smile when she saw the ring.

But William was waiting. He all but attacked Chris when he walked through the kitchen door. When he saw Chris's arms were empty, he stepped back.

"Mom said you went to buy me a present. Where is it?"

"I hid it until the party," Chris said with a grin.

"Aw, Chris." He scuffed his feet back to the living room to watch television.

"Where is she?" Jessica whispered.

"With Sean and Leia being coddled and spoiled. They're trying to teach her to come here."

"At three months old?"

"If anyone can, it would be Sean."

When she turned her back to tend to dinner, Chris fumbled for the ring. Bobby and Meredith's crew burst through the door. The moment was lost...for now.

Chris slunk home for the puppy. When he walked in the door, she recognized him, wiggled closer, and presented her tummy for scratching. Chris, Sean, and Leia laughed at her antics, then returned to Jessica's.

William's jaw dropped at first sight. Chris gently placed the pup on the floor before him. "Happy Birthday."

The puppy wiggled and wagged her stubby tail at the sight of her new pal. William scooped her into his arms as she covered his face with puppy kisses.

"Look in her eyes, William, so she knows she truly belongs to you," Sean told him.

William did so and was rewarded with more puppy kisses. "What's her name? What kind of dog is she?"

"She's a cocker spaniel and you have to pick out a name."

William considered this for a minute and announced that her name was Buffy.

"Okay, then Buffy it is. Now let's try something." Sean took the pup from William and walked a few feet away. "Pat the floor with your hand and tell Buffy to come to you. Be excited about it and say 'Come here, Buffy.' If she does it, give her lots of love." Sean put her on the floor and William did as Sean directed. Buffy wagged her tail and bounced over to William.

"She did it, Sean!" He picked her up and hugged her. "Can we teach her more tricks?"

"I'd say that by the time I get back from California, she'll be ready to learn." Sean gave William a large box. "This present is from Leia and me. It's everything you need for Buffy."

Chris pulled him to his lap. "You have to understand that having Buffy is a big responsibility. You have to take care of her. Feed her, take her out to go to the bathroom, make sure she's clean, and give her lots of love. And you must never hit her. If she does something wrong, just scold her, and that will be enough to let her know it was wrong," Chris told him.

"Also, William," Leia added, "Buffy is just a baby. She needs lots of sleep just like a baby."

"I'll take real good care of her. Come on, Buffy, let's open presents." With the other children circled around him, William tore open packages. As he discarded the wrappings of one present, Buffy pounced on the paper.

Once dinner was over and the children occupied with cake and ice cream, Jessica took a few minutes to cuddle Meredith's baby. Thoughts of the life she carried within her filled her with warmth. She glanced up and saw Chris watching her, his love sparkling in the depths of his eyes. She loved him so much she wanted to cry.

As if by some cue, William, with Jeff and Amanda in tow, cornered Chris. Cake-smeared faces looked up at him.

"I want to talk to you man-to-man."

"Of course, William. What is it?" Chris asked.

"Me and Jeff and Amanda have been talkin' and we think you should marry my Mom."

Chris tried his best to keep a straight face. After all, this was important business. "What makes you think she'd make me a good wife?"

"She's pretty." Jeff dusted cake crumbs off his shirt. "And she's a good cook."

"She's a good story-teller." Amanda twirled one of her pigtails between her fingers.

"And a good Mom," William put in.

"Well, those are very important things, but can she add and subtract?" Chris asked.

Amanda jumped up and down. "Yes, yes, and she knows her ABC's."

"Then let me think for minute." Chris rubbed his chin. "I can't marry her, guys."

"Why?" they demanded to know.

"Well, every time she comes back from the farm she's dirty and she smells." Chris sent a wink Jessica's way. She returned a smirk that promised she'd get even.

"I'll make sure she always takes a shower as soon as she gets home from the farm," William told him.

"Well…" Chris scratched his head. "Okay, I'll marry her."

"Yippee," they cheered.

"But now wait a minute." They stopped and stared at him. "What makes you think she would want to marry me?"

Apparently, this was something they hadn't considered and now converged on Jessica.

"Well?" she asked them.

"Aunt Jessica, he's handsome," Amanda said.

Jessica looked at Chris. "He's not bad to look at."

"He's a doctor and he likes kids," William pointed out.

"And you smile all the time when he's around," Jeff said.

William put his hands on his hips. "And besides that. He's been kissing you a lot. And I think he should marry you."

She laughed and handed the baby to Meredith. "Okay then, I guess I will."

"You will?" they asked, eyes wide with excitement.

"Sure, why not?" She smiled and sat on Chris's lap.

"When?" they demanded.

"Let's let her decide after she sees this." Chris pulled the ring box from his pocket and placed it in Jessica's hands.

With shaking fingers she lifted the blue velvet lid. A sharp intake of breath followed.

"Oh, Chris, it's just beautiful!" She slipped the oval diamond ring onto her finger, then moved it around to catch the light. "Just beautiful!"

"So, when's the wedding?" Bobby asked.

"Soon," they replied together.

"We'll be married in the chapel here on the island. And, Bobby, you can treat us to a party at your restaurant," Jessica said.

Bobby rolled his eyes to the ceiling. "I suppose you want a free hotel room, too."

"A suite will do," Chris said.

Bobby's feigned groan earned him a playful smack from Meredith and everyone else's laughter.

Chris felt a tug on his sleeve and looked down to see William standing beside him.

"Chris, can I call you Dad?"

"You sure can."

"When Jackie married Dan her named changed. Will Mom's name change?"

"Yeah."

"What about me? I want to change my name, too. I don't want to be William Robert Martin. I want to be William Robert Matthews."

Chris looked at Jessica. She nodded a response to his unspoken question.

"Okay, William," Chris said. "You can change your name, too."

"Yippee! We'll be one big, happy family!"

Brian's loss hit Chris anew like a knife between the shoulders. *If only he had lived.* He shook the thought aside. There was no point wishing for things that could never be.

* * *

Edward Chamberlain lifted his glass high. "A toast to the happy couple."

Champagne glasses raised in honor of Chris and Jessica. A staccato clink applauded their marriage. Jessica brought the glass to her lips, but didn't drink. Her eyes glowed with the secret she and Chris still kept to themselves. It would be another month or two before they announced her pregnancy. The last week had been a whirlwind of activity with wedding and reception plans to make. Then there was the last minute decision to live in Chris's house instead of Jessica's smaller one. Jessica was glad to finally be taking a break.

She glanced around Bobby's restaurant. Although there was no private room for their party, Bobby and Meredith took great care to ensure it was the intimate gathering Chris and Jessica requested. Only those closest to them were there: Sean and Leia, Edward and Elaine, Mark and Gina, Dan and Jackie, and, of course, Bobby and Meredith. The long table was in a quiet corner and decorated with pastel roses. A dinner of prime rib waited to be served. To Jessica, it couldn't have been more perfect...until she saw Carolyn Matthews walk into the room, her arm draped through that of her date.

Jessica prayed Carolyn wouldn't see them, but it was like she had radar. Her dark-eyed gaze fell directly to their table. She said a few words to her escort, then breezed toward them.

"I knew it was too good to be true," Jessica said to the others. "Carolyn is headed straight for us."

Gina's salad fork clattered to her plate. She fumbled for a drink of water to keep from choking. Chris slowly turned around, leveling an ugly glare at his ex-wife.

"Don't let her bait you," Sean told his brother.

Chris took a deep breath to quell his anger.

"Isn't this nice?" Carolyn clapped her hands. "A party. I'm hurt I wasn't invited."

Chris's tone was calm, but icy. "Carolyn, I'm sure whomever you're with has paid good money to take you out tonight. Why don't you just go back to your table and let him enjoy his meal. It'll be the only thing he enjoys all evening."

Carolyn's smile didn't waver. She sliced through Gina with a glance. "Mark, aren't you sweet to take Chris's cast-offs. Or are the two of you sharing her?"

Mark's head jerked around to Gina. She blinked back tears and stared at her half-eaten salad.

Carolyn covered her mouth in feigned shock. "Oh, shame on me. Did I let the cat out? Here I thought everyone knew Chris and Gina were lovers."

Gina pushed back from the table to flee. It was Leia who gently held her in her seat.

The maitre d' swooped down upon them, arms full of pastel tea roses. "Mrs. Matthews?"

Carolyn spun around. "Yes?"

"These are for you from your husband," he said, presenting the bouquet to her.

Carolyn reached for them with a gasp of pleasure.

Chris grabbed for Carolyn. Jessica pulled him back. She'd had enough.

"Wait just a damn minute." Slamming her napkin to the table, she pushed away and walked up to the maitre d'. "I'm Mrs. Matthews. I believe those roses are for me."

The man looked at his employer for help. When Bobby inclined his head, he smiled and presented the bouquet to Jessica with a flourishing bow.

The rage in Carolyn's face was a present Jessica would never forget; neither was the smug satisfaction of one-up-manship on Chris's.

"Who the hell are you?" Carolyn demanded to know.

Jessica lovingly set the flowers aside, then faced her opponent, hands braced on hips. "I am Jessica Matthews. Chris's wife."

Carolyn gave a nervous laugh. "Since when?"

"Since about six hours ago."

Carolyn blinked as if she'd been slapped. "I don't believe it."

"I don't care if you do or not. He's married to me. I hold his heart which is something you could never do. And I'll go you one better than that. I'm also carrying his child. Something, again, you could never say you did."

Carolyn's face twisted with rage. "You're a pathetic excuse for a woman. I worked hard as his wife for five years." She jabbed her finger into Jessica's chest for emphasis.

Chris sprung to her defense. It wasn't necessary.

She snatched Carolyn's finger and bent it back until the other woman winced. "You were never a wife to Chris or a mother to Brian. How did you work hard? On your back screwing everything in pants?"

Carolyn jerked free. "Why shouldn't I? He couldn't screw a hole in the wall!"

"He screwed you, didn't he?" Jessica said with a smirk.

Carolyn hiked her nose to the air. "I'm surprised you married him. How did you manage to even get it up?"

"Frankly, Carolyn, I have a hell of a time keeping it down. Maybe the problem is you. You know you do have to do more to excite a man than lay there like a bump on a log."

Carolyn's eyes widened in shock.

"Now, Carolyn, I'm only going to tell you this once. You leave Chris and me alone, or I'm going to send you where all good little whores go—straight to dick heaven."

Carolyn turned on her heel and marched back to her date. "I've never been so insulted in my life. Take me to my room immediately."

After casting an apologetic look Chris and Jessica's way, the man did as he was told.

Chris gently pulled Jessica back to her chair. Pride swelled his chest and put the hint of a smile on his lips.

"Dick heaven?" Bobby laughed at the flush which crept to Jessica's cheeks.

"Forget that." Meredith waved her hand to brush the comment aside. "You're pregnant? You're going to have a baby?"

Jessica closed her eyes, shaking her head at her own carelessness.

"Yes." Chris gave Jessica's fingers a loving squeeze, then laughed when the ladies squealed with delight. Only Gina remained quiet.

"Why didn't you say something?" Leia asked.

Jessica looked up. "We didn't feel it was appropriate yet. We were saving it for later."

"This is all very sweet." Sarcasm dripped from Mark's lips. The coldness in his eyes never once strayed from Gina. "But I want some answers *now*."

"It was a long time ago, Mark," Chris calmly replied. "Does it really matter?"

Mark glared at Gina.

"You're being stupid," Leia told him. "If their affair was all that hot and heavy, why has Gina been with you since the day you arrived? Why is she living with you? Why is Chris married to Jessica?"

Mark wasn't swayed. "Then why did he go to Hurago in the first place?"

Dan Daniels cleared his throat. "I believe we needed a doctor, remember?"

Mark's anger faded. "It still would've been nice to know."

"Good idea." Sean leaned toward him. "Why don't you give her a list of all your old girlfriends and she can—"

Mark held up his hands. "I get your point. I was being a jerk. I'm sorry. Am I forgiven?"

Gina dabbed at her tears and nodded, accepting Mark's kiss to her cheek. When her gaze clicked up, Chris gave an imperceptible jerk of his head, reminding her of the secret she had to share with Mark. She forced a smiled and laced her fingers through Mark's, ignoring Chris's advice.

CHAPTER 14

Carolyn slammed her hotel door behind her guest as hard as she could. "Where the hell have you been? I've been waiting here for hours."

Carlton Evans stared at her in disbelief before mumbling his response. "It took me a while to get the information you wanted. You said to be discreet."

She snatched a tiny notebook from his hand and read. Her forehead furrowed as she flipped through the pages.

A sneer lifted her lip. "A widow with a child. How sad. Such a tragic accident. But how fortunate she was left with so much money to ease her pain and suffering."

She snapped the pad closed and slipped it into her purse. She smiled at Carlton. The man stepped back.

"I have all sorts of ideas. We're going to have great fun." Hands clasped, she paced a circuit to and fro.

He waved his hands before him. "Keep me out of it, Carolyn. I've had it. You're crazy. I don't want anything more to do with you."

Her eyes narrowed to slits. "Oh, you'll do what I want all right. Unless you want me to make a little phone call to that adoring wife of yours."

"You wouldn't dare."

"By the time I'm through, you'll be finished. You play with me or you don't play at all. We're finished when I say we're finished. Do you understand me?" she asked through clenched teeth.

Carlton met her glare with one of his own. "Yeah, I understand."

*   *   *

The telephone blasted Chris and Jessica from a sleep they had drifted into only minutes before. Jessica grappled for the nuisance, muttering a sleepy hello once the receiver was nestled against her cheek. A man's voice hissed out her name in a long whisper. Her eyes flashed open.

"Who is this? What to you want?" Jessica bolted upright.

Chris clicked on the light. "What's going on?"

The voice went on. "Don't tell me you don't remember me? Your long-lost husband? Gone swimming lately? How about diving? Off a cliff maybe?"

She tossed the phone away and clutched the sheet around her trembling body.

Chris snatched up the phone. "Who the hell is this?" There was a click, then the dial tone. He slammed the receiver into its cradle.

"Jessica, honey, who was it? What did they say?" When she wouldn't answer, he grabbed her shoulders and gave her a little shake. "Honey, answer me. You're pale, quivering, and scaring me to death. Who was it?"

"It...was...Bill." Fear-widened eyes focused on the phone.

"What?"

"Bill... It was—"

"You know that's not possible." He caught her chin and forced her to look at him. "Honey, I saw that cliff. It's just not possible."

A loud rattle drifted from the adjoining room of the suite. Jessica huddled further into the bed. Chris jerked on his trousers and stomped to the outer room, startling a young busboy with a delivery cart.

"What the hell is this?" Chris motioned to the covered dishes.

The young man shrunk back. "I was told to bring it up. To use the pass key and not disturb you."

Chris lifted a lid. A pile of soggy seaweed stared back at him. "Who ordered this?"

With a shaking hand, the busboy gave him a card. The only words written on it were, "Love, Bill." Chris slapped the note onto the serving cart.

"Someone had to pay for this!"

"Sir, I don't know. I only delivered it."

Chris jerked his arm toward the door. "Get out and take this with you."

"Yes, sir."

As he wheeled the cart away, the telephone rang again.

"Don't touch it, Jessica. Let it ring."

"Sir," the busboy called to him.

Chris looked up. Just outside the doorway were several bouquets of dead flowers. The indentation of wet footprints marked the carpet.

"Make it stop," Jessica screamed as the telephone bleated out one ring after the other.

He ran back to the bedroom. She was bundled into the farthest corner of the room, her hands pressed to her ears to block out the sounds. Chris grabbed the receiver. The whispered hiss of her name drifted to him. He slammed the phone down, then called Bobby.

"Get down here right away. We're being terrorized."

He didn't wait for a reply. After hanging up, he wrapped Jessica in the haven of his arms. She leaned into the welcome comfort, yet couldn't bring herself to loosen her hold on her blanket. When he dared a glance down, she clutched her necklace in one hand.

Footsteps padded across the carpet seconds before Bobby, Sean, and Mark appeared in the bedroom. Meredith was close behind.

"What the hell's going on?" Bobby asked.

"You saw the other room?" Chris asked.

"Yeah."

"Good. Have that busboy get rid of all that. When it's gone, Meredith, get Jessica out of here. We've gotten phone calls, too."

"I don't understand." Jessica trembled from the shock.

"Yeah, well I do," Sean said.

"Who? What?" Meredith asked.

Chris, Sean, and Mark answered together. "Carolyn."

"But why?" Jessica asked.

"Because she's crazy." Chris helped Jessica to her feet. "You go with Meredith and Bobby. Sean, Mark, and I are going to see if we can find Carolyn and have a little talk with her."

Jessica dug her fingers into his arm. "Don't. Just let it go. We'll go home tomorrow and she won't be able to bother us. Nothing can hurt us there."

The phone began another chorus of rings. This time Meredith picked it up. She listened for a few seconds, then flung the receiver to its cradle. She hugged herself to hide her trembling, but each hyperventilated breath told how frightened she was.

"Meredith?" Bobby gently called.

Her gray eyes shimmered with unshed tears. "He said…he said he's not as dead as we'd like to believe. My God, Bobby—"

He was by her side in one stride. He peeled her hands away from her body, kissed them, and pulled them around his waist. "You know that's not true, Meredith. We both know that."

"How the hell do we know?" Jessica screamed. "There was never a body!" She spun around to Chris. "Dr. Martin landed on the rocks, but Bill was gone. It was like he vanished and now he's come back."

"Jessica, that's stupid. Why wait all these years to come back? Why would he sit by and let you inherit his father's money?"

Again a ring cut the air. Sean yanked it off the hook and hung up without listening. "This is ridiculous. There's only one way to stop this." He called the switchboard. "Don't patch any more calls to this room."

There was a moment's hesitation before the operator replied, "Sir, I haven't received a call all night."

Sean's eyebrows knitted together. *If no calls had come through the switchboard…* "Is there a Carolyn Matthews staying here?"

"I don't show anyone by that name, sir."

"Try Delgado. She's Hispanic, medium height, a body to die for, long black hair. Acts like the world owes her a favor."

There was a snicker on the other end of the line. "We know her well. She's in Room 1512."

Sean thanked her and faced the others. "She's two floors below us."

Chris's jaw tightened. "Then she's about to get a visitor."

*   *   *

"I don't need a bodyguard." Barking at Sean and Mark was useless. They still strode down the hall with him to Carolyn's room.

"If it helps, think of us as witnesses," Mark said.

Chris snorted and rapped on Carolyn's door. It opened immediately. If the man before him was shocked to see them, he hid it well. It was only after Chris demanded to see Carolyn that he started to fidget. His gaze shifted everywhere but to their faces.

"She stepped out."

Sean lifted one eyebrow. "To get more play toys?"

"Mind if we come in?" Chris pushed his way into the room without waiting for an answer. A cursory search revealed Carolyn wasn't in the room. He stared down at the man once more. "I know you. Evans, isn't it? Podiatry?"

He gave a single nod.

"Well, doctor, I can't imagine why you'd get mixed up with Carolyn. Or why you'd help her pull this little stunt of hers. But let me tell you something. My wife is pregnant. This person you and Carolyn are haunting her with is a man who raped and abused her. You can imagine how emotionally upset this makes her. If anything happens to her or that baby, I'm going to haunt *you*." Chris jabbed a finger before Evans's face. "You two leave my wife alone or else."

"Or else what?" Carolyn spit out from the doorway.

Sean and Mark spun around. Chris continued to glare at Evans. "Keep it up and you'll find out."

He turned on his heel and followed Sean and Mark past Carolyn.

"A baby, huh?" she said to their backs. "Cute. Tell me, Chris, is it yours, or did someone get in before you...again?"

Chris balled his fist. The effort to keep calm shook his arm.

Sean watched the pent-up rage color his brother's face. A part of him was ready to hold Carolyn while Chris beat her senseless. The rational side of him knew violence never solved problems.

"Chris?"

Staring ahead, Chris muttered, "It's okay."

"Then let's go." Mark herded them down the hall.

Carolyn's witchy cackle followed them to the elevator. Once the doors closed, Chris unleashed his fury. With a roar, he smashed his hand against the wall, cracking the paneling. He jumped back with a curse, shaking the pain from his hand. "Son of a bitch! Son of a bitch!"

Mark shook his head. "Not one of your brighter moves. You probably broke it."

"I didn't break it," Chris snapped.

He shrugged Chris's anger aside. "You're the doctor. You oughta know."

Sean punched the lobby button. "I don't know about you two, but I could use a drink. Besides, I don't think Jessica needs to see you like this."

He knew Chris wouldn't dispute that. After the evening Jessica had just had, a furious husband was not something she needed to deal with.

Chris cradled his injured hand to his chest. "Just lead the way."

*   *   *

Jessica studied Chris's face. Even as he slept, he frowned. She hated to wake him since he'd just stumbled to bed a few hours ago. He said nothing about where he'd been. He didn't have to—the smell of alcohol said it for him. It certainly wasn't the wedding night they'd planned, thanks to Carolyn.

A part of her wanted to blame Chris for not being with her last night. She could have used his strength to bolster her own. In retrospect, though, she knew he was furious. Anger was the last thing Jessica needed to deal with the night before. So it was probably better this way—each dealing with the torment in a personal way without dragging the other one down, too.

For herself, Jessica was embarrassed. Caught off guard, she'd overreacted. It simply wasn't possible for Bill to be alive. *A little proof wouldn't hurt.*

She shook the thought away and gently nudged Chris's shoulder. "Wake up."

His eyes opened to slits.

"The police are here. They want to talk to you, Sean, and Mark."

"About what?" His voice was nothing more than a scratchy croak.

"They didn't say."

Chris tossed back the covers. The stench of alcohol swirled around him. With a groan, he buried his head in his hands.

"Yeah, I think that's what Sean and Mark are saying now, too."

He looked at Jessica through pain-shrouded eyes as she handed him his clothes.

"They're a little sandy."

Puzzled, he frowned. "Oh, yeah, we went to the beach after the bar closed."

"And had a few more drinks, I suppose. It's a wonder you managed to find your way back here. That's probably why the police are here. They got a report of three drunks on the beach and followed the trail of beer bottles back here."

"It was vodka." He struggled into his pants and fell back.

Jessica had to laugh.

"I feel bad enough," he said. "Please don't pick on a defenseless man."

"Don't expect sympathy from me." She held up her hands. "You're old enough to know better. What happened to your hand?"

Chris glanced down. The knuckles of his right hand were scraped. The hand itself was discolored and swollen.

"I did something stupid." He shrugged into his shirt. "It'll be all right. It's just a little sprain. Let's see what these guys want." Chris paused at the bathroom long enough to brush the bad taste from his mouth and pop a couple of aspirin, then joined the others in the living room.

Sean and Mark sat before the officers, clutching cups of black coffee in their hands. Leia and Gina hovered nearby with Bobby and Meredith. As Chris sat beside his brother, Jessica placed a welcome cup of coffee in his hands.

The senior officer stood. "Where were the three of you last night?"

"When? Where? And...why?" Mark asked.

"Just answer the question."

Mark focused bleary eyes on the man. "In case it isn't apparent to you, we were out getting drunk."

The officer cut a glance toward Chris. "Sir, what happened to your hand?"

"Get to the point and tell us what you're here for." His eyes never strayed from those of the police officer. It was the officer who finally broke contact.

"I understand Carolyn Matthews is your ex-wife?"

Jessica threw her hands in the air. *Carolyn...again.* "Now what? Doesn't that woman ever give up?"

The policeman ignored her. "Last night someone entered her hotel room and brutally attacked her. She claims it was the three of you."

Jessica stared at the trio on the couch. None seemed fazed by the accusation. Chris still nonchalantly sipped his coffee.

"We went to her room at around midnight. She wasn't there. I told her boyfriend I wanted them to stop harassing my wife. As we were leaving, Carolyn returned. Words were exchanged...very briefly...and we left."

"And you came here?"

"No," Sean said. "We went down to the bar for a few drinks. We left when it closed at two. The bartender can vouch for us. From there, we bought a bottle of vodka and went down to the beach to drink it."

Leia sat on the arm near Sean. "They got back at four. I waited up for them."

"I see." He chewed on the end of his pen. "Did anyone see you at the beach?"

Chris rested his head on the back of the couch.

Jessica wrapped her arms around her midriff. This was all too much. Didn't he realize what was happening here? Or didn't he care?

"And I suppose that's when Carolyn was attacked," Chris finally said.

The officer nodded.

"Then what took her so long to report it?" Gina jammed her hands on her hips. "It's nine o'clock."

"She was emotionally distraught."

Her laugh held no humor. "I'll bet. She probably hired someone to rough her up just so she could blame Mark, Chris, and Sean."

Jessica gasped. "Gina, that's a horrible thing to say."

"And something she's perfectly capable of doing. You don't know her, Jessica. She's a first class bitch. She's probably sitting in her room right now eating a box of chocolates."

"No, ma'am, she's in the hospital," the officer said.

"And where is her boyfriend?" Chris asked.

"He's the one who found her."

"Interesting." Chris took a swig of coffee. "If you're going to charge us, do it so we can call a lawyer. If you're not, please leave."

The man snapped his notebook closed. "No charges at this time. We'll be in touch." He gestured to his partner and the two left.

Sean set his mug on the coffee table with a loud thud. "This really stinks. I'd go back to bed, but I'm too damn mad."

"Yeah, I don't blame you," Bobby said. "We'll order breakfast sent up, then go home." He cocked his head Jessica's way. "You okay, Jess? You look like you don't feel too good."

All heads turned her way.

"Oh...I'm fine." She peeled her arms from around herself and forced them to her sides. "Just not hungry...that's all."

She glanced at Chris. Worry creased his forehead. When he stood and walked toward her, she stepped back and waved him away.

"Now don't start fussing over me. I'm fine. I'm just not hungry. Bobby, if you'll loan me your car, I'd like to do a little shopping before we go."

"I'll go with you," Meredith said.

"No!" When she realized she had shouted, Jessica masked her error with a weak smile. "I just want to shop around for a few things. I won't be long."

She darted into the bedroom before her behavior or actions could be questioned.

Chris stared after her. There was no mistaking the look in her eyes when she stepped back from him. It chilled him to the core of his soul. A look of fear...fear of him.

*　　*　　*

Logic drew Jessica to the nearest hospital, hoping she would find

Carolyn there. She wasn't disappointed. In her heart, Jessica wanted to believe Chris couldn't have hurt Carolyn, but she felt the only way she could prove that was to personally confront the woman. To force a confession out of her. To make her say it wasn't Chris, Sean, or Mark.

Jessica crept into Carolyn's hospital room. Even though she had first-hand knowledge of abuse, she wasn't prepared for what she saw. Bill's attacks against her had left bruises where no one would ever see them. Carolyn was not as fortunate. Jessica winced.

Carolyn's eyes were blackened, one nearly swollen shut. Her lip was cut and puffy. One cheek was covered with a purple bruise and bruises ringed her neck.

"Not pretty, is it?" Carolyn managed to say. "What the hell are you doing here? Did he send you to see if I was still alive? What's the matter? You look shocked. Scared of what he might do to you? It's not the first time, you know, just the worst time."

Jessica could scarcely breath. "I don't believe you."

"It doesn't matter. You'll see. In the meantime, you can give him a little message from me. He can stand by because I intend to sue the hell out of him." She rolled her head toward the window, dismissing her company.

Jessica stumbled from the room blinded by tears. She had been so sure of Chris's love and tenderness, yet here was evidence of the cruelty he was capable of. How long before he lashed out at her in a fit of rage? She rested her hand over her belly. She was as trapped as she had been with Bill.

No. She would not live like that again. This time she had money; money Dr. Martin had left her. She never had to live like that again.

When she returned to the hotel, Chris was the first one her gaze fell upon. Seeing him this way, freshly showered and shaved and wearing her favorite powder blue golf shirt, Jessica doubted he could harm anyone. He took a step toward her, reaching out to touch her cheek. It was the scrapes across his knuckles that brought her to her senses.

"How did you hurt your hand?"

Chris stopped and covered one hand with the other. God how he hated to tell her his temper had gotten away from him, but to lie—especially now—would be disastrous.

"I was angry with Carolyn last night. I punched the elevator wall."

Jessica's gaze flitted around the room. Everyone was there, apparently ready for the flight home. She'd be safe enough confronting him in front of witnesses. She tilted her chin. "Were you mad enough to ram your fist into Carolyn's face?"

Chris felt a knife-like pain twist his gut. He didn't quite know what to say. To have her think he would beat a woman, any woman, hurt beyond words. Yet her fear and accusations were staring at him. He had to say something to make her believe he didn't do it.

Gina sprang to his defense. "Jessica, you can't honestly believe Chris would do something like that. I have known him a long time and—"

"I know how well you *know* Chris."

Gina pulled back. The sting of Jessica's words made her speechless.

Sean stepped forward. "Jessica, we didn't go near Carolyn. You don't understand the kind of woman she is. She's capable of anything. You wouldn't believe some of the things she's pulled."

"I know she couldn't have faked this," she said. "I saw her. This isn't a joke."

Chris took a deep breath. "If I was going to beat Carolyn, I'd have done so long ago when—"

"She says you have."

"Then she's lying. I guess it's up to you who you want to believe— me or her. A man who loves you or a woman who'd sell her own child to…"

The realization of his own words slammed into him. "She wouldn't."

He looked at Sean, then Mark, and finally Gina. The same thought hit them at once. Gina covered a gasp with her fist.

Leia grabbed Sean's arm. "What? What is it?"

"A trip to Catalina with her child when she couldn't stand to be alone with him for more than five minutes," Gina said.

"A death without a body," Sean added.

"And a funeral without her parents there," Mark finished.

"She wouldn't." Chris didn't want to believe it. Yet, once before, during one of their many arguments, Carolyn had threatened to take Brian so far away Chris would never find him. She'd sell him to baby brokers if she had to. He sank to the nearest chair and buried his head in his hands.

"She would. My God, she would. Why didn't we see it before?"

"Because it's too horrible to imagine," Gina said. "And the grief of thinking he was dead was hurting us."

Jessica crossed her arms over her chest. "This is hogwash. No one would do such a thing."

Chris looked up at her. The pain in his eyes knotted Jessica's heart. He said nothing to her, but reached for the phone instead. He paused. "I don't know what to do. I don't know who to call."

"Her parents," Bobby said.

Chris nodded and dialed the number. There was no answer. "Now what?"

"Call Mom and Dad," Sean said. "They can hire a private detective to start looking. When Mark and I get there in two weeks, we'll do what we can."

Jessica listened as Chris spoke with his parents. She had been expecting him to have to convince them of his wild theory, but from the conversation she heard, they had no problem believing him. When he was through, he faced her once more.

"I guess all of us are liars...except for Carolyn, of course. Think about that, Jess." He walked away from her to retrieve their suitcases from the bedroom.

"You didn't even tell your parents we were married," she said to his back.

Chris rested his hands on the door frame but didn't turn around. "A half hour ago you looked like I was the last person you wanted to be with. If you're planning to leave me, I'd prefer my parents not know about our marriage. They already know I made one mistake. I don't want them to know I made another."

Jessica swallowed the lump in her throat as he walked on. Who was telling the truth here? The man she loved and took as her husband? Or a woman who had been battered almost beyond recognition? What woman would have that done to herself? What woman would use her son as a pawn? The questions nagged at her throughout the day until Jessica thought she would go insane trying to come up with the right answer.

It didn't help when she watched Chris read William a bedtime story, then lovingly tuck him in that night. She waited until she was certain the boy was asleep before seeking solace from old friends—the statues by the lagoon.

A gentle tropical breeze caressed her as she walked to the statue closest to the ocean. They had a special kinship, this ancient lady and Jessica. Six-and-a-half years ago, this statue had kept Jessica from throwing herself into the turbulent water below.

Jessica settled down in the cleft between the statue's feet. It seemed made for this purpose—a place to sit and let the goddess absorb your problems. How many times had Jessica come to this very spot when married to Bill to ease her tormented mind? Now she was here again. She hoped the statue wouldn't mind. It had been a long time since they had talked this way.

She leaned back and let the warmth embrace her. It wasn't long before the tears came, making silent tracks down her cheeks. In her mind, Jessica let her worries flow, believing the statue would hear her and help.

There was the crunch of footsteps approaching. The sound stopped, and Jessica peeked around the base to see Gina staring down at the water. A wave rolled in, spraying water. Gina didn't move. There was something about the way she stood, so still, so deep in thought. Jessica had been there before.

"Don't do it, Gina," she said softly. "What ever's troubling you can be worked out."

Gina's chest lifted and fell in a sigh. "I just came here to think, that's all. Leia's been spending a lot of time over here. She says it helps to clear her thoughts. I'm pregnant, Jessica. I know I have to tell Mark, but the words won't come. I'd like to think he'd marry me because he loves me, not because I'm going to have his child."

The words stung Jessica. Was that why Chris had married her? She leaned back into the statute. No, they had talked marriage before then.

"Sometimes when I'm worried I'll sit here, too. Everyone wonders what the statues are here for. I think they're to tell our troubles to and help us. They protect us from true evil. At least that's what they did for me. There's room over here if you'd like to join me." Jessica patted the ground beside her.

Gina hugged herself. "I'm not a superstitious person, but maybe just this once. Jessica, you've got to believe us. Chris would never, ever beat a woman. Not even Carolyn, although she certainly deserves to be beaten."

"No one deserves to be beaten."

"And an eighteen-month-old boy doesn't deserve to be deserted in a hospital corridor, but that's what Carolyn did to Brian. That's how I met him…sitting there all alone, crying for his Daddy, clutching his teddy bear. He was such a sad little boy, but his face would sure light up when he saw his Daddy. Chris, Sean, and Mark didn't beat Carolyn. But I'm not surprised it happened. She's made her share of enemies."

Jessica stretched to her feet. "I appreciate you telling me this. I'm going home now. Will you be all right?"

Gina nodded.

Jessica walked away. She glanced over her shoulder to see Gina taking her place at the statue's feet.

Another person helped.

She smiled up into the goddess's face. For a second she thought she detected a sparkle in the eyes, but decided it was only the reflection of the moon. She returned home.

Chris waited on the porch steps. He rose without speaking and opened the door for her. He held his finger to his lips. Jessica saw Sean and Leia on the couch fully clothed and sound asleep.

Once in their room, Chris shut the door behind them. Still he said nothing as he undressed for bed and crawled beneath the covers. Jessica stared down at him, wringing her hands with indecision.

"Would you like me to sleep in the spare room?"

Jessica shook her head and sat on the edge of the bed, but moved no further.

Chris cursed Bill Martin for causing her fear. He cursed Carolyn for Jessica's anxiety now. And he cursed his own ineptitude for not being able to find a way to prove to her that he was not an abuser of women.

He slipped from bed and knelt on the floor before her. His eyes searched hers, and Jessica did not look away.

"I love you. I would never hurt you. I swear it."

He slipped off her shoes and gently rubbed her calves. The circular motion sent a trail of shivers up her legs. Chris kissed one knee, then nipped at the other. His hands drifted to her thighs while his lips slid further upward. With his tongue he drew lazy designs on her inner thighs, inching higher until she could feel the heat of his breath through the shorts she wore.

"I want to love you, Jess," he said, his voice husky with emotion. "God, let me love you."

Jessica knew she couldn't deny him or herself. She eased the shorts and panties from her hips. Chris hooked the garments with his fingers, sliding them off her legs. When he looked up, Jessica pulled her T-shirt over her head. She unhooked her bra. Chris captured her breasts in his hands. He traced the peach-colored tips until they peaked. Jessica closed her eyes and let her head fall back.

Chris's sigh mirrored hers. His warm breath nudged her legs apart. He dropped a kiss there then deepened the caress, drawing his tongue through soft valleys. Jessica cried out, wadding the bedspread in her fists. He cupped her twitching buttocks while his mouth danced over her most intimate areas.

Jessica felt a rush of fulfillment so intense she truly believed she had been propelled to outer space and back. Then he was covering her. Filling her body with his. Making them one. Rocking with the last throes of her orgasm as he rushed toward his own. It came to him quickly and ended on a simultaneous pledge of love.

They lay together for the longest time touching, whispering endearments, and loving once more before cuddling up to sleep. As the fog of slumber drifted in, Jessica remembered Carolyn's threat. She leaned onto one elbow and looked down at Chris.

"She said she intends to sue you."

Chris pulled her back to the crook of his arm. "Then you can bet she'll do it."

*   *   *

It was the day of Sean and Mark's departure that Chris received official word of Carolyn's suit. But it wasn't Chris she chose as her target. It was Jessica. The charge? Alienation of affection. A little antiquated, but Carolyn was after the most money she could get and that would be from Jessica. Chris merely set her attorney's letter aside. His lawyer could handle it in due time.

Chris's main concern was finding Brian. So far, the detective he'd hired through his parents had come up with no leads, but Chris was hopeful. At the airstrip now he felt Jessica slip her hand through his.

"There are two very sad ladies here today." She motioned toward Leia and Gina.

Both women were in the arms of their men. Mark seemed to be the only one not tormented by the separation. After a kiss to Gina, he climbed onto the plane and urged Sean to hurry.

Sean kissed Leia once, twice, three times, then a fourth. Each kiss longer and deeper than the last. Finally, he had no choice but to leave. He kissed her fingers, then her palm before backing up the steps of the plane. Leia held her hand to her cheek, unashamed of the tears she shed.

As Bobby closed the hatch, Chris was almost certain he saw tears in Sean's eyes, too. The plane taxied down the runway and lifted into the air.

"You could've gone," Chris told Leia.

"I know, but I do have work of my own here, and Daddy wants Bobby and me to start easing ourselves more fully into the company. He says he's getting tired." A small smile bowed her lips, then faded.

"But I sure will miss him."

Chris squeezed her shoulder. "He'll miss you, too. Gina, he's gone and since it's just the four of us here, I'm going to ask…"

Gina spun around, her icy blue eyes shooting sparks. "No, I didn't tell him. Just leave me alone." She stormed to the truck, wrenched open the door, and plopped down to cry.

Leia shook her head. "She certainly can't hide this. What's going to happen when he finds out she kept this from him?"

"My thoughts exactly." Chris draped an arm around Jessica and Leia, and led them to the truck.

CHAPTER 15

Chris knew that Carolyn was pretty good at carrying out her threats, but he hoped her attorney would eventually rein her in. That never happened. The charges leveled against Jessica were clear—alienation of affection. In fact, in the last several weeks, Carolyn had added charges against Chris.

First, there was a charge of assault that no criminal court would touch because of lack of evidence. Still it was going to be brought up in a bid for sympathy for Carolyn. Second, Carolyn had discovered about his financial holdings prior to their marriage. She wanted her share. She might win on that one. No prenuptial agreement was made prior to their marriage. Chris recognized it was not one of his smarter decisions.

Then the charges went from ridiculous to absurd. Her attorney intended to prove Chris had willfully neglected Carolyn and Brian during their marriage, left her at a time when she was grieving and unable to make a rational decision about her rights, flaunted his mistress at Brian's funeral to further her mental decline, and conspired with Jessica to ruin Carolyn's reputation and take from her any financial support due her.

Chris did not intend to back down. If it was a fight Carolyn wanted, she was going to get the battle of her life. Chris's California attorney, George Davis, left no possibility open, or so he claimed. Today, traveling with him to the trial in California were other witnesses George had insisted were necessary—Gina, Edward, and Bobby. Meredith was along for moral support. And Leia was there to see Sean.

The trial was scheduled for the following day, but Chris was sure the next few hours of this day were going to be just as dramatic.

According to Sean, their parents were less than thrilled with Chris's remarriage. They were concerned with having to deal with another Carolyn. Chris had no qualms about them meeting Jessica. He knew she'd win them over in a manner of seconds, so he kept their worries from her. He also kept his and Jessica's latest surprise from them. They could see for themselves just how excited she was about the twins she carried.

Gina was another matter. Mark still didn't know he was going to be a father. Gina spent the entire five-hour flight from Hawaii to Los Angeles crying about it. But then, there wasn't a day she didn't cry.

As for Sean and Leia, Chris hoped they could contain themselves until they left the airport. They had missed each other...a lot. As Jessica said, "One more day of watching Leia mope over Sean and I'll throw up."

Chris felt a tap on his shoulder and looked over his seat.

Edward pressed forward as far as his seatbelt allowed. "This is an awfully big imposition on your family. Are you sure your parents want all of us at the house?"

Chris smiled. It was the third time during the flight he'd had to reassure the man. "Mom said she wanted you there. The house has four bedrooms, a family room, and a living room plus two bathrooms. I'm sure Mom wouldn't offer if she didn't feel she could handle it."

Edward nodded as he had every time they'd discussed this. Then he settled back to prepare for landing.

*   *   *

Sean watched his parents from the corner of his eye. The older they got, the more trouble Sean had keeping up with them. They were always on the go. David and Karen Matthews were a handful. He should be so lucky when he reached their age.

Every once in a while the light sparkled on the silver sprinkled through his father's hair. His mother hid her gray. They stood like statues staring down the jet way waiting for Chris. His mother's hands were under her chin as if she were praying. His father jingled the keys in his pocket. Sean shook his head. All this apprehension over one little redhead.

On his other side, Mark waited with an expectant smile and a dozen white carnations. Sean silently cursed him since all he had to give to Leia was himself.

"Mom, will you calm down? You look like you want to bite your fingernails."

"I do."

"I still don't understand why you invited them all to stay at the house."

"I just thought they might enjoy it. I don't care how rich the Chamberlains are, they ought to prefer a house to a hotel."

"Don't let her kid you," his father said. "She was just afraid she might find herself alone with Chris's wife."

"Jessica's one of the nicest people you'd ever care to meet. You'll see, Mom."

Before Sean could defend her further, the passengers filtered toward them. He scanned the crowd for Leia. There she was, politely darting around people until she was in front. Her eyes were bright with anticipation. With a suppressed squeal, she broke into a run.

*   *   *

Leia couldn't reach him quickly enough. During the long separation, she had come to a realization. She couldn't be happy if Sean wasn't a part of her life. She waited all this time to tell him face to face, so there would be no doubt in his mind as to the depth of her feelings. She was inches from him, her arms open to him. Sean swooped her into his arms, swinging her around as they laughed. Their lips joined as he set her on her feet.

"God, I've missed you," he told her.

She pulled back to look at him and captured his face in her hands. "I've missed you. You have to know... I have to tell you... It doesn't matter about Angela's baby. I don't care. I really don't care. I love you."

Sean brushed his thumb across her cheek. "Honestly?"

Leia nodded, and a wide smile spread over his face. "Then, will you marry me?"

Her reply was a breathless, "Yes."

"Oh, David, they do love each other!" his mother exclaimed.

Sean looked up, believing she meant them. But he saw her gazing wistfully past them as if they didn't exist. It was Chris and Jessica who held her attention. They walked toward them, Chris's hand protectively resting on Jessica's back.

"Welcome to the family." She rushed forward, hugging Jessica close.

Jessica laughed and returned the affection.

"You must be exhausted from the trip. Soon as we get home, you rest. We want a healthy grandchild."

"Just one?" Jessica's eyes sparkled. "What should I do with the other one?"

His mother stumbled for words, but none would come.

Chris laughed. "Yes, Mom, twins."

She gave him a playful smack. "Christopher Matthews, just what have you done now?"

Jessica waved a hand his way. "Oh, Chris had very little to do. It was that fertility cave."

"Mom, I was under a lot of pressure from her. She wanted lots of babies...*now*. I needed help fast. What else could I do?"

She laughed and clasped first Jessica, then Chris, in a bone-crushing hug. "This is wonderful. Just so wonderful."

Sean smiled, but it was time he and Leia had some of that attention. "What about us? We're getting married."

"Married? You're getting married?" Meredith shoved to the forefront.

Edward was close behind. "This is wonderful news." He shook Sean's hand, then hugged his daughter. "Your mother has been looking forward to planning an island wedding for you."

Leia jerked away from his embrace. "Island wedding?"

Sean saw trouble dancing in her father's eyes.

"Yes. Of course, we'd have to wait 'til spring when the monsoons have passed."

"Is there something special about an island wedding?" David Matthews asked.

Chris snickered. "Only that you can't touch the bride until after the wedding."

A smirk played upon his father's lips. "So? Isn't that a general rule?" With fingers splayed across his chest, he added, "*I* never got to touch the bride 'til after the wedding."

His mother smacked him. "Liar."

He laughed and gave her a wink.

"What's it gonna be?" Bobby tucked his arms over his chest and grinned. "Gonna let your hormones run your life, or hang tough and have an island ceremony?"

Sean shook his head. There was no way he and Leia would live it down if they refused an island wedding. He twined his fingers around hers, and with an imperceptible lift of his brow, asked her what she wanted to do.

"They don't give us much of a choice, do they?"

Sean turned to the others. "An island wedding. Mark, want to be my best man?"

Mark never heard him. He stared down the vacant jet way, looking like a hound dog who had lost its best friend. "Where's Gina?"

She appeared around the bend at that time, eyes dry but red and puffy from the gallons of tears she'd shed. She clutched her carry-on bag in front of her.

"Gina's been crying," Mark said. "Why? What's wrong?"

No one answered. No one could.

Mark fidgeted while she took those last few steps toward him.

She refused to meet his gaze. Her body shook with uncertainty. Sean hated to see this, wished there was something he could do to ease the ordeal. But she'd brought this all on herself. All he and the others could do was help them through it.

Then Gina was before Mark, staring at the toes of his Reeboks.

"I...got these for you." There was a tremor in his voice as he held the carnations before her. Sean could just about read his mind—Mark was afraid Gina no longer loved him.

"Gina, you haven't... Is there someone else?"

Her head jerked up. "No. Never."

"Then what..."

She took a few steps back and dropped her tote bag. Mark's chin dropped with it. The silence surrounding them was deafening.

"You're...pregnant," he said, as if he couldn't quite believe it himself.

Gina's tears sprang to life.

"But I thought you couldn't have children. And now..." He gestured toward her protruding belly. "Now...we're gonna have a baby." He fell to his knees before her and gently touched her stomach.

She sniffled. "You mean you're not mad?"

Mark laughed. "Mad? Why would I be..." His eyebrows slammed together. "You're damn right I'm mad. Why the hell didn't you tell me about this?"

"I was afraid you'd leave me."

"Leave you? Gina, I love you. See?" He held the flowers up to her.

Gina laughed through her tears. Cradling the bouquet in one arm, she draped the other around his neck to hug him.

"Hey, Sean," Mark called over his shoulder, "I'll be your best man if you'll be mine."

"You got a deal."

*   *   *

The small party gathered to honor Mark and Gina's marriage sat around the Matthews' living room. The couple had left an hour earlier to enjoy a quiet night together at a nearby hotel. The Simpsons had also returned home. Chris watched his family and friends visit like they'd known each other all their lives.

Edward and his father hadn't stopped talking since they'd met. His mother doted over Jessica and Leia.

Chris got up to stretch his legs, wandering to the bay window. As always, the front lawn was perfectly manicured and beautifully landscaped. Security lights protected the darkest corners of the house. His family home. In the past, Chris had missed living here. Now he could honestly say he didn't. Home was Hurago with Jessica, William, and the babies she carried. Only one thing more could make it perfect.

The delicate scent of Jessica's perfume drifted to him. He smiled down at her, pulling her into the crook of his arm.

"I'll be glad when tomorrow is over," she told him.

"Yeah, me, too."

"I saw you talking to your dad earlier. You've been antsy ever since. This isn't the first time you've come to look out this window."

Chris raked his fingers through his hair. "The detective called. Said he'd be back today with some interesting news."

"But he didn't say what?"

Chris shook his head.

They saw a battered Ford station wagon pull into the driveway. Chris held his breath, hoping, praying it would be Brian. A chubby, blonde woman stepped out with a baby.

"We've got company." Chris forced away the crushing disappointment he felt.

His mother rushed to the window and peeked out. "It's Angela and her baby."

Chris glanced at Leia. If Angela's presence bothered her, she hid it well. Chris opened the door. Blue eyes wide, Angela stared at all the people there.

"I'm Sean's brother. Come in."

Casting a wary eye around the room, she stepped inside. "I didn't know there was company. I bring the baby over every two weeks."

"It's okay. We're all family here," he said. "Let's see your little girl."

She jostled the baby until Chris and she were exchanging smiles. As Chris studied the little girl, he bit back the urge to say what was on his mind. The baby that stared at him did so with wide brown eyes. Angela's were as blue as Sean's.

"Angela, could you bring the baby over here?" Sean patted the couch. "I'd like my fiancée and her to get acquainted."

"Your...fiancée?"

Sean turned a smile toward Leia, curling his fingers over her thigh. "That's right. Leia Chamberlain...Angela Jackson."

The ladies exchanged an awkward nod. Then Angela stepped forward and reluctantly placed her baby in Leia's arms. Leia ignored the woman, turning her full attention to the cooing infant.

"She's adorable. Such a good baby."

"And look at her eyes," Chris said. "Aren't they the widest you've ever seen?"

Leia looked at the baby's big, brown eyes. An old lesson in genetics tickled her memory. "Her eyes *are* beautiful." She smiled sweetly at Angela. "Have you and Sean worked out visitation rights yet?"

"Visitation?" Angela asked.

"Well, of course. As her father, he has certain rights. A good father does more than just pay the child support. We'll be fair about this, but it's very important that she know her father and half-brothers and sisters."

"Half-brothers and—"

"Sisters." Leia flashed another smile. "We do intend to have children, you know."

"Yes, well—"

"It's important that siblings know each other," Meredith said.

"Especially at holiday time," Jessica added.

Angela's gaze darted nervously among the three women banded together in front of her.

Chris hid a smirk behind his hand. They were backing her into a corner, trying to force her to admit what they already knew.

"As far as I'm concerned," Leia said, "the results of the paternity test are only a formality. We have no reason to doubt your word. It could take years before we get those results. Years of time that could be spent having us bond with this sweet little girl."

"We'll be fair," Sean said. "Alternate holidays. You can have her this Christmas. We'll take next."

"Where…where will you be living?" Angela asked.

"On the island, of course," Leia said. "Don't worry. We'll fly here to get her and bring her back. Two weeks at Christmas. The whole summer, too. She'll love it."

Angela snapped to her feet. "Give me my baby. This is the most ridiculous thing I've ever heard."

Leia placed the baby in her arms. "We'd hate to have to take you to court on this, but we will if we have to."

"That won't be necessary." She clutched the child to her chest as if she fully expected them to snatch her away. "Sean's not the father."

"You expect us to believe you now?" Chris asked.

Angela whirled around to face him. "It's the truth. I was never with Sean."

"Then why did you lie?"

"I wanted the best for my baby. Is that so wrong?" she asked. "I discovered I was pregnant and panicked. The father took off long before that. I chose Sean because he seemed to have compassion. When he brought me home after that party, I slipped a little something in his beer. I was hoping it would be easier to get him into bed and blame the pregnancy on him. He passed out on the couch."

"And you staged it to look like we slept together," Sean said.

Angela nodded. "I'm sorry. I was just trying to get the best for my baby." Without another word she left, her child still clutched protectively against her.

Leia slipped her arm through Sean's. "I feel sorry for her."

"She'll be all right," Chris said.

"But we won't if we don't get this mess cleaned up," his mother said. "We've got a long day ahead of us tomorrow. Lord knows what that woman has planned."

Later that evening as he lay staring at the dark ceiling in the family room, Chris relived his life with Carolyn. He had to have been insane to spend all those years with her. At the time he justified his actions by saying he did it for Brian. Now he realized it had done both he and Brian more harm than good. Why hadn't he seen that? And where was Brian now? Alive? Dead? Either way Chris blamed himself.

He eased from the sofa bed. If he laid there much longer, his tossing and turning might wake Jessica. He slipped into his trousers and stepped into the living room. He froze, his hand still on the doorknob.

Sean and Leia lay on the couch, limbs entwined, lips sealed. Leia's hand was somewhere under Sean's shirt while his drifted into her jeans.

Chris shook his head and ducked back into the family room.

"Can't sleep?" Jessica asked in a sleepy voice.

"No, but I'll be okay."

"Come back to bed and I'll help you take your mind off your worries."

It was an offer only a crazy man would refuse.

*   *   *

Leia pulled her lips from Sean's, closing her eyes in ecstasy as his kisses drifted down her neck. With one smooth motion, she yanked his shirt over his head and tossed it aside. Her fingers wandered through the golden hair on his chest, drawing circles around his pecs. With Sean's sharp intake of breath, Leia shivered. The buttons of her blouse became casualties of passion as Sean tore the front open. He fumbled with the hooks on her bra and finally gave up. One upward jerk of the frustrating undergarment released her.

Her bare chest heaved with every breath she took, inviting him to taste. With a low growl, Sean captured one breast, sucking so deeply Leia wanted to scream from the wondrous feeling it gave.

"Having a good time?"

They jerked apart to find Bobby and Meredith leering over them. Leia snatched her blouse closed.

"Is it March already?" Meredith asked.

"Why, I don't think so," Bobby innocently replied.

"But it must be. Sean and Leia were going to wait 'til after the wedding."

Leia leveled an ugly glare at them. "Why are you doing this?"

Bobby studied his nails. "Oh, because when Meredith and I got married *someone* thought it was funny to hound our every move. To make sure we behaved until after *our* island wedding."

Leia narrowed her eyes to slits. "So…this is revenge."

"Payback is murder, little sister," he said with a smile. "I'm going to enjoy the next few months."

"The next few *long, hard* months," Meredith gleefully added.

Sean and Leia sank into the cushions. March suddenly seemed an eternity away.

CHAPTER 16

It had finally come to this.

There were no miracles, no last minute reprieves. The battle in court would go on. Chris and Jessica sat at his assigned table waiting for Carolyn and her attorney. His family and friends sat behind in the gallery. He'd spent a sleepless night worrying over this and waiting for a private detective who never arrived. All he wanted now was to get this over.

He looked up when Carolyn breezed in with her attorney. She wore a red dress with a duster jacket. There was a pooch to her stomach. She really did look pregnant. Chris wondered who the poor guy was. Carolyn paused at Chris's table, then with a smirk and a toss of her long, black hair sat down at the table across from them.

Chris squeezed Jessica's fingers. "It'll be okay." A nod was her only response.

The judge entered then and the hearing officially began. "We are here today to hear the case of Matthews versus Matthews. I have read the charges against Dr. and Mrs. Christopher Matthews and respondent's rebuttal to those charges. I'm ready to hear the witnesses. The petitioner may begin her case, Mr. Jamison."

Carolyn's attorney stretched to his feet. "Thank you, your honor. Our first witness is Mrs. Carolyn Matthews."

Carolyn dabbed a tissue at her eyes as she took the witness stand. Chris resisted the urge to roll his eyes heavenward, and leaned back to watch the performance.

"Mrs. Matthews, how long were you married to Dr. Matthews?" Jamison asked.

"Five years."

"There was a child of this marriage?"

Carolyn sniffled. "Yes. Brian. He passed away in January of this year."

"Tell the court what your marriage was like."

She turned sad, dark eyes to the judge. "Things turned bad after I learned I was pregnant. We'd only been married a short time. After Brian was born, Chris was never home. Brian and I hardly ever saw him. He would leave us without any money or food in the house. I had to beg him for everything. His family treated us as if we didn't exist."

Sean fidgeted in his seat. She was lying just like they knew she would, but hearing those lies was almost more than he could take. Only Leia's hand on his arm kept him quiet.

"He'd spend nights away from home—nights he spent with his mistress, Gina Monroe. He was even with her the day Brian was lost. Then at the funeral, she came. I asked her to leave, but Christopher said she was to stay. I was so upset. The next day he moved out of the house. His brother served the divorce papers. I was so grief-stricken, I didn't protest. I went along with it all.

"In May, Christopher came to see me and he stayed the night. He continued to come over for the next two weeks. It was such a lovely time. We decided to give our marriage another try. He came to me one day to say he was leaving for a while to think things out. He asked me to follow him and I did. But I never saw him."

She effected a sob. "Then in August he told me he was sorry but he'd gotten a woman pregnant and felt obligated to marry her. I later learned that he had not divided our property equally. Here I was struggling, living like a pauper, while he lived like a king."

"I know this is difficult for you, but please tell the court what happened after you discovered his plans to marry Jessica Martin."

Carolyn cast her eyes downward. "Christopher, his brother Sean, and Mark Simpson came to my hotel room. When I begged Chris to reconsider, they beat me. The next day Jessica came to my hospital room. I told her I carried Chris's child. She offered me money to stay away and not tell him."

"Your honor, I submit into evidence a notarized affidavit from Dr. Milton Townsend stating that Mrs. Carolyn Matthews is approximately five months pregnant."

He handed the judge a piece of paper and stood before Carolyn once more, hands clasped behind him. "Mrs. Matthews, has Jessica Matthews ever made any slurs against you?"

"Yes. At a restaurant in Hawaii this August. She called me a whore and made threats against my life."

"Thank you, Mrs. Matthews. No further questions."

"This is the most ridiculous—" Leia shushed Sean as Chris's attorney approached Carolyn.

"Mrs. Matthews, I have here a copy of the property settlement from your divorce. It indicates that you were left with the house worth one hundred thousand dollars with a mortgage, your car, all household furnishings, and a bank account containing five thousand dollars. Dr. Matthews received his car, personal effects, a bank account containing ten thousand dollars, all bills and the proceeds from the child's insurance worth twenty thousand dollars. In addition to that, he also paid you a monthly support check of one thousand dollars until the divorce was final. It hardly seems to me that you were living the life of a pauper."

Carolyn made no response.

"Mrs. Matthews, didn't your father promise you a large sum of money upon your marriage to an individual he deemed appropriate?"

Carolyn gave a single nod. "I received a dowry."

"A dowry of fifty thousand dollars. Wasn't this the only reason you married Dr. Matthews? To receive this money?"

Carolyn tilted her chin. "It was a gift."

"Mrs. Matthews, after your son was born, didn't Dr. Matthews sign the appropriate forms so you could have a tubal legation and thereby become sterile?"

Again Carolyn did not answer.

Davis strode to his table and lifted a sheet of paper. "Didn't you have that operation?'

Judge Baxter cleared his throat. "Mrs. Matthews, answer the question."

"Yes, but obviously they grew back together."

"No further questions."

Chris refused to look at Carolyn as she left the witness stand. He was so angry at her lies that he didn't trust himself to meet her cold gaze. In an effort to control his rising anger, he twirled a pencil between his fingers.

"I call Regina Monroe," Jamison announced.

Gina marched toward the stand. When the clerk asked her name, she proudly gave her married name. Her bright smile was directed toward Mark.

After she sat, Jamison strode to her. "Were you recently married?"

"That's correct."

"I see." He paused, then went on. "What is your relationship to the respondent?

"Dr. Matthews and I are friends and business associates."

"Isn't there more to it than that? Weren't you and Christopher Matthews lovers during his marriage to Carolyn Matthews?"

"Yes, we had an affair."

"And how long did this affair last?"

"Off and on for about two years."

"Didn't, in fact, Mrs. Simpson, this affair continue until after Brian Matthews's death?"

Gina's lips thinned. "No, it didn't."

"Yet you were present at the funeral?"

"Yes."

"And Dr. Matthews escorted you home after the funeral?"

"Yes."

"And stayed the night at your house?"

"Yes, but—"

"Didn't Dr. Matthews reside with you after that day?"

"No, he did not."

"Why did you attend the funeral that day, if not to announce your relationship with Dr. Matthews?" His tone demanded an answer, but he hardly gave Gina the time to do so.

She was getting pissed. So was Mark. Sean pulled him back in his seat.

"Out of love for a little boy who had died."

"Love for the boy, not the father?"

"Yes."

"You had an affair with the child's father for two years, and yet you expect the court to believe you loved his child, but not him? Did you not, in fact, attend the funeral for the sole purpose of making a claim on Dr. Matthews? That you, in fact, approached Carolyn Matthews and said, 'Now that the kid's out of the way you might as well kiss your husband goodbye, too?'"

Mark snapped to his feet. "That's a damn lie!"

Judge Baxter banged his gavel as Sean pulled Mark back to his seat.

Gina flashed angry blue eyes at Jamison. "I never said that!"

"Mrs. Simpson, why did you go to Hurago? Wasn't it for the purpose of setting up a love nest for you and Dr. Matthews?"

Gina couldn't help herself. She laughed. "Oh, puh-leease."

"Answer the question, Mrs. Simpson," Jamison told her.

Gina leveled a glare at Carolyn. "I went to Hurago because Carolyn Matthews had been making threats against my life. She harassed me daily by phone and by mail. Leia Chamberlain and I had met in college. I knew the island needed medical people so I went. I did tell Chris how wonderfully peaceful it was there and he eventually followed. But he followed to be the doctor, not to see me."

"No further questions, your honor."

Davis hurried forward. "Mrs. Simpson, how did you come to know Dr. Matthews?"

"He was one of the doctors working out of the hospital where I worked. One day Carolyn came into the hospital with Brian. Dr. Matthews was in surgery. She left Brian with instructions to the nurse on duty that Dr. Matthews could watch his brat for awhile. She left Brian sitting outside in the hallway. He was only eighteen months old."

"And she left him unattended in a hospital hallway?" He ended the question on a high note to stress his shock. "What was the child's reaction?"

"He held his teddy bear and started crying for his daddy."

"For his daddy, not his mommy?

Gina nodded. "Yes."

"What did you do?"

"I picked him up and comforted him. I kept him occupied until Dr. Matthews got out of surgery."

"What happened when he saw Brian?"

"Brian was so happy to see him, he climbed down from my lap and ran to Chris. Chris picked him up and gave him a hug and kiss. He was angry Carolyn had left him. He took Brian into the nurse's lounge and tried to call his parents to come and get him. He had to go back into surgery. He held Brian the whole time he was in the nurse's lounge. Chris couldn't find his parents, so I offered to take care of the boy for him."

"Was Brian with you often after that?"

"Yes. I fell in love with the little guy and asked to watch him a lot."

"Is that when you began your affair with Dr. Matthews?"

"No. It was about four months later. Chris brought Brian over so he could trick-or-treat in my neighborhood. Carolyn wouldn't let Brian go without fighting about it, so Chris and I gave him Halloween at my place. Afterward, Brian fell asleep on the couch. I was upset because my fiancé had just walked out on me. Chris comforted me and one thing led to the other. It wasn't an every night thing, just an occasional thing. We eventually broke it off when we grew tired of the relationship."

"Why did Dr. Matthews spend the night at your house the night of the funeral?"

"He was very upset. He didn't want to return to the house he shared with Carolyn. He didn't want to go to his parents' house. He said he was having a hard enough time dealing with his own grief, and he couldn't handle theirs.

"He asked if he could stay with me, and I said yes. He slept on the couch. I left for Hurago two weeks after that."

Davis stepped away, and Gina was excused.

Sean testified next to his involvement or lack thereof in the attack against Carolyn. When Jamison's questioning didn't net the results he intended, he called Mark. Again, his questioning fell short. Jamison paused for a moment to scan the documents on the table before him.

"The petitioner calls Robert Chamberlain."

Chris frowned at his attorney. Bobby was to have been a witness for his side. After a sidelong glance at Davis, Bobby took the stand.

"Mr. Chamberlain, what is your relationship to Jessica Matthews?" Jamison asked.

"She's my friend."

"And to her son William?"

"My wife and I are William's godparents."

"Isn't there more to the relationship than mere friendship? Isn't it true that you and Jessica Matthews have been lovers for at least seven years? And that you are, in fact, the father of her son William?"

Bobby's response was calm, but the clenched fist held tightly on the rail told how he truly felt. "I most certainly am not."

"Aren't you the father of the children she is now carrying?"

"Objection, your honor," Davis said. "I fail to see the relevance of this line of questioning."

"Your honor"—Jamison snapped his chin up—"this is necessary in order to prove the current Mrs. Matthews manipulated Dr. Matthews, and thereby prevented him from reconciling with Carolyn Matthews."

"Objection overruled."

146

"Mr. Chamberlain, isn't it true that when Jessica Matthews found herself once again pregnant with your child, you and she conspired to have her marry Dr. Matthews?"

Bobby curled a white-knuckled grip over the witness stand railing. "No, we did not."

"Then you admit the children are yours?"

"They're Chris's. And William was Bill Martin's son. I've never had an affair with Jessica."

Jamison paced before him. "Then explain to this court why you and an individual by the name of Daniel Daniels forcibly prevented Bill Martin from entering the delivery room when his wife was giving birth."

"Because he threatened to kill the baby as it left her. Jessica was in hysterics. We had to keep him out."

"And out of gratitude, she made you and your wife her son's godparents. How touching. No further questions."

Davis declined questioning for the time.

Bobby strode from the witness stand and plopped into his seat. He snapped his arms over his chest and sat there stewing with rage. Even Meredith's comforting hand on his thigh did little to soothe him.

Chris didn't dare look Jessica's way. Seeing her upset would destroy what little composure he maintained.

"The petitioner calls Edward Chamberlain, Jr."

Chris whirled around in time to see Bobby bolt upright. No one had seen Eddie sitting in the back of the courtroom, or maybe he'd slipped in after them. In any event, he was there.

Davis snapped to his feet. "Your honor, I object. This man is hardly a credible witness. He's been arraigned on several charges, including rape and child molestation. I fail to see what purpose a man of his caliber has in these proceedings."

Jamison stood. "Your honor, Mr. Chamberlain is not on trial here. He has been released on bail pending his own hearing. I've called him as a witness because I believe he has important testimony to give. That testimony in no way deals with or addresses the charges pending against him."

"Objection overruled. Mr. Chamberlain, take the stand."

Chris stared at the undisguised hatred in Bobby's face. It mirrored his own. Why did the wheels of justice turn so slowly for someone as vile as Eddie? The man should have been locked up long ago.

"Mr. Chamberlain, you were an acquaintance of William Martin,

Jr.?" Jamison asked.

"Yes. We were best friends."

"Were you in contact with him during his marriage to Jessica Matthews?"

"Yes."

"What was his reaction when he learned of her pregnancy?"

"He was furious she'd gotten pregnant."

"Why was that?"

"Because Bill was sterile. He had mumps in college, and they left him sterile." Eddie smirked.

Chris heard a tiny squeak from Jessica. He glanced her way. Tears slipped from beneath lids squeezed shut. He looked back at the others. Meredith held her quivering hands on her knees. Her bottom lip trembled.

"Your honor, I submit into evidence a verified copy of William Martin's college medical records indicating he was, in fact, sterile." Jamison passed the papers to Judge Baxter. "Mr. Chamberlain, did Mr. Martin indicate to you who had fathered the child?"

"Yeah, my brother Bobby."

Davis jumped to his feet, "I object, your honor. That is hearsay."

"I withdraw the question, your honor," Jamison replied. "No further questions."

"No questions, your honor," Davis said.

As Eddie passed the row where Bobby sat, he snickered and sat down across the aisle from them.

"Jessica Matthews," Jamison called.

Jessica shoved away her tears with shaking fingers. Meredith reached forward and gave a reassuring squeeze to her arm. It couldn't erase her devastation. All the nightmares she'd fought were staring her right in the face and she had no choice but to meet them head on. The walk to the witness stand was the longest of her life. She clutched her quivering hands on her lap and waited for her world to explode.

"Mrs. Matthews, when did you meet Dr. Matthews?"

"In late May of this year."

"And when did you marry?

"August of this year."

"That was a very short courtship. What was the rush?"

Jessica's eyes filled with hatred as she stared up at him. "There was no rush."

"Oh really? Mrs. Matthews, what month of pregnancy are you in?"

"My fifth."

"And you've been married for four months. How odd. And Dr. Matthews's divorce had only become final days before your marriage. Mrs. Matthews, did you know Dr. Matthews prior to his arrival on the island?"

"No."

"Were you aware of his son's death and marital difficulties?"

"Yes."

"Did you take advantage of his confused state at a time when he and Carolyn Matthews were attempting a reconciliation?"

"No."

"Did you make a threat against Carolyn Matthews?"

She hiked up her chin. "If you want to twist it around, I guess you could call it a threat."

"What did you say?

Jessica's face flushed with embarrassment. "Exactly?"

"Yes."

"I told Carolyn to leave us alone or I would send her where all whores go—to dick heaven."

To Jessica's further embarrassment, the courtroom burst into laughter. Even Jamison had a difficult time controlling his smile. He recovered quickly.

"Mrs. Matthews, who is the father of your son William?"

"Bill Martin."

"But that isn't possible, Mrs. Matthews. Bill Martin was sterile. Mrs. Matthews, isn't the name on your son's birth certificate William Robert Martin?"

"Yes." She fought back tears. *Please...no...don't let this be so.*

"And didn't Bill Martin complete the information on that birth certificate? Didn't he give the child the name William Robert as a constant reminder to you and everyone else of your adultery?"

"I... No—"

"Mrs. Matthews, I submit that the father of William is none other than Robert Chamberlain. That Robert Chamberlain is the father of the children you are now carrying. That you learned you were pregnant again with his child. That you attempted to find a husband to legitimatize your unborn child and to hide the truth from Meredith Chamberlain. That you purposefully interfered during a time when Christopher and Carolyn Matthews were on the verge of a reconciliation.

"You slept with Dr. Matthews and announced you were pregnant with his child. He thereby felt obligated to marry you instead of carrying through with his promised reconciliation. You caused great emotional upset to an already grieving woman, ruining any chance of happiness for her—for your own financial and personal gain."

Chris jumped from his seat. "That's a goddamn lie! And she knows it!" He jerked his arm toward Carolyn.

"Dr. Matthews, please sit down," the judge ordered.

Davis pulled Chris back into his chair. Chris jerked free of his hold.

Jessica blinked back her tears. Her world— her horrible secret— was crashing down around her. "It's not true. I am carrying Chris's children. We got married because we love each other."

"You're carrying the children of Christopher Matthews and not Robert Chamberlain?"

"Yes." Tears she thought under control sprang to life.

"Haven't you been having an ongoing affair with Robert Chamberlain?"

"No!"

"Then who fathered your first child? You certainly don't expect us to believe in immaculate conception? Who is the father of your first child? Who is the father of William Robert Martin?"

Jessica's tears poured down her cheeks. "If what you say is true, and Bill was sterile, there is only one other person who could have fathered my son."

"Robert Chamberlain."

"No."

"Then who, Mrs. Matthews? Give us another name, if you can think of one."

"I don't have to think of one! I know!" She snapped to her feet. Tears blinded her to all but the horrid truth. "It was him!" She pointed a trembling finger at Eddie. "That dirty, rotten bastard right there!"

"Your son William is the result of your affair with Edward Chamberlain, Jr.."

"No!"

"No further questions."

"No, that's not true!" Jessica turned pleading eyes to Davis. "Ask me! Ask me!"

He hurried forward. "Mrs. Matthews, please explain."

Hands braced on the wooden rail before her, Jessica tried her best to find coherent words.

"On our wedding night, Bill took me by force and beat me up. He locked me in the room when he left. He returned a few hours later with Eddie. He told Eddie I was as close to a virgin as they come. They spent the rest of that night taking turns with me. Not only that night, but for the rest of the week. Each night Eddie came to our room, and he and Bill would forcibly rape me all night long."

"You bastard!" Bobby lunged for his brother. He grabbed Eddie by the shirt and threw him in the aisle. Two security guards rushed forward and pulled Bobby back.

"Mr. Chamberlain, you will control yourself, or I'll hold you in contempt of court. We'll have a half hour recess while everyone gets in control of their emotions."

Chris raced to the witness stand to enfold Jessica in his arms. "My poor, sweet Jess."

He rocked her while her tears soaked his shirt. It was all he could do to keep from joining her. Words? There weren't any. All he could go was hold her. A bad marriage? She'd truly lived in hell.

Sean watched Jamison glare at his client while Carolyn did the same to Chris and Jessica. He hoped the lawyer realized now what a liar Carolyn was. The love between Chris and Jessica was real, not fabricated. Any fool could see that.

He gave Leia another hug while she dabbed at her tears. Knowing Jessica the way he did, it was hard not to cry. Beside them Meredith, despite her own tears, did her best to comfort Bobby.

"Why didn't you tell me, Meredith? You knew, didn't you, and you didn't tell me."

"Because I was afraid you'd kill him."

"But, Meredith, all these years we've been helping to raise William—"

"I know, honey." She leaned against his shoulder and gently rubbed his back.

Edward also sat with his head buried in his hands while Leia tried to comfort him despite her own pain.

Jamison looked their way, and Sean willed him to know what was in his mind. The attorney looked over to where Jessica was now surrounded by Chris and their parents. Sean watched Eddie saunter over to them. He jumped over Leia to reach him before he could reach Chris and Jessica. Too late.

Eddie greeted them with that annoying sneer of his. "A man always likes to know he has a son. Maybe I oughta pay the kid a little fatherly visit."

Chris spun around, grabbing him by the front of his suit. "You'll stay away from my son, or I'll personally make sure you're castrated." Then he shoved him away.

Sean grabbed his arm and pushed him to his seat. "And I'll hold you down while they do it."

Chris took Jessica's wrist to monitor her pulse. "Drink some water and try to calm down a little. I know it's hard, honey, but try."

"Is she all right?" George Davis asked.

"I don't want her to testify any more," Chris told him. "She's been through enough."

"Yes, I'd say she has." Davis turned to leave and caught Jamison's eye. Jamison gave a slight nod.

Sean breathed a sigh of relief and eased into the chair beside Leia. When court was called to order, Jessica was excused from the witness stand.

"Your honor," Jamison said, "the petitioner rests."

"What?" Carolyn slapped her hand against the table. "You can't do that. You haven't questioned him." She pointed to Chris.

"Mrs. Matthews," Judge Baxter asked, "do you wish to obtain other counsel?"

"No, your honor."

"Then kindly resume your seat and remain silent. Mr. Davis, is the respondent ready?"

"Yes, your honor. Our first witness is Dr. Kevin Samuels."

Chris watched his former business partner take the stand. Kevin should be loving this moment since he'd hated Carolyn from the day he'd met her.

"Dr. Samuels, state your relationship to the respondent."

Kevin smoothed his auburn hair and replied, "Dr. Matthews and I have been friends and associates for almost twelve years."

"You and Dr. Matthews were in practice together—a partnership?"

"That's correct."

"He gave up that partnership after his son died. What remuneration did he receive upon turning his half of the partnership to you?"

"None. He said why bother because he'd only have to give Carolyn half of it."

Chris's father was called next. After testifying to Chris's financial holdings, assets, and his grief over Brian's death, he was also excused. Dr. Carleton Evans testified to his involvement under duress in the

August harassment of Jessica. Then it was Chris's turn. After a quick adjustment of suit and tie, he strode to the stand.

Time to nail the lid shut on Carolyn's coffin.

"Dr. Matthews, What made you finally decide to divorce Carolyn?"

"I came home early one day, and she was trying to burn Brian's teddy bear. Brian was four at the time."

"After Brian's funeral, you left. Did you ever consider a reconciliation?"

"Never."

"Why did you go to Hurago?"

"A change of pace. A challenge, a need, a breath of fresh air, a chance to start all over again."

"You've adopted the son of your second wife, correct?"

"That's right." Chris directed a stare toward Eddie. It was the first time since he'd taken the stand that he had looked at someone other than his attorney. "William is *my* son."

"Did you, Sean Matthews, and Mark Simpson assault Carolyn Matthews?"

"No. Although the thought did occur to me."

"Why?"

"Because of the torment she was causing Jessica. I wanted Carolyn to leave Jessica alone."

"No further questions," Davis announced.

"No questions," Jamison said from his table.

Davis cleared his throat. "Your honor, the respondent calls Dr. Milton Townsend."

The balding doctor scurried to the stand as if he were anxious to get past Carolyn before she could reach out and grab him.

"Dr. Townsend, is this your affidavit verifying Carolyn Matthews to be five months pregnant?" Davis held out a document for the man to read.

Townsend merely glanced at it. "Yes, it is."

"Is Carolyn Matthews five months pregnant?"

"I wouldn't know. I never examined her."

"Then why did you sign this statement?"

"About a month ago, I had a short affair with Carolyn. She blackmailed me. Told me to make the statement or she would tell my wife everything. I did. But when I heard what she was using it for, I knew I had to come forward. Dr. Matthews is too fine a doctor and a man to be framed."

"No further questions."

"No questions," Jamison said.

Davis returned to his table. "Your honor, the respondent rests."

A voice from the courtroom entrance startled them all. "Your honor, I have evidence which needs to be presented."

Chris was surprised to find Maria Delgado standing there. Behind her was the private detective he had hired. Chris gripped the arms of his chair so hard his knuckles turned white. The detective smiled, gave a thumbs-up, and ducked back outside.

"Who are you, madam?" Judge Baxter asked.

"I am Maria Delgado—Carolyn's mother."

"You have evidence to present in this court?"

"Yes, your honor."

"For which side?"

"For Dr. Matthews."

"No!" Carolyn jerked to her feet. "The trial is over!"

"Mrs. Matthews, sit down!" the judge ordered. "Mrs. Delgado, please present your evidence."

"With your permission, your honor, I'll get it." She opened the door behind her, allowing the detective to enter with her evidence—Brian Matthews.

CHAPTER 17

"Oh my God, Brian!" Chris's chair skittered across the floor.

"Daddy!" Brian's bright smile lit his brown complexion. Without hesitation, he leaped into his father's arms.

Chris squeezed him tightly, rapidly blinking back the tears that sprang to his eyes. "Brian? Is it really you? God, tell me I'm not dreaming, please."

"Where have you been, Daddy?" Brian sobbed into his neck. "I've missed you so much. I've been so lonesome. I thought you didn't love me any more."

"No, Brian. That's not true. I would never stop loving you."

He cupped the small brown head. Brian was here. In his arms. He hadn't lost him.

"Let me get a good look at you." He stood the boy on his feet. "My goodness, you sure have grown. You know what? I think your grandma and grandpa are having fits to hug you right now." Chris turned him around to see his grandparents.

Brian smiled and ran to them.

"I missed you, Grandma."

"God, Brian, I missed you, too," she cried.

The emotion was too much to bear. Chris glanced away, but everywhere he looked people, strangers, were overcome by the reunion. Even the judge's eyes teared up as Brian greeted each person he knew with a huge hug and kiss. When he was done, he turned back to his father. He studied Jessica, his dark brown eyes falling to the hand held on Chris's arm.

Chris wasn't exactly sure how to break the news to him. He didn't know how Brian would take it. And he could tell Jessica was just as concerned by the way she clutched his arm.

"Brian…this is Jessica. She's my wife now."

His eyebrows shot up. "You mean you aren't married to Mother anymore?"

"Not for a long time now."

"Then we don't have to live with her anymore?"

"That's right."

Brian broke down into tears so heart-rending Chris caught his attorney crying. "I'm glad. Now I can live with you from now on. Right?"

"That's right. No one is ever going to take you away from me again."

"Jessica is my new mother?"

"Yes."

"Is she nice?

"She is very nice. She has a little boy of her own named William. He's my son, too, now."

"Is she ever mean?"

Sean ruffled the boy's hair. "Only to chickens."

Brian studied her face. "She's very pretty."

Chris was reminded of the day William, Jeff, and Amanda had approached him about marrying Jessica. "And she's a good story teller."

"And she knows her ABCs." Meredith brushed away a tear.

Bobby cleared the emotion from his throat. "And she can add and subtract, too."

"And I love your daddy very much, Brian." Jessica let her tears fall. "I've wanted to be able to hold you and love you from the moment 'r daddy first told me about you. I sure would like it if you would ' up in my lap and give me a hug. But you don't have to if you 'ant to."

'a sensed Brian's hesitation and reluctance, and knew how he 't would be hard to believe a new mother would love you ' one didn't. This poor little boy had a long way to go ' trust again.

' about being afraid, Brian." She finger-combed his 'ne I was afraid to let your daddy hug me, but when he finally did, I liked it very much."

It was good enough for Brian. With a hesitant smile he crawled into her lap. Jessica pulled him into her arms and hugged him tightly. She rested her head on his as he nuzzled against her chest. She couldn't stop her tears any more than she could stop the love she felt for him.

"Do you bake cookies?" she heard him ask.

"Any kind you can think of."

He sat up to look at her. "Chocolate chip?"

"You bet."

He then noticed what he hadn't before. As carefully as possible he rested his small hands on her stomach. "You're having a baby."

She held up two fingers. "I'm having two babies."

His eyes widened with surprise as the babies moved under his hand. "I can feel them move. Daddy, are these our babies?"

"Yes, sir." Chris laughed. "These are our babies."

Judge Baxter cleared his throat. "Let's have an explanation. We'll start with this young man." He pointed to the detective who then took the stand.

"I was hired by the Matthews family to find the boy, which I did. We'd have been here sooner, but we had a few car problems along the way. Mrs. Delgado can fill you in on why she had the child. Shortly after the initial assignment, Sean Matthews asked me to find out who'd really attacked Carolyn Matthews. It took some digging, but I learned that three men were hired in Honolulu to rough her up."

"Who hired them?"

"Carleton Evans."

Carolyn whirled around, but he was already making a hasty retreat from the courtroom.

"You may press charges later, Mrs. Matthews. Sir, you may step down."

As the detective passed Chris, the two exchanged a handshake and a smile.

"Mrs. Delgado," Judge Baxter said, "please take the stand and tell us what's going on. You will be under oath."

Maria Delgado sat down, head held high. She refused to look at her daughter. "We only just learned our daughter let everyone believe Brian was dead. Last January Carolyn called us. She said she and Dr. Matthews were having problems, and she was afraid for Brian. We didn't think this was possible, but she is our daughter. A mother likes to believe she can trust her children.

"We agreed to take Brian, and she brought him to San Diego that day. A few days after that, my mother became ill. We went to Mexico to care for her and her farm. We've been there the whole time. It was only when the detective found us that we learned the truth." Her gaze fell to Chris. "I have all of Brian's things in the car. He belongs with you."

Carolyn pushed from her table. "The hell he does." She stormed toward Brian.

The boy recoiled, hiding under Jessica's arm.

"Give me my son." She grabbed for his arm.

Jessica pulled him from her reach and tucked him close. "You'll never take him from us."

Carolyn grabbed for the boy again.

Chris yanked her back. "Sit down."

"If you're through with your outburst, Mrs. Matthews, I'll announce my decision," Judge Baxter told her. "In fact...I've reached a number of decisions.

"The first is in regard to the child, William...A child of rape is not an easy thing for a woman to live with. Yet Jessica Matthews has strived to bring the child up in a loving and caring environment. It is evident the child is also loved by his godparents, Robert and Meredith Chamberlain, and his adoptive father, Christopher Matthews.

"I hereby order a permanent injunction be issued against Edward Chamberlain, Jr. He is forbidden to contact the child or see the child for the remainder of his life. He is ordered to not seek contact with any member of the child's family. Any attempt to do so will result in a jail sentence. Mr. Chamberlain, I hope the evidence against you puts you away for five lifetimes. You deserve it. Guards, remove him from my courtroom and escort him out of the building. If he resists, lock him up."

Judge Baxter glared at Carolyn next. "Carolyn Matthews, I have never met a person in my life more deserving of a flogging than you. The temptation is more than I can stand. You are fortunate we are living in civilized times. You are as contemptible as the man who just left my court, and I wonder if the two of you aren't somehow related. Both of you are evil personified. You have caused great mental anguish for the Matthews family by your actions—specifically to Dr. Matthews and your own son, Brian. I hereby decree that the divorce settlement between you and Dr. Matthews be modified giving Dr. Matthews full legal and physical custody of the child Brian."

Carolyn shoved to her feet. Judge Baxter silenced any protest with a threat of a jail sentence.

"You'll be given what I will call conditional visitation rights," the judge said. "If you violate any of the conditions I set forth, your visitation rights will be permanently revoked. You will be allowed to visit the child for one week out of the year. This week may not be during Christmas, Thanksgiving, or the child's birthday. You may exercise your right by notifying Dr. Matthews in writing two weeks in advance of the week you wish to visit.

"You will be allowed to visit the child only in the presence of Christopher and Jessica Matthews or their representative. The visit will occur only on the island of Hurago. All transportation costs to Hawaii are yours to bear. Transportation will be provided to Hurago as well as lodging on the island.

"This court finds that you have perjured yourself on this witness stand. You will be brought up on appropriate charges. As for your charges against Dr. and Mrs. Matthews—I find them groundless. I find your harassment of Dr. Matthews and his family completely out of line. As for a settlement—Dr. Matthews's property and assets are his now as they were prior to his marriage to you. You will receive nothing."

The judge turned to Chris. "Dr. Matthews, I regret any inconvenience or discomfort this hearing may have caused you and your family. I'm very pleased you and your son have been reunited. I wish you and your family continued happiness and good health. Court is adjourned."

Before he could pound his gavel, Carolyn bolted from her seat. "How dare you?" She stormed toward Chris. "You'll regret this. Mark my words. I'll make you pay for this. That money is mine. And you"— she whirled around to Jessica—"Miss-Goody-Two-Shoes, you just wait. I'll get you and those bastard children of yours."

"Guards," the judge ordered, "lock her up!"

The guards dragged Carolyn from the courtroom as she continued to scream threats of vengeance. Court was adjourned.

Brian trembled in Jessica's arms. She held him close and tried to reassure him. He clutched her in desperation, and she wished she could erase from his mind the pain Carolyn had inflicted. He looked up at Jessica as his mother was taken from the room and quickly gave her a kiss on the cheek before hugging her again tightly.

Chris put his arms around them both. "Let's get Brian's things and get out of here."

*　　　*　　　*

Chris still found it hard to believe Brian was actually with him. Each time he looked at the boy, a lump welled up in his throat and he wanted to hug him as tight as he could. He blessed George Davis for having enough forethought to leave out the issue of Brian's paternity. If he hadn't, Chris might not be so lucky right now.

It was still Carolyn's little trump card though and she could whip it out at any time. Of course, that would mean she'd have full custody of Brian, and the last thing she wanted was to be a mother. Still, she might use the threat to get money from them.

Chris sighed and rubbed his weary eyes. They'd worry about that later. He had a lot to be thankful for now. Brian had accepted Jessica without hesitation. Chris hoped he would get along as well with the other children on the island. He was still a very quiet child. The boisterous bunch of kids might be a little overwhelming for him. At least he seemed to be happy now that he was back with the family, and gladly sat beside Jessica when they ate lunch at the Matthews' house.

Bobby, however, stared into space, his sandwich untouched before him. The events which had come to light in the courtroom left him sick inside. Chris knew how he felt. He couldn't stop thinking about the horror Bill and Eddie had put Jessica through. A shudder went through him as he considered Eddie's visit to the island last summer, and what Eddie had tried to do to Jessica. He wanted to rail at a world that could allow such cruelty.

"I'm really not very hungry." Jessica shoved her plate away. "I think I'll just relax in the living room for awhile."

"I'm almost done. I'll come sit with you," Brian said.

"I would like that." Jessica smiled down at him, then walked away.

"Looks like someone else isn't very hungry either," Meredith said to Bobby once Brian left the room.

"I'm sorry. My stomach is just all tied up in knots. I just can't help but think about—"

"William?" Chris said.

"Yeah. I certainly get new meaning out of the words Uncle Bobby."

"How do you think I feel?" Edward pushed crumbs around his plate with his forefinger. "I don't even know if I should tell your mother."

"Elaine should know," Chris told him. "If you keep it to yourself, it'll just eat you up inside. She has a right to know."

Bobby looked up at him. "And what about William?"

Good question. Jessica wouldn't want him to ever know. And he was much too young to understand any of it right now. "Jessica and I will have to discuss that when he gets older."

Bobby rested his head in his hands. "All these years Meredith and I have helped Jessica raise William. I wonder if I would have treated him differently if I had known."

"Of course not." Meredith rubbed his shoulders. "You would've realized it wasn't William's fault, and you'd have treated him just the same."

"Poor Jessica." Leia shook her head and stared at a spot on the wall. "What a horrible thing to have happened. She had more reason to be afraid of men than any of us ever realized. I can't believe this person is my brother."

Edward snorted and shoved away from the table. "You? I can't believe he's my son." He ducked out the back door. Chris's father followed.

"Did you see how he was smirking at us when we left the courtroom?" Bobby curled his fingers into a fist. "God help me, I felt like I could've killed him."

"I just hope he stays the hell away," Chris said.

*   *   *

Jessica stood at the bay window. She knew Eddie wouldn't stay away. He felt he had a lever against them all, and he intended to use it. It was no surprise he'd followed them home from the courthouse and now sat in his car smoking a cigarette while he watched the house.

He had ruined the lives of so many young girls and had been responsible for the deaths of a few others. And Eddie's testimony had caused a dramatic change in the lives of the Chamberlains and Matthewses. Jessica was stripped of her dignity, and her son's identity cruelly changed by the evil man in the car outside. A sentence of five lifetimes still wasn't long enough to pay for what he'd done.

Turning from the window, Jessica smiled as she watched Brian set up his cars to play—much in the same manner as William and Jeff did. She was glad he could be a part of their lives, even if it did mean putting up with Carolyn for one week out of the year.

She looked back out the window and longed for the security of Hurago. She fingered her necklace and let her thoughts drift to the statues. In her mind she imagined caressing their ceramic finish just as she did the heart shape around her neck. She could almost feel the tingly heat of that touch on her hand. *Safe on Hurago. Away from Eddie.* He couldn't hurt her there, but she prayed for a more permanent solution.

She watched Eddie toss his cigarette butt to the ground and glance up at her. He saw her and smirked. Jessica's stomach churned and tried to calm herself by imagining her touch on the statues and being safe at their feet. It comforted her. They would protect her. She believed.

"I believe," she whispered.

With his gaze still fastened to hers, Eddie stepped into the street. He never saw the pickup truck speeding around the corner. Never even turned around when the truck was inches away from him. Jessica watched calmly as the truck plowed into him. The driver screeched to a halt several yards away. When he did so, Eddie's lifeless body was smashed beyond recognition.

Jessica let the drape fall and returned to where the family was finishing lunch.

"Eddie's just been run over by a truck. He's dead. I'm going to lie down."

Ignoring their gasps, she walked to the family room and stretched out on the couch. Her last thought before sleep overcame her was a gracious prayer of thanks that the statues had helped her out...again. Only one thing more would give her total peace—that they'd never have to worry about Carolyn again.

CHAPTER 18

"I have to do what?" Sean splayed his fingers across his chest.

Dan laced his hands behind his head and cocked his chair back. "I said...tomorrow morning you have to hunt down and kill a pig. It's part of the tradition."

Sean waved his hands. "No one told me that."

Bobby snapped his fingers. "Gosh, must've slipped our minds."

"That's one hell of a detail to forget." He jabbed a finger in Dan's direction. "You didn't do it."

He shrugged. "Didn't have to. My best man brought one home."

"It attacked me." Sean thumped his chest. "Mark and I killed it."

Dan's smile widened. "Yeah, but Bobby brought it back."

Sean tried a different tactic. "I can't go out and kill an innocent animal. It'll...uh...it'll upset the ecosystem."

"Sean, you and I have counted over two hundred pigs on this island," Mark said. "I don't think hunting one pig will screw up the ecosystem. Besides, they're not indigenous to the island and don't belong here anyway. They're the ones screwing up the ecosystem. So, let's face it...you're chicken."

Sean tossed back a laugh. "I am *not* chicken."

"You're scared it'll get you."

"Well, you would be, too, if you'd been gored."

"My poor sweetheart," Leia said. "Let's show everyone your scar so they can see what a close call it was." A mischievous smile lit her eyes as she reached to unzip his jeans.

"Leia, stop it." He playfully smacked her hands away. She reached for him again. Sean caught her wrists, held her hands behind her back, and pulled her close.

Chris wagged his finger at them. "That'll be enough of that."

"Can't you leave us alone for five minutes?" Sean released her with an exasperated sigh. "For the last three months all you've done is pester us."

"You can't give up now." Jessica rubbed the babies that tumbled inside her. "You've only got two weeks left and you can be married."

Dan rocked his chair. "*If* you get that pig tomorrow."

"The way I see it, you owe me a pig." Defeated, Sean tossed his hands in air. "All right, I'll get the damn pig."

"Great. We leave at six in the morning." Dan righted the chair. "You'll need help to carry it back."

"Six is good. Now, can Leia and I be alone for a little while?"

"Well, of course you can." Chris shepherded everyone from Leia's house. "I'll see you back at the house in fifteen minutes."

Sean waited as long as it took them to troop off the porch, or in Jessica's case, waddle. Then he pulled Leia into his arms and burned a kiss into her lips. His fingers crawled up her shirt to caress her breasts.

Leia gasped and arched her back. "I ache for you, Sean. God, how I ache for you."

"We've got to think of something. I want you so much I can't stand it."

"But, how? Someone's always around. The closer it gets, the worse they get. It was funny at first, but now—"

"I know. I'm getting tired of constant bodyguards. At least they haven't argued about us sleeping on Chris's couch. Maybe my parents arriving tomorrow will keep everyone occupied and we can be alone."

"I'd do anything to be alone with you."

Leia shivered as he scorched her lips with a kiss. Then, reluctantly, they returned to Chris's house.

Although Chris and Jessica were active participants in keeping them apart, their harassment wasn't as intense as Bobby and Meredith's had been. In fact, when they weren't around everyone else, Chris and Jessica never bothered them. Sean considered their home sanctuary.

Leia occupied her time helping Jessica who, in the last months of pregnancy, needed an extra pair of hands.

Sean started a new hobby tracking storms in the Pacific. The time-waster caused him no end of teasing from Chris and Leia who quickly dubbed them "Sean's Storms." He didn't care. It was something to do even if their teasing worsened with each plot mark he made. This evening was no better. Only Jessica defended him.

"I don't have to put up with this, you know," he said as he made his notations.

"What are you going to do?" Chris asked. "Take your toys and go play at Mark's?"

Jessica couldn't help herself. She laughed.

"Et tu, Jessica?" Sean feigned hurt.

"I'm sorry." She laughed so hard she cried.

With the impending birth of the twins, two rambunctious boys to care for, the farm to oversee, and Carolyn's annual visit fast approaching, Sean was more than happy to be her comic relief.

"Go ahead, you guys can laugh and pick all you want, but this could be a very important thing to us one day. Let me show you something." He spread one of the maps out on the coffee table.

"Here's our island." He tapped the map. "And look at this storm." He pointed to one of his plot marks. "It carries ninety-mile-per-hour winds. It's been slowly heading this way. Right now it's stalled, but if it keeps moving as it has been, we'll get the brunt of it. What do you do when a storm hits?"

"We've never had a storm here." Leia hovered over the table and studied the map.

"Only the winter monsoons." Jessica shoved herself to the edge of her chair for a look.

"Well, I think we need to come up with some plan in case we're hit," Sean told them.

Leia clicked her gaze up to his. "Are we really in that much danger?"

"When a storm this size hits—yes."

"What do you propose?" Chris asked.

"Let me think about it some more. I don't want to be an alarmist, but I also don't want anyone hurt."

He remembered news stories of coastal areas hit by hurricanes. Flooding and wind-destroyed homes. Where could they go to be safe?

"You're absolutely right." Chris poured over the map. "I'm sorry I teased you. You can count on our help tracking this."

Jessica patted her tummy. "Especially ours. Since my diligent, ever-ready, ever-alert doctor makes me sit all day, all I can do is knit and watch TV."

"Hey, just you remember, I'm the best doctor around here."

"The *only* doctor, honey."

*   *   *

Leia had to admit she was nervous about the pig hunt. It was a ritual she'd just as soon do away with. The animals were incredibly unpredictable. If Sean missed...

She hugged herself in a vain attempt to soothe her overactive imagination. Each step she took on her path back and forth across Chris's porch ticked off another second they were gone.

"Relax," Jessica said from inside.

"I can't. This is stupid. He's a wildlife biologist. How can he hunt an animal?"

Chris came to the door. "Do I have to give you the feral speech again?"

"No." Once was enough. Sean had given it to her last night.

The pigs weren't native to Hurago. They had no natural enemies. If the herd was not culled, it would eventually overtake the island. It prompted their first disagreement. Leia wanted the pigs gone all right, but not at the risk of Sean being hurt.

"Here they come now," Chris said.

Leia jerked to a stop and followed their progress. Tied to the poles was the biggest pig she'd ever seen. Sean, Mark, Bobby, and Dan struggled under the weight. "Good heavens, it's big."

Jessica lumbered to the porch, her hands pressed to the small of her back. "Yeah, almost as big as me."

Leia laughed. Jessica always knew how to lighten her mood. The three of them watched the men until they dropped their load to the ground and sank to Chris's steps.

"Well," Sean asked as Leia sat beside him, "is it big enough for you?"

She was too relieved to see him safe. She didn't trust herself to speak for fear of breaking down into tears.

"He got it in one shot, too," Dan told her. "Where in the world did you learn to shoot like that?"

"My grandfather used to take me shooting. He'd give me a quarter for every bull's eye. I got a lot of quarters. Must've broke him a couple of times, but he was sure proud of me. He'd brag all the time. I'll tell you, his bragging meant more to me than those quarters ever did."

"What did you and Mark do afterward, swim in it?" Chris pointed to their clothes. "You've got blood all over you."

Sean clicked his gaze his way. "We didn't have any prissy white doctor's smock to cover up with."

"My, my such hostility. Wait 'til I tell Mom and Dad."

"I'll make it easy for you," Sean said. "You can spill your guts all the way from the airstrip to the house."

"I'll have longer than that. I'm meeting them in Honolulu. Don't you want to go?"

Sean caught Leia's eye. "No, I'll stay here with Leia and help Jessica with the kids."

She would have hugged him had he been a bit cleaner. It wasn't the promised time alone which lightened her heart. It was the tender way he caressed her leg with the backs of his fingers—his silent way of saying, "I know how scared you were. I'm okay."

*   *   *

Sean checked his watch for the third time that evening. Ten o'clock and Jessica still sat before the television contentedly knitting a baby blanket. Any other night and she would have been in bed an hour ago.

"Jessica, are you sure you aren't tired?"

"Oh, a little. But I wanted to wait up for your parents."

"If you want to lie down, we'll wake you when they get here."

Jessica looked up with a smile, ready to refuse his offer. She opened her mouth, then clamped it shut. Why hadn't she seen it before? She should have realized. Their fidgeting, the occasional inquiries as to how sleepy she might be, the subtle comments on the lateness of the hour—they wanted to be alone.

With Bobby flying the Matthewses to Hurago, and Meredith at home with the children, it was the first opportunity Sean and Leia had had to be together without risk of intrusion. Even their nights were without privacy. Bobby and Meredith, even Dan and Jackie, had been known to pop in unannounced. Jessica and Chris didn't know how Sean and Leia put up with it. If the situations were reversed, Chris would have told Bobby and Meredith where they could shove their interference.

"Thank you. I'd appreciate it. Just don't forget to wake me when they get here." She stuffed her knitting away and waddled to her room.

Sean and Leia waited until they heard the door click shut. Then he drew her into his arms. Their mouths glided together in a sensuous exploration. It was a lazy discovery, heightened by the knowledge they would not be interrupted. They took their time. One kiss melded into another.

Leia stretched across his lap, pulling him on top of her as she lay on the couch. Her fingers breached the barrier of his jeans and she caressed the length of steel she found.

Sean's lips tensed on hers. The effort of muffling his pleasure was almost too much to bear. He raked his mouth down her throat, swathing a path of burning kisses downward. His hand shook as he opened the blouse buttons. He nuzzled his way to her breast, then closed his mouth around the tender flesh.

"Oh, it feels so nice," she whispered against his ear. "I want you now."

He moaned a soft response into her breast, then slid his hand to unzip her shorts. Before the zipper was down, Leia wiggled her hips free.

Sean swept the clothing off her legs. She was bare beneath him, open and ready for his body. He jerked himself free. Their lips sealed together once more, his tongue imitating what he would soon be doing to her. He eased closer, poised on the threshold of making her truly his.

The front door swung open. Sean and Leia jerked their heads around.

Chris muttered an "oops" and ducked back outside.

"Shit," Sean whispered.

"Is it possible to die of embarrassment?" Leia asked.

"If it is, at least we'll die together."

They adjusted their clothing, and Sean opened the door to his family. Their faces were as flushed as his and Leia's. They filed past him without a word, gave an awkward smile to Leia, and sat down.

"Sorry," Chris whispered an apology.

"It's...uh...okay," Sean replied.

It was only after Jessica joined them that the awkward moment passed. But his mother still couldn't look Sean and Leia directly in the eye.

"We're anxious to see this engagement ceremony tomorrow," she said. "Leia's parents said they'll explain it all as it happens."

"I'm looking forward to it, too," Chris said. "I missed the one for Jackie and Dan. That's when I was delivering Meredith's baby."

She clasped her hands under her chin. "This whole vacation is going to be wonderful."

Jessica sighed. "I don't see how it can be with Carolyn due in a few days."

Carolyn's parting shot as they were preparing to fly home after the trial was to have word hand-delivered that she intended to visit Brian the week before Easter. There was nothing they could do.

The hell of it was, Carolyn didn't want to see him. This was just another way of hurting them. Jessica wouldn't put it past her to suggest a settlement of some kind in exchange for her promise to stay away. Hell would freeze over before Jessica gave her a dime.

"Does Brian know?" Chris's father asked.

"We haven't told him yet. We keep hoping she'll cancel."

"She won't," he said. "But if it'll help, we'll go with Chris to meet her. She's less prone to verbal attacks when we're around."

"I'm sure Chris will appreciate that," Jessica said.

"Yes, he will," Chris replied.

*   *   *

"The engagement ceremony tonight follows the tradition we learned from the islanders," Edward said. "Of course, it's been modified a bit to meet our needs. The men sit on one side of the room with the ladies sitting on the opposite side."

He led them to a row of chairs. Leia sat with the women, her maid of honor, Jackie, by her side, hands demurely folded on her lap. The aged headband of hemp was tied around her head so the long strings of beads cascaded down her hair from the top of her head to her shoulders. On her forehead, the bandeau formed a flat heart-shaped knot.

Chris smiled. It looked very much like the necklace Jessica wore. "What's that she's wearing?"

"That is called the betrothal necklace. In a few minutes Sean will..." He flicked his hand in the air. "You'll see. I'll explain as we go along."

*   *   *

Leia watched Sean wipe his palms on his trousers then slip the cassette into the player. She smiled when she heard the first notes of music. This was it. One more step on their way to being together...forever.

On cue Mark walked her way and extended his hand. Danced refused, he moved on. Jackie and Mark had barely reached the dance floor when Sean hurried Leia's way. Her heart beat against her breastbone as he neared. She smiled up to him, then reached behind her to untie the headband. She shook it, placed it around her neck, and took Sean's hand. He was her chosen, her life-mate.

She knew the love mirrored in their eyes as they walked hand in hand to the dance floor. How could it not when she wanted to burst

169

with happiness? As they began to dance, Leia looked deep into his eyes and felt as if she had met herself. As if their souls touched and were one. She only had to look at his face to feel love for him burn inside her. Her lips invited him and he bent to kiss her.

One touch sent hot desire shuddering through her. Time and space were one. There was only the feel of his lips upon hers, and the warmth of his tongue probing deeply inside of her mouth. She wanted this to never end.

Sean had never known such pleasure in a kiss. He wanted to kiss her until their lips ached as much as the rest of them. Slowly, reluctantly they pulled away from each other and realized the music had stopped. Leia hooked her arm through Sean's, and they walked over to the chairs to sit down. Before they could reach their seats, they were besieged by their guard dogs, sorely testing Sean's temper.

Chris shoved his way past the tormentors. "Give it a rest. This is getting old fast. Leave them alone. If you want something to worry about, worry about that storm."

"We haven't had a storm since we've lived here." Bobby gave a sheepish grin. "I guess that's a stupid response, isn't it?"

Sean arched an eyebrow in reply. It was that air of complacency that got people killed. He was glad Bobby realized it on his own.

"It's heading for us, isn't it?"

Sean looped Leia's arm through his. "If it continues on its present course, it'll hit us for sure."

Mark faced the others. "What kind of emergency preparedness plan do you have here?"

Edward hung his head as he shook it. "I'm ashamed to say we don't have one."

"I don't think the buildings here will adequately shelter us from a storm like this." Sean studied the community building. It might hold up if they boarded up the windows. Then again, it might not. It was a risky chance to take.

Dan snapped his fingers. "That's what the caves are for, remember? You said that yourselves." He spun around to Sean and Mark. "I remember my dad telling me about the day they found this island. A storm blew them off course and when they turned they saw the islanders coming down the pathway to the bridge."

Bobby rubbed his chin. "Yes, that does make sense."

"And they can easily hold everyone on the island." Mark reached for a napkin and started to make notes. "What we should do is make cave assignments so everyone knows which cave to go to. That would also allow us to do a head count once we're all there."

Ideas and plans flew back and forth. Meetings were planned. Provisions and medical supplies listed. A work force and check list were added. There was just one issue they avoided, or maybe no one thought of it. Sean hated to be the one to bring it up, but...

"What happens if Gina and Jessica go into labor during storm?"

Chris cut off his own conversation in mid-word. "Bite your tongue. I'm nervous enough about these births without thinking about that."

"Nervous about adding to your already blossoming household?" Meredith asked with a laugh.

He scratched his head. "Well, we'll definitely have a full house."

"Wasn't that the plan? But before that happens, if there is a storm on the way, there are things Bobby and I have to do at the hotel. Would it be too much trouble if we left the kids with you for a day or two?"

"Of course, I don't mind. Leia and Sean are there to help. If it's all right with Jess, it's all right with me."

"Thanks, Chris. We'll fly out tomorrow when you leave to get Carolyn." She kissed his cheek and wandered over to Jessica.

Leia sidled up to Sean and whispered in his ear. "Did you hear that? The watch dogs will be gone."

"I've already got the time and place picked out."

CHAPTER 19

"Hey, Grandma, Grandpa, watch what Uncle Sean taught Buffy to do," William said.

"Not now," Jessica told him. "You'll be late for school."

"Aw, Mom. It'll only take a minute. I won't be late and even if I am, Dan and Jackie won't mind."

"Well…all right." What harm would it really do? If the rain started up again, there would be little chance for dog and boy to run off excess energy.

William pulled his shirt over his head and tossed it to Sean. "Hold Buffy now."

Sean smiled and picked up the dog. While the six-year-old went to hide, Sean let the dog get a good whiff of the shirt. He put her on the ground and let her sniff the shirt again.

"Where's William, Buffy? Buffy, find William."

Sniffing the air intently, then the ground, Buffy zoomed to a nearby tree.

William laughed and scooped her into his arms. "Good girl, Buff. Good girl." Her body wiggled at the lavish praise.

Chris's mother clapped her hands. "That was wonderful."

"Now you and Jeff scoot to school," Chris told him. "It looks like it might rain again any minute."

The boys ran off, and Chris eyed the gathering clouds, renegades from the hurricane. "You sure we'll be able to fly out?"

"Yeah. Roger has the plane ready to go. The sky is clear from here to Honolulu," Bobby said.

Chris raked his fingers through his hair. There was no avoiding it. "Damn, let's get this over with."

"We'll wait out here while you tell Brian," his father said.

Chris and Jessica found the boy where they'd left him ten minutes before, sprawled on his belly watching cartoons with Amanda. They'd hoped Carolyn would change her mind at the last minute and Brian wouldn't have to be upset. As far as they knew, she was waiting for Chris in Honolulu.

Chris sat on the couch next to Jessica and tried to dredge up the courage to break Brian's heart. There simply was no easy way. "Brian, Mom and I need to talk to you for just a minute."

The boy scrambled to his feet and tucked himself between Chris's knees. His face fell with the news.

"I don't want her here. You tell her no."

Chris held his small shoulders. "I can't do that. The law says she can come see you."

He jerked away. "No! I won't see her! I won't! I hate her!"

Amanda ran from the house, crying for her father.

Brian stomped his feet into the carpet. "I won't see her! I won't! I won't! I won't!"

Brian kicked the coffee table over, scattering magazines across the floor. He fell on top of them, kicking and screaming. The outburst was frightening.

Chris yanked him to his feet. "Stop it right now or I'll spank you."

It was a harsh threat under the circumstances; one Chris had no intention of carrying out. But he couldn't think of anything else to do.

Jessica reached out to calm the boy. "Sweetheart, please—"

With a growl like that of a caged animal, Brian swung at her.

Jessica caught his arm and gave him a stern shake. "Stop it. Now."

Brian broke down into sobs and threw himself into the comfort of her arms. "I don't want her to come here. I hate her." He sobbed against her chest. "She doesn't love me. She never gives me any hugs or kisses. She never tucks me in. She doesn't even make me chocolate chip cookies. And she always yells at my daddy."

Chris couldn't stand it any more. As Jessica rocked the sobbing child, he took the coward's way out and left. He prayed this wouldn't be an indication of how Carolyn's visit would turn out.

"That went really well," Bobby said when Chris stepped out to the porch. Amanda's face was burrowed in her father's neck as she cried.

Chris rubbed her back. "It's okay, Amanda.."

"No, the witch is coming," the five-year-old wailed. "Brian said she was a mean, old witch. Brian wouldn't lie to me. He's my best friend in the whole world."

How could Chris argue with such logic? Especially when he knew first hand just how big a witch Carolyn really was.

"It's only a week, Amanda," Meredith told her. "She won't hurt anyone while she's here."

Amanda looked up, her brown eyes wide and wet. "That's right. The statues will protect us. Aunt Jessica says." She scrambled from Bobby's arms and ran inside. She returned almost immediately with Brian in tow. Hand in hand the children darted in a straight line to the statues.

Meredith rolled her gaze heavenward.

"What's it going to hurt?" Bobby asked her. "If it helps them get through this week, then isn't it worth it?"

Meredith shrugged. "I guess so." She turned to Chris. "You sure you can manage all the kids for a few days?"

Sean answered for him. "Relax. It'll be okay. Leia should be back from the farm soon. After I load more supplies into the cave, I'll be here. And if Jessica has a problem while Chris is at the airport, she can call Mark to come help. You know he won't be far from Gina until their baby's born."

Still she hesitated. "Well…"

"Let's go." Bobby steered her toward the truck.

"Good luck," Sean told his brother. "And remember, patience is the greatest weapon you can use against Carolyn."

"Easy for you to say."

Chris kept Sean's words in his head when he and his parents met Carolyn. If the visit was to be disastrous, it would be through no fault of his.

*   *   *

Leia swam from behind the curtain the waterfall made and saw Sean standing by the pool of water. "You're late."

He answered with a smile as he stripped down to his swimming trunks and dove into the water.

Leia looked around to see where he would surface. Sean snuck up behind her and lifted her from the water. She squealed when he tossed her back into the pool. He dove again. She warily scanned the water. He surfaced in front of her and took her by the waist, then pulled her into shallower water until their feet could touch the bottom.

It was precious time alone. There was no one who could disturb them. Yet the long abstinence made them impatient. As their tongues twined together he pulled her bikini bottom down. Leia did the same for him, releasing him to her touch.

Sean gasped. "God, honey, I can't wait any more."

He pulled her leg around his waist, the strong band of his arm held her steady. Then he stabbed his flesh into hers.

Leia cried out, tossing her head back in ecstasy. He nipped at the curves of her breasts as he struggled to hold back the rush he felt. Leia twitched against him, anxious for the pleasure he could bring her. Sean thrust forward, his jaw tight. She clutched his shoulders, her nails biting into his flesh as he stroked her. She arched against him as the first wave of pleasure washed over her. Her soft cry echoed in his ear. Digging his fingers into her buttocks, he seated a final deep thrust.

They held each other for several minutes, wrapped in the wonder of the moment. Then they pulled apart for a slow swim to the waterfall and back. At the shore he pulled her close for a kiss.

"Do you suppose the island gods are angry with us?" she asked.

"No." He helped her to a large rock. "How can they be mad when we love each other so much?"

They stretched out on the rocks to warm themselves while the sun played peekaboo behind the clouds. Leia heard a strange buzzing, and turned to see what it was. Next to a red hibiscus were two hummingbirds.

"Male and female," Sean whispered to her.

She watched the tiny birds with interest. "Are they mating?"

"No. You see, males are very territorial. That hibiscus is the last one in the immediate area. She's hungry, but he won't let her have any of the nectar. Now...look...she's starting a courtship flight. He'll share the nectar with her as her mate."

"In other words, she's telling him she'll give him all she has to give if he'll share with her." Leia looked deep into Sean's eyes.

"And he would gladly give her all he has if she'll just be his." He gently took Leia's mouth with his.

*   *   *

Jessica felt the mild contractions shortly after Chris's departure for Honolulu. Under the circumstances, her only alternative was to lie down. She trusted Brian and Amanda to play quietly and watch television while Rachel occupied her time in the playpen. But with the storm pending, little tempers flared and minor disputes broke out among the house-bound children.

Jessica looked forward to nap time. Immediately after lunch, amid gripes and complaints of being too old for naps, she made everyone lie down. Then she crawled wearily into her own bed. Someone would be there soon. William and Jeff from school, Sean and Leia from their work. Maybe even Chris. All she wanted to do was rest until they arrived. An hour later she stretched herself awake and walked to the living room to check on Rachel.

Shock rooted her feet. A small mountain of mud sat in the middle of the light blue carpet. Bored with being confined and unwilling to take a nap, Brian and Amanda had decided the rain had made the dirt outside perfect for making mud sculptures. Knowing they weren't allowed out in the pouring rain to play, they decided to bring the dirt inside. They sat side by side chattering away while they worked, oblivious to all.

"What in the world have you two done? You both know better."

She marched to the kitchen and snagged her wooden spoon. Amanda's eyes widened. She tried to dart into the bedroom, but Jessica was too quick for her. Three solid whacks reminded her of her manners. Turning angrily toward Brian, Jessica administered the same to him.

"Now the two of you clean this mess up and clean it up now, or I'll spank you again."

"But, Aunt Jessica, we put down newspaper," Amanda wailed.

"Now!" She jerked her arm toward the mess. Still bawling, they scooped mud into their pails.

Jessica eased herself into a nearby chair as a contraction overwhelmed her. The front door opened. *Thank God someone is here.*

William and Jeff stood in the doorway, mouths wide at the mess. She handed him the spoon. "William, put this away. Then the two of you help with this mess."

Moments later he ran back into the room, tears streaming down his cheeks. "Mom, come quick! Buffy's bleeding! I think she's dying!"

Jessica waddled to the kitchen and found spots of blood on the floor. Buffy was in heat. And Chris was in serious trouble. She'd been begging him for weeks to have her spayed. Each time he put her off. *"I'll take care of it, Jess."*

Yeah, right.

"She's all right. It just means she can have babies now."

"I don't believe you. Buffy's dying and you're scared to tell me."

He clutched the dog in his arms as tears doubled.

"Aunt Jessica, come quick. Rachel's throwing up," Jeff shouted.

Jessica braced herself against the table and breathed through the pain. *Where is everyone?*

Using the wall to support herself, she made her way back to the living room. At least Jeff had the sense to pick Rachel up and not leave her in her mess. Sick, uncomfortable, and very unsure of who held her, the baby wailed at the top of her lungs. Jeff was more than happy to give her up.

Still, her cries were nothing compared to the fight brewing between the five-year-olds. Nose to nose and at the top of their lungs, each blamed the other for their trouble. With the baby in her arms and the boys hanging by her sides, Jessica desperately tried to restore order between them.

It was hopeless. She snagged Brian's arm to sit him in one corner. Amanda picked up a fistful of mud and hurled it his way. It hit him square in the face.

From the corner of her eyes, Jessica saw the front door open again. Taking advantage of the distraction, Brian pulled free of her hold and scooped up a handful. Amanda ducked. The ball of mud sailed past her and connected with Carolyn's white silk dress. Jessica didn't know whether to laugh or cry.

Chris slammed the door behind them. "What in the hell is going on in here?"

The children jerked their heads up. Before Jessica had the chance to answer, another contraction seized her.

"Give me the baby and sit down." Chris reached for Rachel. "Now, what is going on?"

Rachel threw up again, missing Chris and hitting Carolyn behind him. "That answers that question. What else?"

"Buffy's in heat. There's blood all over the kitchen. And William won't believe she's all right." Jessica rubbed at the pain. "As you can see, Brian and Amanda have decided to bring outside in."

"When did you start having contractions?"

"Shortly after you left."

He briefly considered lecturing her for not calling for help, then thought better of it. Judging from the fire in Jessica's eyes, she was none too happy about the dog. The wrong word now and she might just come after him with her infamous wooden spoon. And he certainly didn't want Carolyn to hear them fuss.

"Are the contractions regular?"

"No, every now and then."

"You've been on your feet too much. Sofa or bed for you. No place else." He pointed to the children. "Have those two been punished?"

"Yes." Again her eyes shot him daggers.

If he didn't get himself out of trouble soon... "I'll set up an appointment with the vet right away."

"Thank you." With one final glare, she shoved herself to her feet and walked to their room, slamming the door behind her.

Chris heaved a sigh and turned back to the other problems.

"Brian, Amanda, get this mess cleaned up right now. I don't want to hear another word out of either one of you. William, get that dog back into the kitchen. I don't want blood all over the furniture. And start cleaning up the floor in there. Where the hell are Sean and Leia?"

"Right behind... Oh my G—" Mouth wide, Leia gasped at the mess in front of them.

"Carolyn, if you still intend to begin your visit immediately, I suggest you sit down and get out of the way," Chris told her.

"If you don't mind, I'll wait 'til tomorrow. I wish to be taken to where I'll be staying."

"Dad, get her out of here."

"I refuse to ride one more foot in that hideous truck," Carolyn said. "Have the hotel send someone for me."

"There is no hotel," Chris said. "There are cabanas for visitors on the beach."

"How am I supposed to manage? What am I supposed to eat?"

Leia parked herself in front of Carolyn and tucked her arms under her bosom. "Eye of newt? Witch's bane? I'm sure you could conjure up something."

Chris's mother snickered. Sean was less discreet—his laughter carried him to the kitchen.

"How dare you," Carolyn shouted. "You are deliberately trying to chase me away."

Chris pulled Leia out of the way. "Believe me, Carolyn, no one knows better than me what an impossible task that is. Now stay and help or go, but quit your bitchin'."

The bedroom door swung open behind him, and he heard Jessica's weary sigh.

"Chris...please."

Her quietly spoken entreaty eased his rage somewhat, if only for her benefit. He stepped away from Carolyn and placed the baby in Leia's arms.

"Carolyn, Leia will show you where you can clean up your dress," Jessica told her. "After that she'll give you a sponge and a bucket so you can help carry out the mud."

With a snort Carolyn pivoted on her heel and stomped from the house.

"I thought as much." Jessica shut the door.

Chris massaged the ache in his temple. "This is going to be a lovely week."

*   *   *

Doctor's instinct made Chris leap from his bed. He was momentarily dazed as he haphazardly donned his robe, trying to figure out what woke him. Another, louder knock at the door cleared his head. He glanced at the clock. Five. Gina's baby?

Why didn't they call?

He wrinkled his nose when he entered the living room. It still smelled like mud. The stench was so bad even Sean and Leia opted to sleep at Dan and Jackie's. He rubbed his nose and whipped open the door. Concern turned to irritation when he saw Carolyn standing there.

"Do you have any idea what time it is?"

"I've come to see Brian. I only have a week, and I intend to use every bit of it."

"Two can play at this game, Carolyn. Come on in. If you want to see him, you'll just have to watch him as he sleeps."

She slithered up to him and made a move to caress his chest. Chris smacked her hand away.

"Don't you even think about it." He stalked to the bedroom to dress, careful not to disturb Jessica.

Upon his return, he chose to ignore Carolyn and use the time to settle down in his chair with a cup of coffee, and catch up on his reading. It didn't take Carolyn long to take offense. Her verbal assault was quick in coming.

"Are you always so rude to your guests?"

"You aren't a guest. You're an intrusion," he replied without taking his eyes off his magazine.

"You invited me into your house."

"Only because I knew if I didn't, you'd continue to pound on the door until everyone in the house was awake."

"I'm exercising my right to visit my son."

"You are, as usual, making a fool of yourself. You're using Brian to get to me so you can continue to make my life miserable. I don't want you here and neither does Brian. I'm allowing it only because the law requires me to do so. If you upset Brian in any way, I'll see to it your visiting rights are revoked."

She stuck out her lower lip in a pout. "The least you could do is offer me a cup of coffee while I wait."

"The least you could do is get out of here and let me get back to sleep." From the corner of his eye he watched her draw breath for another volley.

Thankfully, the telephone's ring stopped her. He was more than grateful for the reprieve and silently hoped whoever it was would provide him with respite from Carolyn. Mark's frantic announcement Gina was in labor answered his prayer and put a smile on his face.

"I can't do this, Chris. I'm too scared."

Chris heard Gina snatch the phone away from Mark. "Chris, I'm nowhere near ready to deliver."

"Why don't you and Mark come over here? Maybe that'll put his mind at ease," Chris said.

"We'll be right over."

"What's going on around here?" Jessica asked groggily as she entered the living room.

"Gina's in labor, and Mark's a nervous wreck. They'll be here soon. I'll just monitor her here." He went to hug her. "How are you feeling?"

"Tired. I see you've started your morning early, Carolyn. If you're here to see Brian, you've got a long wait. He won't be up until about eight, then he and Amanda are going to the farm with Leia to collect eggs. If you intend to visit him, you're going to have to be prepared to follow him around. I won't have his life disrupted while you're here."

Carolyn perched her hands on her hips. "And just who do you think you are?"

Tired, uncomfortable, and more than a bit on edge, Jessica refused to be bullied. "Carolyn, may I remind you that you're a visitor in my house? While you're in my house, you will not raise your voice to me. I'm also Brian's mother and responsible for his well-being and care. I repeat, I will not have his life disrupted during the week you are here."

"You're trying to turn him against me."

"You've already accomplished that by your prior treatment of him. He doesn't want to see you. Nevertheless, he has been told he has to, and I assure you, he'll show you the same respect due to any other adult."

Jessica left Carolyn standing there, dressed as quickly as possible, and returned to the living room as Gina and Mark arrived.

Mark was truly a nervous wreck. Each time a contraction came, he winced as if he were experiencing it. One by one the children woke and eyed Gina curiously. To keep Mark occupied, Chris put him in charge of breakfast while he cared for Rachel and Gina. By the time breakfast was over, the word was out that Gina was in labor, and the family and friends slowly filtered in.

The first to arrive were Sean and Leia with his parents close behind. "We've come to take Amanda and Brian off your hands for a while," his mother said.

Jessica wasted no time reminding Carolyn she would have to go with them if she expected to visit Brian. She wanted her gone as much as Chris did and was just as determined to help her leave, one way or the other.

"This is the most ridiculous thing I've ever heard of. You actually expect me to follow the child around?"

"Isn't that the purpose of visiting him?" Jessica asked.

She hiked her nose in the air. "I will not go near a bunch of dirty chickens."

"Then sit in the truck." Chris struggled in vain to control his mounting anger. "You either go with them, or you go back to your cabin. You will not sit in my house all day long."

She reluctantly went with the children and his parents, while Leia stayed behind to help Chris.

Sean boasted a mischievous grin as they left. "I think I'll take the three boys backpacking tomorrow."

"That's dirty, Sean," Chris replied with a smile, "but I love it."

CHAPTER 20

Chris smiled as Mark and Gina marveled over their daughter's tiny fingers and toes. The baby nuzzled into her mother's chest and quieted.

Mark's hand shook as he reached out to touch her. "Isn't she great? What a little miracle? She's as beautiful as you, sweetheart."

Leia plumped up the pillows behind Gina. "Does this little girl have a name?"

"Rebecca Ann...Becky." Mark traced the back of his finger over his daughter's cheek.

Chris didn't understand how they could have waited this long to find out the sex of their child. He and Jessica had wanted to know right away. Unfortunately, one of the twins wasn't cooperating. All they knew was that one of them was a boy.

But Mark and Gina swore Chris to secrecy and never once tried to drag the information about their child out of him. All they wanted to know was that the baby was healthy.

"Ready for visitors?"

They nodded, but Chris wondered if they actually heard him.

Sean was the first one through the door. "Well, what was it?"

"A daughter," Gina said.

He edged closer, straining for a peek. "A daughter. Wow! Guess Mark will be needing a shotgun."

"No need," his friend replied. "She won't be allowed out of the house 'til she's thirty."

Chris watched the joy and awe in the new parents' faces and all he could think about was soon that would be him and Jessica.

"This was a sneaky thing to do." Meredith was poised in the doorway, hands jammed on hips. His mother and Bobby stood beside her.

Chris chuckled. "How did the visit to the farm go?"

"Good for us. Bad for Carolyn." His mother snickered. "She wasn't watching where she was going and stepped into mud up to her ankles."

Sean tossed back a laugh. "She's going to love backpacking tomorrow."

"You're taking her with you?" Bobby asked.

Sean shrugged and lifted his palms. "She insists on being with Brian his every waking minute. I'm just making sure she is."

"Then I'm going with you." Bobby rubbed his hands together.

Chris wasn't sure how smart it was to antagonize Carolyn. It only made things worse. True, she brought her woes on herself, but she lashed out at others because of it.

He herded them all toward the door. "It's time to let this new mommy rest."

Once he was confident Gina and the baby were settled, he followed the others to his house. He was more than irritated to find Carolyn there. From the tight set of Jessica's lips he could tell she wasn't happy about it either. Murderous intent backlit her eyes.

Amanda squealed when she saw her parents and tossed herself against their legs.

Meredith hugged her, then held her back. "I understand you and Brian had a talk with the wrong end of Aunt Jessica's wooden spoon yesterday."

Amanda gave her mother her most endearing apologetic look while Brian stared at the floor.

Carolyn jumped to her feet and whirled around to Jessica. "You beat my child? How dare you. My poor little darling." She smothered a hug into the boy.

Brian struggled for release.

"I'll report you to the authorities for abuse."

"Go ahead." Jessica shifted that deadly glare her way. "Bobby will be glad to fly you out right away."

"How dare you treat this so lightly! My poor baby." She cupped Brian's face and forced him to look at her. "Mother's sorry your mean stepmother beat you so badly. Mother will make sure it never happens again."

He shoved away. "She's not a mean stepmother. She's a nice one. And I love her. I love her more than you. I hate you. You're mean. I hate you. I wish you were dead." He spun around and threw himself into Jessica's arms, while sobs shook his small body.

What little patience Chris had left. He narrowed his glare Carolyn's way. "Your visit is over for today. If you wish to visit with him tomorrow, he'll be leaving after breakfast for a backpacking trip. Get out."

With a haughty toss of her long, black hair, she stormed from the house.

Chris closed his eyes against a pounding headache. *How many more days?* It didn't matter. This was what it would be like once a year for the next thirteen years.

Jessica set Brian on his feet and patted his bottom. "You kids go play for awhile." She held her smile until they dashed out the door, then collapsed wearily in her chair.

"I can't wait 'til Friday morning."

Chris squatted before her and rested his hand on her knee. "We know she wants money. Let's just pay her to stay away and be done with it."

Jessica looked like she wanted to cry. She turned it around to a sad laugh and caressed Chris's cheek. "Because whatever we give her will never be enough. She'll always want more."

Chris kissed her palm. Jessica was right. If she could be strong, so could he.

Sean sidled up to them. "Don't you worry. She'll be on that plane if I have to hog tie her and carry her away. I'm sick of this. I'm sick of her. And I'll be damned if I'll have her interfering with our wedding."

Unfortunately, the hurricane had other ideas. By Thursday evening, it had moved closer, right between Hurago and Oahu. No one could get in and no one could get out... including Carolyn.

Jessica tried to take the news in stride and prayed the storm would move before the wedding preparations. But although the island weather was clear, the hurricane stayed where it was. They were stuck with her for the duration.

At least Carolyn showed the good sense not to interfere with the festivities on this sunny Saturday. As the fathers of the intended couple, Edward and David built the altar on the peninsula while Elaine and Karen decorated it and the aisle with hundreds of plumeria and tube rose blossoms.

Forbidden to lift a finger, Jessica lounged outside on a lawn chair, reading, sipping lemonade, and watching the activity. From time to time someone stopped by to visit her, and she generally enjoyed the attention even if she did hate being idle. How could she really mind when she was protecting the tiny lives inside her?

As the day wore on, the preparations slowed and everyone settled around her for a break. They laughed at nothing in particular and everything in general. They watched the children play and Sean teach Buffy the logistics of fetch-the-stick. And, generally, just enjoyed each others' company.

Jessica glanced toward the statues to thank them for such a perfect day. Both pulsed with energy. At least that's what it felt like. They were brighter, the colors more vibrant. Joy radiated to Jessica.

Carolyn's approach spoiled the moment. Jessica watched her slink over and found herself wishing the ground would open up and swallow her.

"Isn't this a cozy family gathering?"

Chris didn't spare her a look. "Carolyn, your visit was officially up yesterday. I've put up with your crap all week long, and I'm not going to anymore. You've made everyone miserable. Now leave us alone. Trust me, you'll be on the first plane out of here."

Buffy bounced over to visit the family. Seeing Carolyn, the dog stretched out to tentatively sniff her leg. Carolyn screamed and kicked the little dog. Buffy's yelp brought William running to her aid.

"You mean lady. You kicked my dog." He reared back and whacked her in the shin.

She screeched. "You wretched little street urchin!" She slapped him hard across the face.

William fell back with the force of her blow, toppling to the grass. A growl curled the dog's lips.

Chris snatched Carolyn's upper arm and shoved her against the side of the building. "If you ever touch him again, I swear to God I'll kill you. Do you understand me?"

"You're hurting me!"

"Answer me!"

Sean curled his fingers over his shoulder. "Chris, stop. She's not worth it."

He threw her away from him and squatted down to William, who sobbed in Jessica's arms, while Leia held Buffy at bay.

"You okay?"

William looked up and nodded, then put his arms around Chris's neck.

Carolyn sneered behind his back. "Always the ever-loving, ever-caring father." She slowly rubbed her arm.

Chris handed William back to Jessica and faced Carolyn. "And it's a damn fine thing, too, for Brian's sake."

Brian ran up to Jessica, wrapped his arms around her, and buried his face in her neck. She tucked both boys close, wishing she could deafen them to the harsh words.

"All you ever cared about was him." Carolyn jerked her finger toward the boy.

"I will not discuss this with you…now or ever."

Jessica watched the fury rise in Chris's face. It was a mystery to her how he kept calm.

"Why? Too busy with your baby factory? Your little harem?" She perched her hands on her narrow waist and sneered. "Or should I say your little whores?"

Chris raised his hand, then pulled it back down. "Who in the hell do you think you are? You've ruined the lives of everyone you've come in contact with. And you have the nerve to stand there and talk trash."

He pulled in a deep breath. "You're finished, Carolyn. You'll never come back here again. You'll never see Brian again. And if you want to take me to court for that you go right ahead, because I'll have Brian tell the judge exactly how he feels about you."

A smile lit her dark eyes with evil intent. "Oh, I don't think you really want to do that, do you? *I'll* be the one making sure *you* never see him again."

Jessica's heart raced. Carolyn was going to challenge paternity. Panic stole her breath. She prayed Carolyn wouldn't see her fear; wouldn't notice the tears that threatened to pool. This couldn't happen. She couldn't take this dear little boy. If it meant giving her every last dime she had, Jessica would do it. Anything to keep him.

She opened her mouth, ready to make her offer.

A piercing siren cut the air. People froze and searched the area, confused at where the sound was coming from.

"It's the statues," Mark shouted above the din. "It's coming from the statues." As soon as he said the words, it stopped.

"What in the world?" Bobby scooped Amanda into his arms.

"I'm scared, Daddy," she said.

"Don't be, sweetheart."

"Mom, what was it?" William asked.

Jessica stared in awe at the giant ladies. "I have no idea."

"It's the mad words," Brian said against her neck. "They don't like it. They want it to stop."

"You're probably right," Leia said. "Tomorrow will be a busy day. Let's go home and have some dinner."

Jessica patted the boys. "Come on. Get Buffy and we'll go."

Cradling his dog in his arms, William raced Brian home.

Jessica eased to her feet. Her gaze never left Chris's face. The thought of losing Brian sickened him. Jessica felt like slapping Carolyn all the way to Honolulu. She had to reassure him. No one was taking Brian. With a tender smile that came straight from the heart, she walked toward him.

Carolyn's leg shot out. Jessica saw her intent too late.

Time moved in slow motion. She was vaguely aware of other people rushing forward to help her as she plummeted toward the ground. A hand darted out and missed her arm. Chris dove forward to cushion her fall. She landed on him with a dull thud. Knife-like pain pierced her belly.

Jessica clutched at her stomach, eyes squeezed shut against the pain. She refused to cry out no matter how much it hurt. When she opened them, it was to find Chris's worried face hovering above as he cradled her.

Chris rested his hand on her belly, feeling the contraction as it eased.

"This is it, isn't it?" she asked.

"I'm afraid so."

"I think they're coming fast, too."

"Then we could use your help, Leia." He helped Jessica to her feet, then he and Gina led her to the infirmary.

Thirty minutes later she pushed their son into the world. Chris choked up as he placed the infant on Jessica's stomach while he cut the cord.

"He's beautiful." She caressed the tiny head.

There was no way Chris could describe the myriad of emotions that filled him. They were too overwhelming.

"Jessica, he's perfect," he somehow managed to say. "Steven is perfect. Thank you for giving him to me. Gina, we're ready for you to take our son. Don't drop him."

Gina laughed lightly as she took the baby. "Relax, brand new daddy. I haven't dropped a baby yet."

Leia stole a peek. "He sure looks like you, Chris."

Once Gina cleaned him up and swaddled him, she placed the baby in Leia's arms. "He can go in the bassinet now."

Leia gave her an absentminded nod and made it as far as the nearest chair. Chris chuckled. He knew how she felt. If there wasn't a second child on the way, he and Jessica might be fussing over who got to hold him.

They had barely had time to settle Steven when the next baby arrived.

"It's a girl," Chris said with a laugh. "Looks like her brother, but with a tinge of red in her hair. Wonder where she got that. Name?"

Jessica looked over at Leia. "I'd like to name her Shawna Michelle."

Leia beamed her approval at the feminine version of Sean's name. "I like that name."

"I wonder why." Chris placed the baby in Gina's arms. "Jessica Matthews, you're a doctor's nightmare."

"What do you mean?"

"Don't you ever deliver babies that fast again."

Jessica giggled as the first tremors of after-birthing overcame her. "I'm not worried. Not when I have the best damn doctor around."

Chris laughed. "Ah, you finally discovered my true value."

"I discovered that long ago, my love." They exchanged a loving kiss.

"Let's get you and our babies all fixed up. I'm sure we'll have lots of visitors soon."

*   *   *

Carolyn glared as family filed from the building. The broad smile on Chris's face galled her. She wanted to cause them pain, not happiness. She'd fix them. She'd fix them all.

She grinned at the cleverness of her plan. It was perfect. They could deny her nothing then. All she needed was the opportunity to do it.

CHAPTER 21

The sirens blasted the island awake early the next morning. Jessica jumped as she nursed Shawna. The baby never flinched. "What do you suppose it means?"

"I don't know." Chris diapered Steven, then cuddled him. "Everyone on the island seems to think you're the expert on these statues. You have more of a communion with them than anyone else does."

"Well, maybe so, but this is a little scary. It's six o'clock. They went off at six last night. Why are they doing that? *How* are they doing that?"

He traded babies with her so she could feed Steven while he put Shawna in the crib.

"Maybe if I could sit with them for awhile I'd know."

"Go ahead." He jerked his head toward the door. "You know you won't rest until you do."

Jessica smiled. He knew her too well. If they had this strong a connection now, she wondered what they'd be like in twenty years.

Once the infants were fed, she wandered down to the statues and sat in her niche by the feet, staring out to sea. A feeling of danger overcame her—a danger so great it could kill. *But from who or what? Carolyn?* Evil *was* her middle name. She closed her eyes and leaned back, trying to hone in on the threat. *Please don't let her take Brian.*

"Shouldn't you be resting?" Edward asked.

Jessica opened her eyes and found him standing beside her. He, too, scanned the ocean.

"I'm fine. I only gave birth. I didn't undergo major surgery."

Edward smiled. "Yes, but you gave birth to two at once. And I suspect if you had major surgery, you'd bounce back the next day. You amaze me, Jessica, you always have. You've lived through so much...hell. You come through with your head high. I'm as proud of you as I would be if you were my own child."

"Thank you, Edward." The praise humbled her. She didn't know what else to say.

"We haven't talked about it, but you don't know how ashamed I am of what Eddie did to you. I wish there were some way I could make up—"

"It isn't your fault." And she didn't want to talk about it. It might be out in the open now, but it was still the biggest nightmare of her life.

Edward sighed. "I think sometimes if Elaine and I had raised him differently. But, then, he was brought up the same way as Bobby and Leia. I don't understand. And, William... Funny, I always thought he looked like Bobby. I'm ashamed to say that once or twice I thought... You know."

"Yes, I know."

"He's a wonderful boy. Elaine and I have always loved him. Chris is a fine young man, Jess. He'll be a good husband and father."

He looked up at the statue as he caressed the porcelain surface. "You feel it, too, don't you, Jess?"

"The danger?"

He nodded.

"Yes. But I don't know what it is."

Edward stared across the lagoon. "Maybe it's the storm. Look at how high the tide is and how rough the waves are."

"Well, you know as well as I do that the storm is going to kick up the ocean a bit," Jessica said. "The weather report says it should hit Oahu by night. If it changes course, we'll know. And the caves are stocked with everything we'd need."

"Yeah, we're prepared. Thanks to Sean. It would just help to know for sure if we'll be hit."

He extended a hand to help her to her feet. "I'll walk you back home. You should rest while you can. You don't want to miss the wedding."

Jessica smiled. "No, I definitely don't want to miss that."

*   *   *

"Will you two hurry up?" Sean paced the length of Chris's living room for what seemed the millionth time. "How long can it possibly take to get ready?"

"You're forgetting we have more than ourselves to dress," Chris shouted from the boys' bedroom. "Relax, she's not going to get married without you."

Sean could have smacked himself for his inconsideration. He apologized and went to help Jessica with the babies. He found her staring solemnly into the crib. The twins lay sleeping side by side.

"Something wrong?"

"No...not really. Sean, would you be terribly offended if I didn't go to the wedding?"

New Mother Syndrome. "Of course we won't mind. You can watch from the porch."

Jessica thanked him and gave a smile that didn't quite reach her eyes.

"We're ready," Chris called.

Sean kissed Jessica's cheek and dashed out.

He and Chris walked to the community building where the family waited to begin the traditional walk to the altar at the peninsula. Flowers strung together in an ornamental garland lined the pathway.

Sean fidgeted. The sooner this was over, the better he'd feel. He tried to tell himself he had caught Jessica's jitters, but it was more than that.

The air hung about them like a heavy blanket. The normally azure sky was mutating to a nasty slate gray. Except for the murmurs of the crowd, there were no other sounds. No birds twittered. No bees hummed. It was eerie. If Sean were the superstitious type, and he was, he'd call these things bad omens on a wedding day.

Chris nudged him. "Here comes your bride."

Sean looked up. Leia's smile settled his nerves. She wore a silky halter-type dress of white that swirled delicately around her calves as she walked. In her hair was a single red hibiscus flower. Around her neck were pink and yellow flowered leis. She stood before Sean and placed one of the leis from her neck to his.

"I'm glad you remembered about the hummingbirds." He cupped the hibiscus.

"How could I possibly forget?" Linking her arm through his, they turned to follow the family procession down the flowered walkway.

A breeze stirred as they stood before Reverend Blankenship.

Solemnly, they took their vows, exchanged rings, and traded leis. Then, as Sean drew Leia close to kiss her, the atmosphere was ripped in two by the sirens.

The volume increased as the breeze turned into a wind.

Jessica raced toward them, pointing to the sky. "It's the hurricane." Her voice was barely audible above the wind and sirens. "The news report just said it veered away from Oahu early today. It's heading right for us."

As if to verify her statement, a wave slammed into a bridge pylon. Water shot into the air. A woman screamed and darted for the bridge.

Bobby snagged her elbow and yanked her to a stop. "Panicking isn't going to help anyone. We planned for this. Now let's calmly walk to the caves. Everything is there and waiting for us. No pushing or jostling. Families gather together and stay together."

But the resounding crash of a wave against the peninsula brought more screams, and the crowd raced for safety.

"Get the hell out of our way, Chamberlain," a man yelled. "You don't give the orders where our lives are concerned!"

Others roared their approval and stormed the bridge. Chris yanked William and Brian from the crush and shoved them toward Jessica. "Get back to the house. Bring the van around. I'm not taking the kids through that mess. We'll go around through the mesa meadow and take the path to the caves."

He motioned Gina and Mark to follow Jessica, then pushed his way into the melee. He could hear Amanda scream for her mother, and saw Meredith's frantic attempts to reach her. She was close, but the forest of bodies made it impossible to find her.

Edward plucked Jeff from the crowd and seated the boy on his shoulders. Chris's father grabbed his mother in one hand and Elaine Chamberlain in the other, while Dan and Jackie Daniels pushed a way clear for them. Then they darted to the community building.

Suddenly a space appeared and Chris saw Amanda huddled on the ground. In one sweeping motion, he scooped her into his arms. Then, after grabbing Meredith's hand, Chris pushed them free, and shoved Amanda into her arms.

"Get Rachel and get to my house. Take the truck and van and go around."

"What about Bobby, Sean, and Leia?"

Chris scanned the mob. The three seemed hopelessly ensnarled at the bridge's entrance. "Go on without us. We can make it across. Those children and babies can't."

Meredith hugged him. "God, Chris, be careful."

Chris fought his way forward. Although Leia was sheltered between Sean and Bobby, the crowd still threatened to smother them. Twice Chris was shoved back. A third time he pushed forward. When the surge of people tried to sweep him aside, he felt strong fingers clamp around his wrist.

Chris wrapped his fingers around Sean's arm. It was a bond more forceful than any frenzied crowd. He pulled himself forward, and Leia wrapped her arms around him.

"Let's stay together and get the hell out of here," Bobby said.

The progress across the bridge was slow. Leia clung to Sean. Rain slashed against them like wind-driven needles. Out of the corner of his eye, Chris saw a huge wave approach them. Leia turned to look. The wave crashed over the bridge a few feet behind them. She screamed and buried her head in Sean's chest.

"Come on, honey," he said. "We're almost there."

They pushed on. A figure dashed by, shoving them aside. Leia stumbled backward. Only Chris's quick reflexes kept her from falling into the water. He glanced up and saw Carolyn run into the woods.

"Come on." Sean wrapped his arm around her waist.

"No, I can't do it." Leia dug her heels in. "I'm afraid." She was six years old again and on a ledge overlooking a rough high tide.

"Leia, we're almost there."

"No!" Tears streamed down her face, mixing with the rain.

"Leia, this is no time to argue. Cross that bridge."

"No! I can't. You go without me. I'll follow later."

"The hell I will." He tossed her over his shoulder and walked on. Bobby and Chris flanked him to ensure he kept his balance. Once on dry land, he set her on her feet, and they hurried on to the caves. The rest of the family were already there.

"Is everyone accounted for?" Bobby asked Dan.

"Yes, plus one." Dan jerked his head toward Carolyn.

"Well, let's get settled in," Bobby said. "I'll pass out the sleeping bags."

Chris picked up two blankets and threw them at Carolyn. "You almost killed Leia back there. If you know what's good for you, you'll keep as far away from us as possible. Understand?"

"Perfectly clear." Using the edge of the blanket she fluffed her hair dry.

He spun away from her. "How are the babies?"

"I got a nice warm fire going," Mark said. "All the little ones are near it and safe. The road was a mess. I saw at least one tree fall behind us. If that bridge doesn't hold, we'll be here for a while."

Chris followed him to where the ladies sat with the children and infants. After checking his tiniest patients, he sank to the sleeping bag beside Jessica.

"Well, at least one mystery of the statues is solved." Bobby propped a blanket behind him and leaned against the cave wall. "Their purpose was to warn islanders of approaching storms. We got a twenty-four-hour warning, a twelve-hour warning, and a warning when the storm was actually here. I'll bet when it's safe to leave, the sirens will stop."

"What do our two amateur archaeologists think?" Chris asked.

Sean and Leia didn't answer. The couple sat as far from the group as they could. They were cross-legged in front of each other, holding hands. Leia still cried from the ordeal.

Chris rubbed his weary eyes. *Let them have their time alone. They earned it.* He stretched out to rest. A few minutes later, the sleep he'd missed the night before and the exertion of fighting to reach the caves caught up with him. With a blanket tucked under his head, he let himself fall asleep.

*   *   *

Sean held Leia's hands in stunned silence. How could he reassure her when he was having the same doubts?

"Don't you see?" she whispered. "This is all our fault. We flaunted the island's traditions. We were together before the marriage and still had the island ceremony."

Sean nodded. It made sense to him. The statues had warned them the day before, then the morning of the ceremony. Sean and Leia had ignored it. The island wedding went on as if they had every right to it. The island was angry. The giant ladies called the hurricane as punishment.

"What are we going to do?" Leia asked. "How do we say we're sorry?"

Sean thought about that for awhile. There seemed only one solution.

"We'll ask Jessica. If anyone would know, she would."

It was several annoying minutes before they could catch her attention. Once they had, she hurried over and sat beside them. She didn't scoff or tease as the others might. Their concerns were real for her because they were bothered by them. Afterward she smiled.

"You're putting a lot on your shoulders. The storm was headed this way anyway. It was merely a matter of time before it hit. I don't believe the statues purposefully called it. And if they did, I doubt it was to punish two people so obviously in love. There is another force here far more unsettling. If they wanted to punish, that's who they would punish." She glanced toward Carolyn.

"But what if it *was* us?" Sean asked. "What could we do to ask forgiveness?"

Jessica sighed and rubbed the back of her neck while she thought about it. "Well, another place the islanders revered was the fertility cave."

"That's it," Sean said. "The fertility room is in this cave. We'll consummate our marriage there—tonight."

"You know what it means if you do," Jessica said. "I can attest to the fact that it works *very* well. I think if you corner Gina long enough, she'll agree."

"It's the only way I know of to prove our respect to the island," Sean told her.

Leia nodded her agreement.

Jessica patted their knees. "It seems your decision is made. I'll leave you to think about it and make sure no one disturbs you."

They waited until Jessica had everyone settled down for the night. Then, with candle and sleeping bags in hand, they found their way to the fertility room.

Leia placed the candle in a niche in the wall while Sean put the bags over the goddess on the floor. He extended his palm to Leia and she took it. They kicked off their shoes and sat between the fertility goddesses.

Sean pulled off his shirt. The candlelight shimmered against his bronzed skin. When Leia started to undress, he stopped her. He pulled her close, kissing her cheek, neck, and throat while he slowly unzipped her dress. Leia ran her hand through the golden hairs of his chest. Sean sighed. His lips wandered to the curve of her breast.

She dropped the top of the dress and pulled his head to her nipple. He gently sucked the tiny bud into his mouth. The sensation brought shivers from them both.

He couldn't get enough of her. He kissed her throat and suckled her breasts, then left a trail of fiery kisses down to the band of her panties. Licking and kissing her belly, he slowly slid the silky garment off her hips. As they neared her feet, she kicked them into a corner.

Leia's heart quickened as he removed his trousers. God, how she loved him. If they could never be together physically again, she knew she'd still love him just as much. She reached for him, her hands grazing muscle-cut arms.

Sean brought his lips to hers as he slowly guided himself deep within her heat. She was tight around him like a velvet glove. *Heaven. Love.* He could live forever and still not find the right words to describe it.

Soft words of love fell from her lips, encouraging him to brand her his with a pounding thrust. When he did so, she held back a cry of pleasure and wrapped her legs around his waist.

He cupped her buttocks, lifting her higher to reach deeply-hidden places. With her throaty moan, he lost what little control he had. He clasped her closely, pounding hard and fast until she exploded beneath him. Then he, too, finally found his pleasure.

They whispered endearing words of love to each other, accentuating each one with gentle little kisses. He stayed deep inside of her, not wanting to leave, then moved slowly, hardening again with the motion. Leia sighed as his mouth drifted to the other breast. Again they loved. Then again, until exhaustion over took them.

Reluctantly they dressed, gathered their things and returned to the main room. With tender words of love and gentle kisses, they cuddled together and fell to sleep.

*   *   *

Carolyn grimaced as she gazed at the couple, then at Chris and Jessica curled together. It sickened her. Nothing had turned out as she had planned. She hated the Matthews family now more than ever. This was the perfect time to carry out her revenge. As morning arrived, and with it the passing of the storm, she crept over to the sleeping babies, picked up her target, and left.

*   *   *

Buffy's growl jerked Jessica awake. She saw Brian run to the entrance and struggled to her feet.

"You can't take our baby," he shouted.

Chris bolted upright and raced Jessica to the clearing. The others followed in his wake. Carolyn stood on the far side of the clearing, a baby nestled in her arms, Brian before her.

A snarl curled her lip. "I can do whatever I want."

Jessica clutched Chris's arm. "She's got Steven."

He didn't question how she knew from this distance.

196

Brian blocked her way. "Give me back our baby, or I'm telling Dad."

"That's far enough, Carolyn."

She jerked to a stop. Brian yanked free of her and ran to Chris. The glint of metal flashed in the corner of his eye. Chris glanced in that direction and saw the rifle poised in Sean's hands.

"Give him the baby now, Carolyn. You know I'm a dead shot."

Fire blazed in Carolyn's dark eyes when she saw the weapon. She strode toward them and plopped the baby into his arms. "Here's your bawling infant."

She spun away from them and started down the path to the lagoon.

Chris passed Steven to Jessica who cuddled him close and began to nurse him.

Sean walked over to them. "Good thing she didn't call my bluff. It's not loaded. Is he all right?"

"I think so." Chris caressed Steven's soft little cheek with his finger.

Jessica lovingly cradled the baby as he continued to nurse.

Sean watched with a smile. It seemed so right, so perfect. Jessica wasn't bothered by her audience. For her, it was simply a part of nature. It made him want a child of his own. He caught the tender smile Leia gave him. She felt it, too. If the legend was true, they'd get their wish in nine months.

"Better tell him to save some for his sister," he said softly to Jessica.

"He's just about through," Jessica replied. "See. He can hardly keep his little eyes open."

They watched the baby drift to sleep, releasing his hold on the nipple as he did so. Shawna demanded her turn.

"You might want to hurry," Leia said. "She's trying to nurse off me."

Laughing, Jessica switched babies and met her daughter's demands while Leia marveled over the bundle in her arms. Once Shawna was satisfied, Jessica quickly rearranged her clothing.

Chris wrapped his arm around her. "Let's go home." If they had homes to go to.

No one spoke. They simply moved toward the bridge. They were relieved to find it intact and proceeded across, anxious to be home. The ocean was calm, gentle waves rolled in.

The remains of Edward's beloved boat were washed on the shore.

Other debris scattered the shoreline among a few fallen palms. The visitors' cabanas were gone. Chris imagined Carolyn would find some way to sue them for the loss of her possessions. Most of the buildings sustained damage of varying degrees, but had been spared major damage.

He breathed a sigh of relief to see the infirmary had sustained no apparent damage. From his position on the bridge, he couldn't see his house.

As they neared the peninsula, he saw a palm tree had fallen on Leia's home. She sucked in a gasp. Sean patted her hand reassuringly. They were safe and that was all that mattered.

Then he saw Carolyn. She waited for them on the peninsula, fists clenched at her sides.

"You stupid people. You stick together like thieves. I'll make you pay. I'll make you all pay!" She picked up a coconut from the ground and hurled it at them.

"Stop it, Carolyn. Haven't you done enough damage for one day?" Chris wasn't in the mood for any more games.

"I haven't done near enough damage. You want to see damage?" She picked up a rock and threw it at the statue, hitting her target squarely.

"Carolyn, stop it!" Sean hurried toward her. "You don't know what you're doing!"

"You sound worried. You mean I've finally done something that concerns you? These stupid statues are nothing but junk!" She picked up another rock and threw it, again hitting the statue.

"Stop it!" Sean sprinted toward her.

"Get back!" Carolyn glared at them as she picked up a large stick and raced to the statue on the point. She was possessed. Evil twisted her face and gleamed from her eyes.

Jessica clutched Chris's arm. "My God, Chris. She's insane."

If there was any doubt before, there certainly wasn't now. Chris patted Jessica's fingers and ran toward his ex-wife.

Carolyn threw herself against the statue and beat the stick into its surface. The statue emitted a low hum. Carolyn's eyes widened with fright. She backed away, mouth agape. The hum grew louder.

She glared at them. "This is a trick of yours. Well, it won't work."

Laughing, she jerked her arm up for a new attack. The motion pulled her off balance. She teetered for balance on the edge of the bluff. The ground crumbled beneath her feet. She screamed and fell into the ocean below.

Chris and Sean raced to the edge. It was too late. They gazed into the churning, deep blue water below and saw nothing.

Footsteps beat the ground behind them. Chris glanced over his shoulder to Bobby, Mark, and Dan.

"She's gone. We need to call the Coast Guard and get a rescue squad out here."

"Chris, if she's still alive, she won't be by the time they get here."

Bobby was right. There was only one other solution.

*   *   *

Leia shut herself away in Chris and Jessica's house. She refused to watch, much less condone what Sean and the others were about to do. He couldn't blame her. He was nervous too about the rough water. But Sean also knew he couldn't sit back if someone was in danger, even when that someone was Carolyn.

"Ready?"

Mark and Dan nodded. With scuba gear in hand, they hurried to the bluff where Chris and Bobby waited with the fathers for some sign of Carolyn. After tying guide ropes around their waists, they eased over the side. The last thing Sean saw before he slipped beneath the waves was Leia staring down at him. She blew him a kiss. He gave her a thumbs up and dove.

The water teamed with life. Fish darted out of their way as they edged along the bottom. The water was clear, visibility excellent despite the current that surged and pulsed around them. If Carolyn was here, she'd be easy to spot.

Sean felt a tap on his arm. Dan motioned him to a cave several yards away. Mark was already headed in that direction. It was pitch dark, like the yawning mouth of a hideous monster.

He shook the image away, switched on the light strapped to his wrist, and followed the other two. The opening widened. The water calmed into a pool then shallowed. Black faded to dusk gray.

They surfaced in unison and found Carolyn's body washed to the rock ledge before them. Her vacant eyes recorded the horror of her last few minutes. Sean crawled from the water and closed them.

Mark cast his light around the subterranean room. Skeletons lay sprawled everywhere, some on top of each other. It was hard to tell just how many bodies were here.

Dan edged closer to one and stooped for a better look. He dropped his head and slowly shook it. "Bill Martin."

The wrist watch on the skeleton's arm left no doubt.

"What do you make of it?" Mark asked as he looked around.

Dan stretched to his feet. "It's quite a find. I wonder if the islanders made human sacrifices to the statues."

Sean shook his head. The answer was clear. "Nope. Jessica was right all along. The island takes care of the truly evil."

EPILOGUE

Chris watched the babies and toddler play in the middle of the dance floor. The three nine-month-olds crawled among themselves, exploring here and there with intense curiosity and a stream of unintelligible sounds while Rachel walked among them on wobbly legs. Each baby had a unique personality. It was amazing to see them grow.

He glanced over at Sean and Leia who marveled over their own twins born three days before. Then at Dan and Jackie who were expecting their first in a few months. And finally at Gina who was just beginning to show with her second. Chris couldn't imagine a life other than this. Before Jessica, before Hurago, he had no life. The island, the statues had truly blessed him...them.

The caves and the underwater cavern caused quite a stir in the archaeological community. Hurago bustled with scientists from all over the world. Theories were tossed around, but most were content to believe Hurago took care of its own and had for centuries. Some of the remains were thousands of years old. It was quite a discovery.

Edward waved them all to the center of the room. "If everyone would please gather around, I have an announcement to make."

It took a few minutes for everyone to settle down and get the children corralled.

"I'll make it quick. I have an early Christmas present to give." He hesitated for a moment before he continued. "I'm giving my island to you."

"To whom?" Bobby asked.

"To you and Meredith, Dan and Jackie, Chris and Jessica, and Sean and Leia."

Bobby frowned. "But why? Dad, are you all right?"

Edward laughed. "Of course, I'm all right."

"I don't understand," Jessica said. "This island is yours."

"Which means I can give it to anyone I choose. Actually, one way or the other the island would eventually fall into Bobby's and Leia's hands. But I wanted to pass it on in much of the same way as I received it."

"But why?" Sean asked.

"For several reasons. Whether any of you realize it or not, all of you have been running this island for the last year-and-a-half. I haven't done a thing, and I've enjoyed that. You're all very close. There isn't anything you wouldn't do for one another. And you'd do it without any questions asked. You care for the island and will keep it as it should be. With all the work you've done and all you've brought to the island, why shouldn't it belong to you? If I give it to you now, you can enjoy it while you're still young. And I get to watch you enjoy it."

"But what will you do?" Bobby asked.

"The same thing I've been doing for the last year-and-a-half. Working with you all on the island, going out on my boat, and watching my grandchildren grow." Edward looked at each one. "You don't have to give me an answer today. Think about it for a few days."

"Dad, if this is truly what you want to do, then I'll go along with it," Bobby said.

"Leia and I would rather have the island this way, than to have you die first," Sean told him.

Edward turned to Dan. "I really feel that since your father and Jackie's father were also the original owners, you rightfully should own part of the island now."

Dan considered this for a moment, then nodded, "Thank you, Edward. We accept."

"And what about you two?" Edward asked Jessica and Chris.

Jessica looked to Chris for an answer. He squeezed her hand.

"Edward, if you don't mind, we'd like to discuss this with you later."

He lifted his hand, silencing Chris. "Before you say another word, I want you to know this isn't out of guilt. I'm doing this because I feel you and Jessica have made very valuable contributions to the island.

This little lady here has a love and appreciation of this island that no one else does. She's even managed to make our own island honey and also, thanks to her, the feral pigs have been rounded up for domestication."

Chris scratched his head and tried to hide a smile. "Actually, I think Leia had more to do with that than Jessica."

Laughter tittered through the group.

"Be that as it may, we couldn't manage without her. And you've given Jessica something no one else could. William, too."

"That works both ways, Edward," Chris quietly replied.

"I really want to do this, Chris. I feel you both deserve it. What do you say?"

Chris and Jessica exchanged another look. The choice was hers.

She pulled in a breath. "All right. We accept. We feel honored to be owners of your island."

That evening as Chris and Jessica lay together, they talked of all the things which had come to pass.

"It all seems like part of someone else's life," Jessica said. "So remote and unreal. Yet every moment I've spent with you is preciously etched in my mind. Two years ago, if someone would've told me I'd become a mother again, I'd have told them they were crazy. And look at me now."

Chris leaned toward her and pulled her close. "Want to start working on another one?"

Jessica laughed and ruffled her fingers through his blond hair. "Of course, but this time, let's have them one at a time."

CATHERINE SNODGRASS

Anything Is Possible!

That's Catherine Snodgrass's motto. Blessed (or cursed) with a vivid imagination, Catherine has learned to turn that "talent" inward. She grew up reading Victoria Holt, Phyllis Whitney, and others, and loves to "go places" in her writing. Readers should expect different locales and deep emotions in Catherine's books. She also believes that life is to be lived not watched, and has done some inner exploring of her own— hiking a new path, learning a new skill, and even conquering a life-long fear of singing in public to take a turn or two on the stage of the local community theater. Her work as a paralegal in family and tax law has helped her tune in to the emotions of others and further deepen that aspect of her writing. Having set her children off in the world to explore their own paths, Catherine lives in the beautiful desert of Southern California with her husband (a genealogist) and the animals she loves.

AMBER QUILL PRESS, LLC
THE GOLD STANDARD IN PUBLISHING

QUALITY BOOKS
IN BOTH PRINT AND ELECTRONIC FORMATS

ACTION/ADVENTURE	SUSPENSE/THRILLER
SCIENCE FICTION	ROMANCE
MAINSTREAM	MYSTERY
PARANORMAL	FANTASY
HISTORICAL	HORROR
YOUNG ADULT	WESTERN

AMBER QUILL PRESS, LLC
http://www.amberquill.com